Chris Kraus is the author of the nove
Summer of Hate, as well as *Video Gre*
Nothingness and *Where Art Belongs*. A
teaches writing at European Graduate School and lives in LA.

PRAISE FOR *TORPOR*

"Chris Kraus writes about the strangeness of the world in a clear American prose
filled with emotion, but with no vapors of style ... Chris Kraus is a great writer"
— Michael Tolkin, *Artforum*

"Feelings about messed-up relationships cut back and forth with painful prod-
dings of historical events, all rendered in a kind of open prose that allows a dirt
road to lead to Desert Storm and end up in an analysis of *Thirtysomething*. The
effect is so startling that it resuscitates words long fallen out of fashion: *Torpor*
is honest and true"
— Alex Kitnick, *The Believer*

"*Torpor* takes aim at the traditional bourgeois novel about marriage and family
and delivers a book full of bullet-holes: the death of the novel, the fall of
Europe, the end of the family, devastation of the arts. What is left standing? A
battle-scarred but indefatigably hopeful *I-Love-Lucy-esque* Chris Kraus"
— Michael Silverblatt, *Bookworm*

"Kraus is at work on a kind of philosophy ... It is possible, she finds, to turn
on in ourselves the bright light of the interrogation room ... to expose all experience always to direct and sustained evaluation ... Through the intention,
perpetual effort to comprehend it, existence is transformed from a series of
events ... and therefore the world in which it is lived is something within our
power to comprehend"
— Elizabeth Gumport, *n+1*

"[*Torpor*] has more heart than any intellectual of the author's caliber has gotten
away with having since Celine. And, like Celine, she knows that life, alas, is not
about feelings"
— Gary Indiana, author of *Three Day Fever*

PRAISE FOR *I LOVE DICK*

"The intelligence and honesty and total originality of Chris Kraus make her work not just great but indispensable – especially now, when everything is so confusing, so full of despair. I read everything Chris Kraus writes; she softens despair with her brightness, and with incredible humour, too"
  —Rachel Kushner

"*I Love Dick* is a classic. Here pain is the aphrodisiac and distance is the muse. Unrequited love is transformed into a fascinating book of ideas"
  —Zoe Pilger

"I know there was a time before I read Chris Kraus's *I Love Dick* (in fact, that time was only five years ago), but it's hard to imagine; some works of art do this to you. They tear down so many assumptions about what the form can handle (in this case, what the form of the novel can handle) that there is no way to re-create your mind before your encounter with them"
  —Sheila Heti

"Tart, brazen and funny … a cautionary tale, *I Love Dick* raises disturbing but compelling questions about female social behavior, power, control"
  —*Nation*

"Ever since I read *I Love Dick*, I have revered it as one of the most explosive, revealing, lacerating and unusual memoirs ever committed to the page … *I Love Dick* is never a comfortable read, and it is by turns exasperating, horrifying, and lurid, but it is never less than genuine, and often completely illuminating about the life of the mind"
  —Rick Moody

"*I Love Dick* is one of the most important books about being a woman … Friends speak of Kraus's work in the same breathless and conspiratorial way they discuss Elena Ferrante's novels of female friendship set in Naples. The clandestine clubbishness that envelopes women who've read and immersed themselves in the texts shows how little female desire, anger and vulnerability is accurately and confidently explored in literature and culture … the book reveals far deeper truths than standard and uncomplicated love plots tend to"
  —Dawn Foster, *Independent*

TORPOR

CHRIS KRAUS

TUSKAR ROCK PRESS

First published in Great Britain in 2017 by Tuskar Rock Press,
an imprint of Profile Books Ltd
3 Holford Yard
Bevin Way
London
WC1X 9HD

First published in the USA in 2006 by Semiotext(e), South Pasadena, California

1 3 5 7 9 10 8 6 4 2

Designed by Hedi El Kholti
Printed and bound by Mackays of Chatham, Kent

The moral right of the author has been asserted.

A CIP record for this book can
be obtained from the British Library

ISBN 978 1 78125 898 9
eISBN 978 1 78283 377 2

CONTENTS

FOREWORD BY FANNY HOWE   vii

CHAPTER I   THIRTYSOMETHING   I

CHAPTER 2   THE ANTHROPOLOGY OF UNHAPPINESS   23

CHAPTER 3   WELTSCHMERZ   47

CHAPTER 4   THE REVOLUTION WILL BE TELEVISED   77

CHAPTER 5   BERLIN DEATH TRIP #1   101

CHAPTER 6   THE NIGHTMARE OF HISTORY   121

CHAPTER 7   BERLIN DEATH TRIP #2   135

CHAPTER 8   WHO'S PEAKED?   149

CHAPTER 9   FUTURE ANTERIOR   163

CHAPTER 10   PRAGUE DISASTER   191

CHAPTER 11   EDGE PLAY   205

CHAPTER 12   DEPECHE MODE   221

CHAPTER 13   END GAME   233

CHAPTER 14   WORSE   249

CHAPTER 15   BETTER   263

AFTERWORD BY MCKENZIE WARK   274

To my parents Ruth *and* Oz Kraus

A Great Ride

From the description below, you will not get how deep and devastating this novel is. Sylvie and Jerome have houses that they own but no home. They head to Romania to adopt a child and never make it to the orphanage. Jerome is a philosopher and cultural critic with a traumatic childhood. Sylvie is much younger, a filmmaker and writer who is deeply insecure. She is also hilariously funny and it is her view of the passing world that drives them along, her self-deprecating, ironic but naïve certainties about what they are doing going to Romania. They love a dog in common. But abortions haunt them as signs of the torpor that is the state of the novel.

They share an aesthetic in their work of buying houses to fix up and rent. They want the most bourgeois kind of smug nostalgia imaginable, the kind that is embellished by kitsch from thrift shops. The dog Lily helps.

"Look, Jerome!" Sophie would have exclaimed, "this is Lily's season." Lily's small rust-colored body would have blended perfectly with the fallen leaves. "Ahhh," Jerome would have replied, "she is a dachshund," although they both knew well that like them, Lily was a mongrel. Each of Jerome's approving utterances about the little dog would have brought the couple closer. Their rhapsodies about the dog were practice in the basic words of parenting, a language which—it was becoming clearer every day—they'd never speak first-hand with each other.

For Jerome "History was a code-word for Holocaust." His childhood was detoured by war, in France, as a boy, when his parents disappeared and he was taken into foster care and made to change his name. His life is like a fairy tale, one of the early and perplexingly surreal Grimm stories that seem to prophecy the sadism to come. The grotesque figures and obstacles in those stories characterize his life, and have set him on a permanent course with no fixed resting place. He hates everywhere. He "sees a prescience of horror in the disjointed texts of Georges Bataille and Simone Weil; Artaud, Celine. It's as if these people had experienced, alone and in their bodies, events that would be massively played out a decade later." Sylvie mistrusts almost everyone, especially people in the art world, and so Jerome and she are perfectly matched, and a thoroughly modern comedy team to travel with.

A road of prose is unknown in advance. Where it goes is both the reader's and the writer's guess. When you set out on such a road, the words write the words to follow. If you have an intention, it quickly gets lost in words you never expected to see in the first place. It is as if you have taken a wrong turn onto a wide toll highway, with a destination in mind at first but now missed. The wrong miles stretch ahead of you and you may not have enough money to pay the toll to turn around and go back again. Your ever-accumulating outrage and alienation turn into the content of your journey now. The prose becomes a story about the progress of a hope.

If a dog crosses the highway, it becomes part of the prose road, because it is by now a story where there are contingencies, surprise entries, relations. The story is like the driver of a car who is lost. The driver has heightened, even burning consciousness of the weird, the accidental, the dangers of weather and health. The driver laughs by herself. Surreal flash-memories of her known life take on a comic dimension. She curses herself as an idiot who, despite everything, wants things to control the world. She wants that so much she might think, "I meant to get lost."

She might pause by a cliff and consider suicide. Feel the gravity haul at her bones when she stands at the ledge of air. But she backs away and drives on. She never mentions this episode to anyone. The reader might pause at the same time and think of abandoning the book, but be unable to do so. It would be too intentional in the situation of complete randomness in which she and the heroine are living for this time. Such a long error with repetitive surges of hope and disappointment, the error becoming the actual fate (perhaps even the pre-determined one!) can develop into a metaphysical desire or stay wholly modern. In this latter case, there is little distinction between living people outside the book/car and imaginary people inside the head/car of the driver/writer. Not only a dog might wander by, but also Michael Jackson or Vaclav Havel. There is nothing metaphysical here, only the developed world bouncing on air.

The marriage of Sylvie and Jerome, grudgingly agreed to, over the issue of health insurance, actually seems to be a marriage of something deeper, funnier, sadder, truer than romantic love. It is of course tested on this strange erroneous journey where the future is worse than empty, not a place to which you are going, but a study of tread-marks, skids, spilled oils, infertile fields, a Chernobyl landscape….these are what you pass and enter simultaneously. All experience moves in a cocoon, as if swaying back and forth on a stick, rather than in a direction. Is No Time the New Time?

They travel to Germany where he has work (an unwritten book she calls "The Anthropology of Unhappiness") and then on to Central Europe to look for orphans. It is here we enter the desolating perplexity of modernity. "We are the last generation to whom things really matter," said Gilles Deleuze. It is 1991. The Serbo-Croatian war is brewing. Peace-keepers are fleeing. Sylvie and Jerome pass through Prague as tourists and head on to Austria, not knowing where it is. She doesn't want to go; they argue; they go. And then the journey fizzles before they return to New York.

"There was a gorgeous Rheingold sign above the bar: a large electric clock featuring an autumn scene, with two red setter dogs looking up above the blazing maples at a pheasant. Each smiling dog had one of its front paws pointed. Outside sanitation trucks thudded over potholes onto West Street, but on the Rheingold sign the pheasant soared against the sky's heroic turquoise plastic surface."

What is torpor outside of this brilliant, entrancing and heart-rending novel called *Torpor*? A condition in which not even collapse or entropy occurs. A fertile field wreathed in yellow watery matter where Yes, Maybe and No rub together without consequence. You have to read this book to get the great ride it gives. A ride where torpor steams in all directions without interruption, minimal will or curiosity; torpor is the name of the spirit of the leftover world.

CHAPTER I: THIRTYSOMETHING

THIRTYSOMETHING

"The Sugar Maple is easily distinguished at any season of the year. In winter the cone-tipped branches are distinct and characteristic. In spring the beautiful yellow-green blossoms in pendant clusters are different from those of any other Maples. In summer the broad leaves with their rounded sinuses enable one to identify the species at a glance. And in autumn the key-fruits and brilliant yellow, orange and red leaves serve a similar purpose. In woods, the trees grow straight and tall, and in open situations they develop a wide expanse of foliage, which makes them ideal for shade."

— *Our Trees: How To Know Them*, copyright 1936, Clarence M. Weed, D.Sc., Teacher of Nature Study in the Massachusetts State Normal School at Lowell

THERE IS A BROAD dirt path behind Brant Lake that slopes up gently through the woods along the ridge between Hawk Hill and Sand Beach Mountain. The path begins where Ike Hayes Road dead-ends. Originally a wagon trail, it was used later as a logging road, but now no one uses or maintains it.

On this mid-October Wednesday afternoon, Jerome Shafir and Sylvie Green, two rootless cosmopolitans who split their time between investment rental properties in the depressed upstate New York town of Thurman and Springs, East Hampton, are walking on this path with their little dog. Though Jerome is a professor at Columbia University, the pair can no longer afford an apartment in New York City. Their two "homes" are seven hours apart, in quaint rural slums adjacent to resorts. Both locales involve a grueling four-hour drive from Manhattan. Still, they find this arrangement preferable to living in a cheap apartment in Hoboken or Park Slope. At least, they think, they get to see America.

It is a classic bright fall day: the kind of picture that still gets cranked out on the mimeograph machine by teachers at North Warren Central School in the picture-postcard town of Brant Lake Village. Incorporated in 1838, this southern Adirondack town boasts a duck pond and a water-mill, a white clapboard Episcopal church, a granite Roman Catholic church, and an unreconstructed general store called Daby's that still sells hardware, blankets, cigarettes and groceries. Brant Lake is one of Thurman's richer cousins, and Daby's is the kind of store that will soon inspire product lines by Tommy Hilfiger and Ralph Lauren. Hunting season hasn't started yet. The town has emptied out for autumn.

It is 1989 or 1990. George Herbert Walker Bush is President of the United States and the Gulf War has just begun in Saudi Arabia. "Collateral damage," a military term coined to describe the accidental wasting of civilian populations, is just beginning to crossover into self-help therapeutic terminology. Somewhere in the Persian Gulf, civilians cower in the rubble while in New York, Sylvie's friends discuss the "collateral damage" of their break-ups. Everywhere, there is this yearning for simplicity.

The most popular TV show for Jerome and Sylvie's white, college-educated, 28–54 demographic is *Thirtysomething*, but they rarely have a chance to watch it, because they're never in one place long enough to rationalize spending $40 a month for cable. *Thirtysomething* is a well-written, well-performed ensemble drama about lives of people like Jeff and Carla, the nice young couple who are subletting Sylvie's small, rent-stabilized East Village tenement apartment. Carla, a model, is taking classes in fine furniture restoration because at 28 she wants to *keep her options open*. Jeff quit his band three years ago and now makes money doing high-end apartment renovation. Like the cast of *Thirtysomething*, but unlike Jerome and Sylvie, Jeff and Carla lead lives that they are invested in, where cards like Marriage, Family and Career are played closely to the heart, and small decisions matter.

Sylvie is amazed by the tremulous sincerity that grips these people when they talk about their futures. Having grown up with Iggy Pop and the Sex Pistols, she remains faithful to a philosophy so brilliantly contained in just two words: *No Future*. The only thing that really matters to her is their small dog, Lily, who is bundled up this afternoon in her cable-knit blue sweater. October days up here get chilly after sunset. Beneath their feet, the trail is softly bedded down with tiny hemlock cones and pine needles.

"The 30s are all about *heart*," Melanie Griffith confided recently to *People*. She meant, of course, that decade of her life, and not the century's. Melanie and her formerly-abusive husband, Don Johnson, have just gotten back together. After completing residential rehab programs in Boca Raton and Minneapolis, respectively, the pair bought a 200-acre ranch outside of Aspen, Colorado so that the children of their blended family (two of their own, two from Don's last former marriage) could have a "normal" childhood. Melanie's scaled back on her career to try and be a better mom: "I'm learning now how much family really matters."

Meanwhile, her rugged husband Don stumps around campaigning for the re-election of George Bush I, because, he says, "I like his strength and character."

Likewise, each week on *Thirtysomething*, new parents, Hope and Michael, and their best-friends, Elliot and Nancy, move backwards through a poison fog of culturally-induced reflexive irony towards a New Traditionalism. The births of their amazing off-spring have led these former hipsters to rethink everything. As the network TV season advances, their childless former friends move closer to the fold. Ellyn, Gary and Melissa (a city planner, college teacher and photographer, respectively) begin to recognize the foolishness of thinking they can fulfill themselves through careers in education, art or social activism. Unlike these three, alpha-couples Hope and Michael, Elliot and Nancy have had the courage to *grow up* and come to terms with the empty, idealistic posturing of their Princeton student days. They no longer want to change the world. Now, they are *creating families*.

Post-punk, pre-grunge, the United States stands behind its President to Support Our Troops somewhere in a Persian Gulf sandstorm. Sylvie and Jerome have never felt so alienated. Because the world itself is now unfathomable, the only complexities that really count are small moments of domestic life that combine to trigger deep emotion. There is no longer any way of being poor in any interesting way in major cities like Manhattan.

It is the beginning of the New World Order, which means that wars can now be fought and won without any US military casualties. Yellow ribbons line the road on trees from Brant Lake to New York City. Yellow ribbons—a symbol of America's Norman Rockwell past salvaged just in time by Reagan speechwriter Peggy Noonan—had long ago bedecked front porches, mailboxes and office doors during the First World War. In those times, the yellow ribbons symbolized a nation's willingness to put aside its minor differences (racial lynchings, union busting, the accumulating wealth of trust conglomerates) and join hands across the great divide to pray Our Boys Will Come Home Safely.

And then again, after the Black October stock market crash of 1987, the *Ladies Home Journal* leapt to restyle itself as the bible of "The New Traditionalism." Full-page color ads appearing everywhere depict the soft, expressive face of a female Ivy-educated Thirtysomething. Once a lawyer or a stockbroker, she has re-thought her choices. A banner headline runs above her earnest, pretty brow:

She was looking for something to believe in… And guess what she's found? Her family, her home, herself.

Sylvie herself has flirted briefly with the New Traditionalism. A punk-formalist film and videomaker in her early 30s, she's in Brant Lake to do a Warren County Artist-in-the-Schools residency. It's the only grant, or job, she's had this year. Since they've moved upstate, she mostly lets Jerome support her. When Sylvie isn't writing applications for grants she'll never get, or in bed, depressed and reading, she decorates their "homes" with ideas adapted from *The American Girl's Guide to Handy Homecrafts*, a 1920s book she discovered in a thrift store. Jerome has little interest in these "homes." He only grudgingly agreed to marry Sylvie so she could be on his medical insurance. Happily, Columbia matches his payment on her premium, so without having to petition anyone for a raise, he can extract another $150 a month from the institution. Jerome has little interest in the bittersweet significance of family life. French, and 18 years older than his "wife"—a term he never uses without airquotes—he's never heard of *People* magazine, much less of *Thirtysomething*. Jerome stopped listening to contemporary bands around the time that DNA broke up and Lydia Lunch retired. Joy Division left him cold, with their earnest, pretentious pop lyricism.

It would have been Jerome's 53rd or 52nd birthday, that day when they were walking in the woods: the height of autumn foliage upstate, the 15th of October. Although Jerome doesn't use the word "upstate." Instead, he calls it "upper state New York," in phraseology borrowed from Edith Wharton, and F. Scott Fitzgerald. Though he's lived in America now for almost thirty years, his English remains defined by the expat-Englishmen who taught at the Sorbonne when he was a student in the 1950s. He fills his drug prescriptions at the chemist, speaks derisively of the Middle West, and gets his shoes fixed by the cobbler. Verbs like "make" and "give" continue to bewilder him, despite all of Sylvie's best efforts to correct him. He "makes" a party, "gives" some phone calls. It's as if for 30 years, he's managed to not hear a thing.

Birthdays, for Jerome, had never been a cause for celebration. Each new and passing year just sucks him farther from the source of who he really is, though who he really is, is hard to say, and no one guesses his identity. Born on the heels of Crystallnacht in Paris, 1938 to two bewildered Jewish immigrants from Poland, Jerome imagines he *is* history. He is the fall of France to Nazi Germany in 1942, though France will always be a country that he hates. His father was deported two years later, thanks to the collusion of the French, and all of Jerome's early years were spent in hiding. His father died at Auschwitz, and Jerome is hiding, still. Before he says his name, Shafir, few people even realize that he's Jewish. Jerome has light brown hair and ice-blue eyes. He speaks a soft and traceless French, and pronounces his name *Chezfaire*, a little private joke.

Jerome observes Sylvie's dabbling with the symbols of the New Traditionalism with blank stupefaction. It is ridiculous, her notion of a happy home. His home will always be the camps, but no one—not even Sylvie—knows this. Like most of her ideas, this domestic mania comes straight from television. Gathering pinecones in a plywood bushel basket to put beside the woodstove, making scalloped window treatments out of plywood dowels and sheets she buys at thrift stores, putting up two dozen quarts of zucchini pickle… Jerome cannot imagine why she bothers. For him? They have no kids, it's hardly worth it.

While Melanie Griffith has two children with her husband Don, and *Thirtysomething*'s Hope and Michael have their daughter Janey, all Jerome and Sylvie have is Lily, an aging temperamental lapdog Sylvie rescued from the City Pound. Part dachshund, part cocker spaniel, Lily was abandoned at age 7 in a feeble and emaciated state. The dog is arguably the only thing they'll never sell or give away, and now she is 11.

Recently it's occurred to Sylvie she could turn this New Traditionalism into a cottage industry, renting out their two unhappy homes to happy couples who could afford to pay top dollar. When Jerome's mother sold the two Israeli seaside condos purchased for her by Yvette, Jerome's vivacious, self-made older sister, Sylvie thought long and hard. Yvette, a graduate of secretarial school, had saved her whole extended family from poverty by making real estate investments. The $100,000 given by his mother to Jerome wouldn't even buy a small 2 bedroom co-op in their gentrifying East Village slum. The monthly maintenance fees alone would be higher than the rent in her rent-stabilized apartment. Why not fix the apartment up, then rent it out, and use the rest to make down payments on two houses in the country? She'd rent the Long Island house for summer, and live there in the winter while renting out the Thurman house to skiers. These rents would more than cover up both mortgages!

It was a profitable scheme, but consequently, the pair are homeless. Because Jeff and Carla are still living in her renovated slum apartment, and when the Thurman ski idea had not worked out, she'd had to rent the house at cost through May to a family of locals. So when the Long Island summer renters offered another $3000 to stay on through the fall, Sylvie took it. Consequently, to do the Warren County Artist Residency—which after all, paid *less* than the Long Island rent—she'd had to scramble for an off-season upstate autumn lease. The Brant Lake cottage that she found belonged to two gay women who'd built the place from scratch and taught at SUNY Albany.

With nowhere else to go, Jerome comes up and stays there with her several days a week. Tuesday through Thursday, he's in New York to teach his classes at Columbia. On Tuesday and Wednesday nights, he crashes on a graduate student's sofa.

It would have been the height of Adirondack autumn, and they were walking on the path over Hawk Hill that Sylvie had discovered within a stone's throw of the freezing cottage. She wanted to bring Jerome up to the clearing at the summit that she'd found. Standing on it, you could see all the way across Brant Lake to First and Second Brother Mountains.

"Look, Jerome, a Balm of Gilead tree," she would have called excitedly. A conversation would have then ensued on arboreal etymology. Gilead, Jerome would have recalled, was a mountain town in ancient Palestine that had been annexed, a century ago, to Jordan. "Gilead" meant "rugged" in ancient Aramaic, which was originally the source of Hebrew and Arabic.

These languages diverged, Jerome would have continued. "But," asked Sylvie, "why did they call the tree a balm? Does it have medicinal properties?" The leaves were shiny-smooth, a distant cousin of the poplar.

Sylvie would have wondered what Ike Hayes and his neighbors had been thinking when they named the things around them. The Balm of Gilead tree, First and Second Brother Mountain. She imagined them alone in snowbound huts, with just two books to last through an entire winter: Grimm's *Fairy Tales* and the Bible. The trail they walked on would have run beside an old stone boundary fence. That afternoon the woods were very stately, glorious. White birch, silvery and smudged like naked skin, flashed between the thicker trunks of oaks and maples.

"The day is warm," Sylvie would have observed as they moved higher up the mountain. At 3 p.m., the sun would hover up above the crest of Second Brother, and they might make the sunset, still. Warm light filtered through the leaves and a fiery iridescent maple would have cast deep shadows.

"And yet, the bottom of the air is cool," Jerome would have replied. This utterance expressed Jerome's affectionate familiarity with Sylvie. It was the key-line to *fond de l'air*, one of the word-exchange routines they'd made up together. *Fond de l'air*—top and bottom of the air—was one of Sylvie's favorites in their current repertoire. While other couples had careers and homes and babies, Jerome and Sylvie had a handful of routines that echoed the repetitive games they'd played as children.

Since they were not children but full-grown intellectuals, these routines transcended fart jokes and took in everything they knew. Their routines giddily embraced an entire panorama of world consciousness.

The *fond de l'air* routine originated with a phrase Jerome remembered vaguely from his childhood. The expression was *so very French*—the idea that you could taste the air the way you taste the cheese. Typically, *fond de l'air* had several variants. Some days the bottom of the air was warm, the top was cool. On other days the hierarchies of air were indistinguishable. As a child, he'd been embarrassed and confused: *fond de l'air* was the kind of thing that French adults would say to teasingly 'educate' Jerome, a child of Polish immigrants. But now, with a PhD from the École des Hautes Études, Jerome fully understood its nuances. Didn't *fond de l'air* originate in the 18th century lexicon of French rationalism? The notion that the world could be contained by *classifying*…

Together, he and Sylvie recalled the Comte de Buffon's *Encyclopedia of the Animals*, ca. 1752, in which the Count described exotic beasts according to the things that they were not. There was Charles Fourier's mad utopia, and then, of course de Sade—the way he ranked his slaves by age in color-coded dresses. Mostly, though, Sylvie liked *fond de l'air* because it was so "French." When she'd met Jerome she'd been a gutter rat, and she liked that he could teach her things about French culture.

It was Jerome's birthday, and Sylvie would have wanted for him to be happy. She would have rushed home from Bolton Landing School at 2, and filled a red plaid thermos that she'd bought at Daby's General Store with fresh hot apple cider. Though Sylvie's faith in the possibility of Jerome's happiness was waning, she still believed in perfect days. She loved all things seasonal and occasional.

The Brant Lake woods this afternoon would have reminded her of a plastic sign for Rheingold beer. In the years before she met Jerome, she spent most Saturday afternoons at the Ear Inn bar on Spring Street. Since she'd started topless dancing, she had plenty of free time, but not many ways to fill it. There was a poetry reading series there, and she liked to go and be around the poets. At that time, she was studying to be an actress. The poets were an elite and cliquish bunch, and at the readings no one talked to her.

Terrified of sitting uninvited at a table, she stayed mostly on a barstool. There was a gorgeous Rheingold sign above the bar: a large electric clock featuring an autumn scene, with two red setter dogs looking up above the blazing maples at a pheasant. Each smiling dog had one of its front paws pointed. Outside sanitation trucks thudded over potholes onto West Street, but on the Rheingold sign the pheasant soared against the sky's heroic turquoise plastic surface. While Sylvie spaced a 12-ounce beer between three cigarettes, she thought about the Perfect Life unfolding somewhere in the north, without her. She couldn't rent a car—she had no credit card or license. And even if she had the money for the bus, she had no friends to go with.

But now the promise of the sign had been fulfilled. She had a dog, a car, a husband: proof it might be possible to get everything you want, providing you wait long enough.

Jerome, for his part, distrusted everything autumnal. Autumn meant the onset of another academic year. He's been a tenured professor at Columbia for almost twenty years. The fact his salary's been frozen roughly where it was when he began, increasingly defines everything. He is the non-custodial parent of Laura, a 14-year-old who hates him.

Laura, an only child, lives with her mom in a spacious Central Park West apartment. Ginny, Laura's mom, is an heiress and a former hair model. Her trust fund pays the rent, but it doesn't pay for everything. Consequently, half of Jerome's pre-tax salary goes to pay tuition at his daughter's private school, where her hatred of him grows increasingly informed, articulated. He also pays for Laura's horseback lessons, ski vacations and child therapy.

"Daddy, why," his daughter's asked, since she could first put two words together, "can't you live closer to us, in our neighborhood?" Since after meeting these expenses, Jerome can't afford a faculty apartment, much less one on Central Park, he is condemned to play the guilty absent father. Once, in a moment of self-sacrifice, he'd offered to give up his nomadic life. He'd move to some Brooklyn neighborhood with a decent public school. Laura could move in with him and Sylvie. Both notions were absurd. "Brooklyn" soon became a running mother-daughter metaphor for Jerome's cheapness.

Jerome believed he'd finally overcome his past when he started dating Ginny. His mother, a diehard communist, wept at Stalin's funeral. Ginny, a one-time hair model, had no politics at all. But now her very idleness, which once seduced Jerome, enables her to spend her energies in making his life miserable.

She clubs 'til 4, gets up at noon, and when she isn't talking on the phone, she combs the *New York Times* and *Psychology Today* for ways to get Jerome to spend more money on their daughter.

Currently, Ginny is obsessed with Laura's *puberty*. She's bought their sensitive, shy daughter thongs and push-up trainer bras. She's had Laura's hair tinted, styled and highlighted. Still, the child remains oblivious to boys. Clearly this is Jerome's fault: his absence has deprived her of an essential stage in Oedipal development. It's common knowledge, girls of Laura's age need to *test their sexuality* by *flirting safely* with their fathers. Perhaps Jerome would like to take her on a father-daughter tour of Italy for the holidays?

Bewildered, Jerome mostly pays and stays away. He knows that for their lives to attain the bland perfection of the Rheingold sign in

Sylvie's dreams, he would have to either a) find another job, or b) abandon Laura. Both possibilities are impossible. The War taught him blood was blood. He couldn't dispossess his child. Blood was the only thing that mattered. But to find another job he would have had to play the game and be taken seriously by his academic colleagues. This would entail years of writing academic books and articles, a thing that didn't interest him at all. He'd given up on academe when he received tenure at Columbia and met Ginny.

What Jerome liked best was to think that he could act behind the scenes of the culture. He was too interested in ideas to confine himself to dreary textual analysis. He preferred to be an agent provocateur, a producer. Towards this end, he publishes a magazine and arranges meetings between philosophers and rock stars. He stages summits and events with terrorists and pedophiles, historiographers and sex workers. He plays chess with John Cage, has tea with Natalie Sarraute, and shows up at department meetings bare-chested in a leather jacket after doing coke all night with William Burroughs. These actions make him a downtown celebrity and a pariah in Columbia's Department of French Literature and Philology. .

Through this, Jerome has found *interviews* to be far more telling than any textual analysis. He conducts rambling in-depth interviews with French theorists and culture heroes. Jerome lives within the pauses and the jump-cuts. He finds that once you draw a person out enough, you will uncover inconsistencies. Acting as a broker-spy enables him to move perpetually without ever being held to any single viewpoint. By working all the time, he manages to be quite well known while remaining essentially invisible.

Sylvie, whose only thought is how she might become more visible, is similarly trapped. Since giving up on acting she's made experimental films and videos, but these are so unwatchable the only place for her is the Cinema Studies Department of a university. Since she has no qualifications or degrees, it's unlikely she'll be hired.

Jerome dreads the beginning of each academic year. He also dreads vacations. While his colleagues spend their summers writing pointless academic tomes, he's charged with shuttling Laura between his mother's Paris tenement, a horse camp in Dordogne, and Ginny's Southampton summer rental.

Last summer's camp had turned out to be an absolute disaster, like everything else he undertakes for Laura. Ginny had decided Laura's 13th summer should be spent mastering French. She'd read a *Times* science article about how a child's ability to learn languages exponentially declines when she enters puberty. Ginny herself spoke flawless French: she'd grown up in a boarding school in Switzerland. The only hope for Laura now was full immersion in the language. French, after all, was the language of Jerome's family—a *bond* between him and their daughter—so it made sense that he should pay for Laura's language camp in France all summer.

This was dreadful news. French camps for rich Americans could cost upwards of $5000, and on September 1, he'd have to pay for Laura's fall tuition back at Breaerly. All winter he procrastinated, hoping Ginny would forget it. But by April when she didn't, it dawned on him that French people also send their kids to summer camp. These might not be as expensive. With Yvette's help, he found a perfectly authentic summer camp along the Dordogne River, where ordinary French kids slept out in tents, rode horses, practiced archery.

Ginny was right about their daughter's French deficiency. Laura didn't speak a word of French, and no one at the camp spoke English. Miserable and exiled in a buggy tent with nine other girls who laughed at her, Laura called her mother collect—the bill for this was still on Jerome's desk—and he was charged with dropping everything and going to Dordogne to rescue her.

Compared to this, Jerome is numbingly content as he migrates between Brant Lake and his student's New York sofa. *It could be worse*, he chuckles. He wasn't dead. Although all his life, he's wanted to be. Jerome has studied death in depth, invented death-classes at Columbia: *Death and Sexuality*, *Death and Literature*, *Death and the Disembodied Signifier*. It pleases him that while others see him as a man constantly in motion, he has succeeded to a very great extent in his ambition to be dead. He's visited morgues throughout the New York area; he's read textbooks on embalmment. He'd once dated a cosmetologist who made up corpses for a funeral parlor.

The rodents in the woods that summer would have been similarly active. Chipmunks and red squirrels would have scampered through the woods with nuts between their little teeth, anticipating winter. Jerome and Sylvie loved all things diminutive. Lily, in her best approximation of an Irish Setter, would have bounded off the path in a brave attempt to tree a helpless squirrel.

"Look, Jerome!" Sylvie would have exclaimed, "this is Lily's season." Lily's small rust-colored body would have blended perfectly with the fallen leaves. "Ahhh," Jerome would have replied, "she is a dachshund," although they both knew well that like them, Lily was a mongrel. Each of Jerome's approving utterances about the little dog would have brought the couple closer. Their rhapsodies about the dog were practice in the basic words of parenting, a language which—it was becoming clearer every day—they'd never speak first-hand with each other.

A spirited debate would have then ensued about the origins of the word "dachshund." While "dacha" was the Russian word for "country house," "hund" meant "hound" in German. Their little dog was born to live in country houses! The whole idea of *dachas* was incredibly appealing. Democratized by the Soviets after Chekhov, the old haunts of the haute-bourgeoisie were bestowed on Party bureaucrats and *college professors*. Sylvie imagined them loading up their Lada for the weekend. He, the rumpled intellectual, she the pretty, former-actress wife. She'd wear stretch pants and an Italian mohair sweater, and of course she'd hold the little dog. In this film, the dacha would be some reasonable commuting distance along scenic roads, not a five-hour drive up the New York State Thruway. With the squirrel now completely out of sight, Lily would have jumped and clawed the tree. Clearly, she was born to chase small mammals.

Climbing further up Hawk Hill, they would have stopped and rested. Sylvie would have taken the red plaid thermos out and poured the still-hot apple cider. Fingers stiff with cold, heads close together, they would have passed the small red plastic thermos cup back and forth. The taste of apple was a sacrament that marked their shared exile to this region.

Words were practically redundant now but in an effort to maintain the illusion they were actually two separate people, Sylvie would have asked Jerome:

"Have you heard anything from François?"

François was one of Jerome's oldest friends but since his new book on Georges Bataille came out, he was fast becoming Jerome's enemy. During their student days, through both their first and second marriages, François had been the reckless one, wild and irresponsible. Now François was a department chair, married to a woman his own age, also a prominent New York intellectual.

"I left a message for François," Jerome would have answered petulantly. "But he did not return my call."

Their last visit had been at Sylvie's rehabbed East Village tenement, and François had actually wiped his fingers with a handkerchief in the hall after touching the stairway banister. And now François' new book on Georges Bataille had just come out, and everyone considered him the leading specialist. Jerome found something deeply flawed in François' reading of this great philosopher.

Why does François ignore Bataille's relationship to the Holocaust? Jerome has never written anything about Bataille, but he's read and taught his work for twenty years. He knows Bataille was deeply drawn to fascism. In 1936, the year Jerome's parents fled from Nazi Poland, Bataille was writing rapturously about the primitive, collective thrill of Nazi demonstrations. What does this mean? Bataille was not an anti-Semite; he'd studied sociology with the Jews, with Marcel Mauss and Emil Durkheim. In fact Bataille's most famous formulation, that of "sacred sacrifice" came directly *from the Jews*, who'd pioneered the field of structural anthropology. *The need for roots*. Bataille loved fascism because it was the most ecstatic antidote to rootless, 20th century European urbanism.

What was a "sacred sacrifice"? Within five years Bataille's dream of "sacred sacrifice" had started coming true, and on a massive scale, all over Europe. Ironic that it originated, as a concept, with the Jews. But did the mass extermination of the Jews really constitute a "sacred sacrifice"? In order to be sacred, the sacrificial victim had to *will* his immolation, but the Jews were sacrificed precisely because they were no longer human.

Listening to Jerome brought tears to Sylvie's eyes. "Jerome," she would have said, "you really ought to write about this."

The sky above Brant Lake was now that turquoise Adirondack blue, the color of the beer-sign. Sylvie was awestruck by the force of

Jerome's argument. François, the child of a wealthy Catholic French provincial family, had poetically observed the way Bataille's texts evoked "the smell of war-time." Jerome knew first-hand that *stench* was much more like it. Jerome was so intelligent, thought Sylvie, so well trained in analytic thought. If he could only find a way to *use* this training to externalize the things he knew, his writing would be absolutely brilliant. And then François and all his other colleagues would have no choice but to admire him. They would no longer be unhappy. His salary would be unfrozen, he could find an even better job, and they could move back to New York and have a baby!

But to do these things, Jerome couldn't know the things he knew, because this knowledge left him paralyzed and empty.

"No one can write about the war," Jerome shot back resentfully. "Do you think that Primo Levi's books begin to tell the horror of the camps?"

Sylvie didn't know.

"They are so elegant"—he spat this out—"so utterly composed, so distant."

Well yes, she knew what Jerome meant, but still, that kind of, spareness—wasn't that what Maurice Blanchot meant when he talked about *a language that is deprived of power?*

"Blanchot was not a Jew!" Jerome countered. There was something so remote, so formalized about Blanchot. His prissy and meticulous desire to define a 'language of disaster.' The camps were blood and shit. Just like François, Blanchot had no idea of how it felt to be a dirty Jew, despised and banned from using public pools. He could only look at horror from a distance.

But Jerome can't do this either: put the words 'I am' before 'despised.' The only way he can approach this numbing cavalcade of suffering is through the works of the crazy modernists he teaches.

Anybody who survived the War was struck too numb to actually convey its horror. But Jerome sees a prescience of horror in the disjointed texts of Georges Bataille and Simone Weil; Artaud, Celine. It's as if these people had experienced, alone and in their bodies, events that would be massively played out a decade later.

Jerome recalled a word, *malheur*, that Weil used often in her notebooks. The word stood out, because in French it couldn't be grammatically applied to any person. *Souffrance*, or suffering, was mine or yours: it could be preceded by a pronoun. But *malheureusement*—"unhappiness"—was a state, an abstract noun so huge it stood alone. *Malheur* defied the boundaries of the person.

Years later, after Sylvie left Jerome, she tried explaining to a friend why the writer Marguerite Duras left her husband after finally arranging his release from Dachau. Duras suffered horribly through each day of his incarceration, but she filed for their divorce as soon as he'd recovered from diphtheria and starvation. "But don't you see?" Sylvie exclaimed. Her friend did not. "He was no longer *the same person.*"

But on that afternoon in the Brant Lake woods, Sylvie would have still believed in the possibility of Jerome's happiness. Because there was a moment, then, when everything came together into promise: the thermos and the trees, the little mongrel dog who'd never be an Irish Setter, let alone a human child, the disappointment of her husband's birthday. There was a link. Jerome had lived through this intensity for all these years for some good reason. He could explain it now, move on. This fact struck her with great certainty.

"You'll write a book," she would have said, "about the War." "You'll call it *The Anthropology of Unhappiness.*"

CHAPTER 2: THE ANTHROPOLOGY OF UNHAPPINESS

THE ANTHROPOLOGY OF UNHAPPINESS

FEW THINGS ARE more ridiculous than a childless middle-aged couple traveling alone with a miniature longhaired dachshund. This thought crossed Sylvie's mind as she, Jerome and their now 13-year-old little dog approached the International Hotel Astoria and stepped out of their rented Ford Festiva. It was August 1991 and they were in the civil war-torn city of Arad, the western-most provincial capital of Romania. Eighteen months ago the Romanian Revolution had erupted thirty miles from here, in Timisoara.

Sylvie wore a sleeveless French-blue linen dress, topped off by a gray-market pair of Versace sunglasses. They were in Romania to adopt a child—at least, this was what they told each other.

She'd planned the outfit thinking that the rhinestone glasses would throw the bourgeois respectability of the linen dress into insouciantly witty airquotes. When she got out of the car holding the little dog against her chest, a dozen sullen cab drivers stared at her. Eighteen months ago their dictator Nicolae Ceausescu had been eliminated and Romania was open, once again, to western tourists. Though judging from their stares, Jerome and Sylvie were perhaps the only western tourists that these men had seen.

During his three-decade reign, Ceausescu had succeeded in transforming an entire country into a huge ghetto. With his supremely paranoid grandiosity, Ceausescu most resembled Joseph Stalin on a methamphetamine binge. Two hundred thousand unwanted children—the living legacy of Ceausescu's demographic engineering policy—languished in Romania's state-run orphanages.

Jerome and Sylvie had spent the past week driving southeast from Berlin thinking they ought to have one. The road trip cost much less than two airfares from Berlin to Bucharest. They didn't know much more about Arad than that. Or Romania, or orphaned babies.

It was early evening when they reached the City of Arad. Jumbles of summer foliage topped the squalor of the boulevards. They'd only driven fifty miles that day from southern Hungary, but they'd been stopped for several hours at the border. When they finally crossed, all the road signs were written in Romanian and they became immediately lost. Zigzagging around the entrance to the city, they finally pulled up in the parking lot of the International Hotel—a tourist mecca, so it seemed, though they did not see any other foreigners.

At 10 a.m. they'd left Szged, the Hungarian paprika capital of the world, after having breakfast at the Hotel Tesla. At 20 bucks a night this once grand hotel was a fantastic bargain and they could have stayed forever, sampling the charms of southern Hungary. Jerome would have been happier if they'd done this. But they'd been drifting through the former Soviet bloc for an entire week, and Sylvie was desperate now to reach their destination.

This "destination" had originally been Romania in general—the charming backwardness of Transylvanian mountain villages; the old Greek Orthodox cathedrals—but they'd scaled down this plan as soon as they crossed the border. Fuel was scarce and sometimes unavailable. Horse and donkey carts outnumbered cars and no one spoke anything except Romanian. There was no express bus or rail service between Romanian cities. Electric service in Arad, Romania's third largest city, shut down at 9 p.m., and a decrepit railway crawled between the western towns at 15 miles an hour.

That morning at the Hotel Tesla in Szged, their trip still seemed like an adventurous vacation, albeit one that had lasted several days too long. Jerome was in his element preparing their departure, rolling cheese and bread and apples, sliced meats from the buffet tables, into stolen napkins each time the wall-eyed peasant waitress turned her back. To Sylvie's great embarrassment, Jerome did this everywhere they went. And she protested vigorously—Jerome's actions hardly matched her dress—but he insisted, as he stuffed their bags and pockets full of stolen food, that it was wise to be prepared because they really didn't know how bad the situation might be in Romania.

"But its such a beautiful hotel," persisted Sylvie. And didn't it shame Jerome a little bit to steal? The hotel service staff were probably poor, you didn't see them filling up their bags and aprons.

"The Hungarians are pigs!" Jerome replied. "It is well documented." He was thinking about the War, of course, as always. "Did you know that the Hungarians were second only to the Poles in their eagerness to turn Jews over to the Nazis?"

Obediently, Sylvie slipped into her role within their well-worn Holo-banter. "For this you blame the waitress? Jerome, she wasn't even born!"

"Ahh," he shrugged, "you know so little about the War."

"I know it happened fifty years ago, and you'd better just get over it."

"Have you read about the Hungarian transport?" Jerome asked, as he gestured for a refill of his coffee. "This happened just six months before Germany surrendered to the Allied Forces. It was a Sunday afternoon, late fall. The German Occupation officers received orders to round up every Jew in Budapest. The Jews of

Budapest were not peasant cobblers from the schetl. These were doctors, lawyers, bankers. Women in fur coats—whole families of assimilated Jews—were dragged by the Hungarian police from concert halls and put on trains to Dachau. Where they were, of course—" he finished with a tight smile—"gassed upon arrival."

"But what about Cambodia? El Salvador and Palestine?" Sylvie countered earnestly.

"That's not the point! Don't you see? The Germans knew that they'd already lost the War. Budapest was the most strategically unnecessary of all the Nazi transports. Which makes it reprehensible—" But there he paused, realizing he'd stepped into a Nazi conundrum, a quagmire. Was it possible to quantify brutality? Can there ever be a valid measurement of human life? The Holocaust had made it ethically impossible to ever say *If A is true, then therefore B...* because to understand it is to no longer believe in rational causality.

Jerome collected Holocaust statistics the way others traded baseball cards. He catalogued and applied them to his daily life like Uncle Remus homilies. Pleased with himself, Jerome stuffed one last stolen roll into his bulging pocket.

"Just *stop!*" she begged. And then they squabbled.

"I'm very organized," Jerome said in self-defense, to end the argument. *Organized* was his own most special phrase. It described the pain he felt when caps were left off pens, or Sylvie failed to fold his t-shirts in a certain way. *Organization* was an invocation against the chaos that threatened to engulf him every day. But better still, used as a verb the word alluded to the underground economy of the camps. "If you pass this message to my wife in Birkenau," the enterprising *macher* whispers to the *musselman*, "I will organize you half an egg."

Sylvie didn't like to eat and she never thought about the future until after it arrived. Her spaciness and frailness moved Jerome to organize her diet and Sylvie loved to be protected. Sylvie's helplessness made him powerful and stronger. "Holocaust" was the very best of their routines. With her, he could be a *macher*.

Since the pair had read that Romanian conditions could be very 'harsh' that summer, before they left Berlin Jerome organized the tiny rental car as if they'd be crossing the Sahara. There were five-gallon jugs of water; German army surplus jerry-cans of gas; a primus stove; non-perishable food; a dozen rolls of toilet paper. There was his laptop, so he could continue working on an essay that was already three months late; a universal plug-adaptor; all of Sylvie's clothes; and a dozen cans of food for Lily. Throughout the trip, he added to their cache by swiping hotel towels and bathrobes.

In between her clothes, Sylvie had packed Lily's wardrobe—a selection of her doggy sweaters in case the Transylvanian nights were cold. She couldn't really choose, so she took the pink one and the blue one.

The only thing missing from their luggage was a stuffed bear for their orphan. They'd fought long and hard about the bear. Sylvie had wanted to bring one. The bear would be a traveling companion for the baby's long trip to America. And if they had to leave the child behind to go home and get the paperwork in order, the bear would give the baby hope that they'd be coming back. Sylvie knew the child would understand. Like most of Sylvie's passions, Jerome found this charming and ridiculous.

Weeks before they'd left New York, Sylvie tried to organize an outing with Jerome in search of the right bear. They'd go to FAO Schwartz on 59th Street. This shopping trip would yield a double pleasure. There'd be the happiness of finding the most perfect bear, and then of course, the secret triumph of convincing Jerome to go along with this. Because once he did, he'd see just how adorable the accoutrements of "child" could be.

But in the end, Jerome had been too busy. She'd pleaded with him, wept and badgered, until eventually he agreed she could bring the little sea-green baby sweater trimmed with white angora. They'd bought it at a thrift store several years ago during one of their aimless drives in eastern Pennsylvania.

Jerome's willingness to purchase it that afternoon had brought them so much closer. She'd held the sweater out and nuzzled up to him, a powerful erotic proof of what their love could be. But still, it constituted the entire contents of her hope chest.

Having studied the range of plush stuffed animals extensively, Sylvie left New York determined to pick up the question of the bear in Germany. Perhaps she could get Jerome to buy a German bear, a Steiff, the kind that cost $200. She'd seen them in the boutique baby stores around the Upper East Side and East Hampton. These were the bears that promised future lives of private schools and storybooks and sailboats. The very image of these bears made Sylvie melt into a fantasy of complete protection. But in Berlin, Jerome was even less inclined to humor her.

"What would a screaming infant puking formula in an unheated Romanian orphanage want with an 80 dollar bear?" he wondered.

"But still," she said, "I want to give the baby something to remember me."

And Jerome had gruffly, realistically remarked how it was pointless to buy a bear for a child they'd never seen, and anyway they'd have more time when they were on the road, in Berlin his time was back-to-back with meetings, his text was three months late, but Sylvie wondered anxiously how plentiful the choice of bears might be in a country where, the papers said, it was impossible to buy gasoline. But this time Jerome prevailed, and the Ford Festiva left the Berlin Ku'damm bear-less.

IT WAS AUGUST, 1991. Gypsy campfires fanned along the road that ran from Szged to Nadiac, the first small town across the Romanian border. Forty miles southeast, the war had just begun in Yugoslavia.

For the past week, Sylvie and Jerome had been zigzagging southwards from Berlin through Eastern Europe. Jerome understood this trip would be his final chance to experience the Europe that he knew.

When the Berlin Wall fell in 1989, all his friends who held opinions about these things had said it was the ending of an era.

Because after the Berlin Wall came down, there was a miner's strike in Warsaw. The Communist Party was disbanded, and Lech Walesa became the president of Poland. Vaclev Havel led Prague's Velvet Revolution, and then Czechoslovakia split in two. When Tito died, Milosevic succeeded him, and now it seemed as if there might no longer be a Yugoslavia. Romania, the Soviet Bloc's last domino, fell in 1989. By 1991, only Mikhail Gorbachev hung on to keep communism alive within the Soviet Union.

Jerome and all his friends believed that history would soon be disappearing. ("History" was defined by them as the continuity they knew.) Jerome had only a passing interest in Romanian orphans, but he was glad to have the chance to witness, one last time, the European landmarks that he knew. Their reality could not withstand the rising flood of Body Shops and Bennetons.

There was a former-Czech hotel Jerome and Sylvie liked a lot outside of Bratislava. Built for attendees of conferences on Communist Modernization, ideology and People's Art, it was still ten bucks a night. In place of widescreen cable, the rooms had desks and reading lamps. Homemade tartan curtains framed the windows; above the desk there was a woodcut *in the manner of Georg Grosz*. The room also had two low-slung single beds, as narrow as a ship's berth, that offered them a true vacation from the nagging difficulty of sex. Sex had followed them throughout the former Soviet empire like a thunderhead, threatening to explode into a declaration that, in a certain sense, *they couldn't stand each other*, and so instead they marveled at the Spartan graciousness of Soviet décor. These rooms posited the worker as an active thinking subject, ventured Sylvie.

Thousands of Croat refugees were piled up at the Hungarian-Croatian border. Jerome would have liked to take a day trip down to Bosnia, just 40 miles away, where there would almost certainly be fighting. To his great disappointment, both sides had closed their borders. The Yugoslavian Army had just attacked the newly-independent Bosnia to prevent Muslims there from interning half a million Serbs, or so they said, and 10,000 people had already been killed. Jerome longed to see some action, find out for himself what was really happening.

Southwest Romania bordered on a section of the former Yugoslavia, but curiously, there were no attempted movements among refugees across that border. Perhaps the Slavs preferred remaining in a war-zone to entering Romania? Jerome and Sylvie only thought about that later. Instead, they marveled at the ancient gypsies camped in Calistoga wagons all along the Szged road.

"Look, Jerome," squealed Sylvie, pointing out the window, "real gypsies!" She begged Jerome to stop. There was still another 40 miles before they reached Romania, but for the last two hours, Lily had been humping her right leg in the cramped front seat and it was not a dry hump.

Sylvie's views on interspecies sex were mixed. Allowing their little dog to hump her leg was probably perverse, but still, she wanted to be a conduit for canine happiness. When she'd adopted Lily at the city pound six years ago, the dog was nearly blind and starving. She'd obviously suffered terrible ordeals, and Sylvie wanted to believe that misery could simply be replaced with happiness. Time was a straight line, stretching out before you. If you could create a golden kind of time and lay it right beside the other time, the time of horror, Bad History could just recede into the distance without ever having to be resolved. This theory had worked well enough with Lily. Sylvie couldn't understand why it wasn't working with Jerome.

Jerome grunted as he parked the Ford Festiva. Gypsy horses grazed beneath a clump of alder trees set back from the road. Outside the car, there was only heat and distance. The gypsies and their caravans did not belong to any country. Before the War, their mountain village had been Romanian but they became Hungarian when the border was redrawn. Or was it the other way around? And did the gypsies even know the difference?

Each week, the gypsy men traveled to the market in Szged. Coming down the mountain, they bore a heavy load of chalky powder—a kind of pigment ground with ox-pulled mortars in a rough stone quarry. The journey took three days. In Szged, they sold the powder to the paint factory, spent the money at the market, then traveled three days back to fill their wagons up again.

For the gypsies, travel is a means of standing still. For Sylvie, travel is a way of moving forward into an imaginary world. The future is a promise that's been deferred so long you've nearly given up, but it can be suddenly fulfilled. The turquoise Rheingold sign above the bar can turn into a sky above Brant Lake, providing you wait long enough. But how to fill the years spent waiting? All the saddest songs, she thinks, have happiness inside them.

Jerome only wants to travel backward. For him, everything that counts is rooted in the past. The gypsy caravans remind him of the Turkish steppes he'd lived on during his early 20s. At that time the Algerian War was raging and he didn't want to fight in the French Army. To avoid the draft, he'd taken a job teaching at a remote outpost Turkish-French lycée. Jerome identified completely with the Algerians as quarry. Like them, he loathed the French. As a Jew, he'd undergone a kind of psychic torture at Sorbonne academic parties. During his student days in the decade following the War, he quickly learned that if he announced his Jewishness he'd be ridiculed for 'flaunting' it. But if he concealed it, he ran the risk of being called a 'sneak' when his French hosts cracked a Jewish joke or two.

Since that time, he's trained himself to scrutinize the names of everyone he meets in search of hidden Jewish origins. He studies names like others study palindromes. He sees the Goldfields and Lavines as the Goldbergs and Levines they really are. Do they see him? To Jerome, all Jews are friends. The French— as well as all the Poles, the Austrians, Ukrainians, the Italians, the Greeks, the Lithuanians, Czechs, Hungarians, Romanians, and of course the Germans—are enemies. And the Swiss are not as innocent as they seem.

Sylvie's so excited by the gypsy caravans she forgets about the baby. All her life she's longed to travel. Jerome flags down a gypsy wagon and she holds onto his sleeve. The gypsy driver doesn't speak any of Jerome's seven languages, but when Jerome opens up a pack of Kents and takes the lens cap off his camera, he's more than happy to oblige. Jerome gets busy snapping photos. There's one of Sylvie and the gypsy and their little dog! She's wearing the blue sleeveless linen dress and the fake Versace sunglasses. When Jerome gives the man another Kent, the gypsy drapes his arm around her. Sylvie arranges her thin lips around bad dental work, but the gypsy and her dog are beaming radiant and toothless smiles. Jerome quickly changes film to a more authentic black & white (Kertesz!), and gets a great shot of the gypsy and his horse beside the wagon.

Jerome and Sylvie like to think they're going to Romania to adopt a baby, although they have no contacts and no applications pending with any adoption agencies or lawyers. In the unlikely event they find an orphan, they have no idea what kind of forms they'll need to get the child out of Romania. They don't know what kind of documents they'll need to bring a foreign child into America. Beyond the City of Arad, they have no idea where they are going. Sylvie is 35 years old. Jerome is 53.

But after all, Jerome reasons, they've often snuck their little dog through customs in a nylon zipper bag, and at 14 pounds, the dog is somewhat larger than a baby. Beneath the jerry-cans of gas and hotel souvenirs, the empty zipper bag is folded up, expectantly.

Sylvie and Jerome don't know that foreign adoption has been outlawed in Romania since the beginning of the summer. But everybody knows Kent cigarettes are still the universal currency of Eastern Europe. So even though Jerome had nixed the bear, when they'd loaded up on Kents before leaving the Berlin Ku'damm, Sylvie took it as a sign of hope. How many cartons would it take to get a baby?

SANG-FROID. Jerome and Sylvie have become a parody of themselves, a pair of clowns. They are Bouvard & Pecuchet, Burns & Allen, Mercier & Camier. But were they always? And if not, how did they become this way?

Given the number of viable pregnancies of her own Sylvie has already terminated, her desire for a third-world infant is as arbitrary as the use of Kent cigarettes as currency. Why not Parliaments, Pall Malls or Winstons?

But always, if you look hard enough, there is a reason. "When a death occurs, there is always a reason, you just have to find the reason," Jerome declares at the end of *How To Shoot A Crime*, a movie he and Sylvie made together. It is a movie about death, Jerome's favorite subject. But it's unclear to Sylvie which death he is talking about: his father's, which occurred, to the best of Jerome's knowledge, in 1943 at Auschwitz? The recent death of a Frenchwoman known as Madame Carmen who'd hidden Jerome, Yvette, and several other Jewish children in her home throughout the German Occupation? Given Jerome's obsession, Sylvie was surprised when Jerome declared himself "too busy" to attend Carmen's funeral. (But then again, not one of Carmen's wartime 'children' managed to be there.)

The death that fascinates Jerome most is metaphorical: his own. In the movie, Jerome asked his police videographer friend, George Diaz, to videotape him lying face down on his bed, as if he were the victim of a drug lord execution. It's as if by being killed symbolically on film, Jerome can embrace the death that's been his life as long as he remembers.

If he can do this, there is a chance he can prevent it. But in order to escape completely—and here, Jerome's thinking takes on the circuitous claustrophobia of a nightmare—he has to *find the reason* for his death, but since it can't be separated from his life, the answer continues to elude him.

Jerome has always been attracted to the exotic rituals of the primitives. He spent a sabbatical year in Africa, riding camels with the Bedouins. He noticed that the tribal Bedouins were bound together by the symbolic weight they give to certain actions. The Bedouins had ten steps for making tea. They had a special means for grooming camels. These routine actions were repeated so meticulously that they became ingrained, like dances.

Like the Bedouins, Jerome enjoys many ritualistic fetishes. He steals food from buffet tables, he swipes toilet rolls and uses slugs for subway rides. He licks his plate, hordes plastic bags and swipes little plastic packs of condiments from fast-food restaurants. But since these fetishes are entirely his own, they only reinforce his image of himself and end in stasis.

Jerome's fetishes neither comfort him nor guide him. He's right in thinking that he needs to understand his death in order to escape it, but the fact that he's already dead makes understanding it impossible. *No one has ever felt like this before*. He wants so badly for his death to be completely singular.

In the video, when Jerome asks George Diaz how he shoots his crime scenes, he replies: "You've got to keep your eyes moving. So long as you keep your eyes moving, you keep the shock of it, you keep the horror, to a minimum."

And this is how Jerome sees his life: a crime scene. Like the primitive systems of exchange described by structural anthropologists, Jerome's death is a code that can't be cracked: an anthropology of unhappiness.

WHEN NICOLAE "Count Dracula" Ceausescu was ritually executed on Christmas morning with a short-range bullet to his head, Romania joined the free world of democratic nations. For the first time in thirty years, the country was accessible to foreign journalists and aid workers. Since his ascendancy in 1965, Ceausescu ruled the starving nation with an iron fist, outlawing imported food and merchandise, foreign films and rock music, contraception and abortion. Socialist Romania's reproductive policy was based on primitive arithmetic, and not on moral grounds. If every female citizen bore five children, reasoned Ceausescu, Romania's scant population would be doubled in a decade. With 60 million workers, Romania would no longer have to beg for import credits or sell its soul for foreign aid. The country would be wholly self-sufficient.

Food and fuel were scarce throughout the 1980s. Not all of Socialist Romania's gold-star moms were able to support their five state-mandated children. And so the tribe of Ceausescu's children—infants abandoned within hours of their birth to state-run orphanages—was born.

During the months that followed Romania's liberation, foreign journalists discovered 200,000 of these nearly feral children languishing in makeshift dormitories. Horrified, they discovered infants crippled from continuous confinement to barred iron cribs; children with skin covered entirely by rashes caused from wallowing for hours, even days, in their own excrement and urine. They discovered orphan-stalags built to house the "unrecoverables": children with mild deformities like club feet, crossed eyes or protruding ears. Conditions in these camps were so severe that half the children died each winter from exposure and starvation. Still, each year these dead children were replaced with new ones. AIDS was rampant because Ceausescu's Minister of Health, one Teodor Nicelescu, believed that infant malnutrition could be treated by transfusing blood. The only problem was, Romania could not afford to import western-style disposable hypodermic needles, so 3000 children were infected after 'sharing' nationally manufactured dirty needles.

When photographs of these children beamed around the world, foreigners from many walks of life mobilized to help them. Michael

Jackson toured the Turnu Rasu orphanage bearing gifts of food and clothes donated by his fan club. Ogilvy and Mather (UK) produced a series of pro-bono TV ads to raise funds for "Ceausescu's Children." The Red Cross and Doctors Without Borders set up bases near the orphanages. Ad hoc groups of German carpenters and plumbers traveled at their own expense to install running water, heat and sewer lines in the substandard filthy buildings. Everyone assumed that since the orphan problem was a consequence of Ceausescu's crazy reproductive policies, it would soon be solved.

By the year 2000, abortion and contraception had been legalized in Romania for a decade. Free market capitalism had long since replaced the dictator's isolationist brand of communism and most of 'Ceausescu's children' were adults now. But somehow, these children had replaced themselves. Food and fuel were scarce as always. Eleven years after Ceausescu's fall, there were still 200,000 children living in Romanian orphanages.

Even though Jerome had nixed the Berlin bear, Sylvie Green was not totally bereft in the stuffed animal department. There was a bear at home she loved, named Honey. Jerome had won him for her at a fair, though at the moment she could not remember in which box of which garage the bear was stored in. Honey was a plush toy of the $2.99 variety. He was a 10-inch bear, with Ethiopian-brown glossy drops of plastic for his eyes.

The way that Honey entered Sylvie's life was a kind of miracle, the way that something happens when you've given up all hope. With a shiny gold acrylic ribbon tied into a bow around his neck, Honey was a pure sentiment: a not-quite living sign that Jerome, sometimes, could be aware of the need to smooth symbolic balms of happiness over his and Sylvie's bottomless despair. With his rough acrylic fur and stitched-on grin, Honey Bear was such a symbol.

IT WOULD HAVE BEEN an evening during one of the torpid migratory years of Jerome and Sylvie's marriage. It would have been the weekend after Labor Day, when all the New York artists are arriving back in town from Provincetown, the Catskills or the Hamptons. The air's already cooling off, and everyone is looking forward to the new fall season. Such weekends were the time when Jerome and Sylvie traditionally packed and moved their things between their upstate rental house and the East Hampton rental house they spent their winters in. Driving back along the LIE through Nassau County, they've been on the highway for six hours with just another two to go. Throughout the trip, Jerome would have been seething in a vague unspeakable resentment. Another summer gone, and he had nothing but a folder full of notes to show towards the progress of his book, now titled *Modernism and the Holocaust*.

They'd been fighting since they missed the turn-off from the Major Deegan Thruway two hours ago. Another fight about his daughter Laura—it was white noise to Jerome. Laura was coming out next weekend for a visit, and when he'd made the plan with Ginny she'd remarked *Does Sylvie have to be there?* In Ginny's mind apparently the answer should be *No*. Jerome had no opinions on this subject, but when she'd put Laura on the phone and Laura sobbed, *Why can't I spend some time with you alone*, Jerome saw no good reason why his wife couldn't just unpack her bags and catch the Jitney back to New York City. Sylvie, for her part, saw this as another crisis in co-parenting. All the airplane magazines had articles about *blended families*. Besides, her East Village place was rented, did Jerome expect that she would *leave her own home* and crash out on the floor at one of her girlfriend's studio apartments?

Sylvie wept. Her weeping brought her to a deeper and more ancient sadness until she was completely inconsolable. She scratched the soft skin of her forearm, she saw no way outside of the car. Why couldn't Laura accept her as a part of Jerome's family? Why didn't he insist? All summer she'd been so absorbed in Jerome's anguish with his book she'd hardly registered the fact September was approaching. Her old East Village friends were arranging dance recitals, readings, shows, but she had nothing going on, no screenings of her films, no grants, no teaching jobs or residencies. She was marooned in this strange life that she'd created with Jerome, from which she could be exiled upon Ginny's every passing whim.

At first, she tried to reason with Jerome. Then she mocked him for his weakness. Jerome maintained his discipline. He didn't hear her. He simply could not keep up with the demands of these three women.

"Why do Ginny and your daughter hate me?" Sylvie asked. She asked this several times. Jerome looked for a diplomatic way to broach this. "Well cherie, Ginny thinks you're not my type." Sylvie knew the rest, and it was dreadful. Back in the downtown club days, Ginny had been friends with everyone that Sylvie'd wanted to be friends with. Ginny had done coke in bathrooms with a crowd of people who strategically ignored and despised Sylvie. "Ginny thinks I ought to be with someone who is ummm, more conventionally pretty."

This was the worst! Now everything was wrong. Ginny was rich and she was poor, and she'd never be as social or as beautiful as Ginny. She was awkward, shy, a dork. Her own *husband* thought so! Emotion was the only thing that gave a contour to her days, and emotion was completely formless.

It would have been a cool September dusk as they were driving eastbound into Suffolk County. They would both be sitting silent for a while, when Sylvie would see the colored floodlights of a County Harvest Fair beckoning beyond the highway.

Jerome detested mob events, especially ones that harked back to a false Americana. Still, he would have seen this as a chance to cheer her up. He would have gotten off the highway and paid the parking lot attendant $5 without wincing. Then he'd take her by the hand and walk her through the fair gates, past the Ferris Wheels and bumper cars and popcorn stands. Suddenly, everything would have been alright, now. She and Jerome were entering another world, and it was precisely in these other worlds that they could be together. Cheering up, she'd point out a cotton-candy vendor. She loved the way pink strands of cotton-candy sugar melted on her tongue, and Jerome would take out another bill and buy one.

Colored lights and gunning motors in the distance made Sylvie think their misery might simply disappear amongst the rides and brawny men in fishnet t-shirts, fat women tottering on stilettos. Music pounded all around them from the portable loud speakers, and Jerome would put his arm around her haltingly and he'd whisper in her ear, *One of these days you're gonna miss me, Honey.*

This anthem was his favorite in their current repertoire of stock routines. The song's sentimental lyrics ricocheted around the novel *Nausea*, Jean-Paul Sartre's classic ur-text of depression. Jerome and Sylvie had both memorized whole parts of *Nausea* at age 13: he in a Paris café, five years before her birth, in the 1950s. She'd read the novel later, in the Connecticut factory town she was imprisoned in before her family immigrated to New Zealand. This coincidence was further proof that despite their different lives and ages, she and Jerome were actually *the same person*.

The Sartre routine gave Sylvie Green a triple rush of happiness and pleasure. She loved to coax Jerome into shedding his professional, professorial detachment and become, like her, an amateur! A fan! Someone who was just dumb and sentimental. And then again, the image of the young Jerome reading *Nausea* at the Deux Mag-gots Café (in the presence, maybe, of the real Jean-Paul Sartre, Simone de Beauvoir) reminded her how far she'd really traveled since her Bridgeport days, into some remote proximity with her heroes. And then there was the joy of finding that her childhood loneliness could be shared with him two decades later.

Sylvie would have spotted Honey on the middle shelf of an arcade as they walked past the beanbag toss and rifle ranges. While Honey sat beneath the top-shelf Panda bears and dinosaurs, he was definitely *above* the packs of playing cards and key rings. Honey stood right out with his seductive mix of being something both desirable and attainable.

"I want the bear!" Sylvie would have pleaded, and Jerome would have agreed to take his chances at this money-wasting game, which consisted of discharging artificial bullets into moving metal duck-like targets. He would give the carnie guy two bucks, shoot six rounds, and miss. Sylvie's spirits would have been com-pletely crushed when the attendant handed her a key ring. Was this not emblematic of her entire life? "Go back to the car," Jerome would have commanded gruffly. "Take care of the dog. I'll meet you there." This would have been so unlike Jerome: confi-dent, mysterious, decisive. Ten minutes later he would come out to the parking lot, holding Honey. Sylvie would never know if Jerome had won the bear, or slipped the guy a twenty, but either way it didn't matter.

Honey wore a baby-t that ended halfway up his midriff. He was a bargain bear. Unlike the more expensive Swiss and German bears, whose bodies were as smooth and pliant as the flesh of chil-dren, Honey's small body was extremely stiff and rigid. Still, his fur was nappy smooth: a gorgeous amber honey-mustard color. No attempts were made to render him with any mammal-authenticity. His baby-t only served to emphasize his total lack of bearness.

In compensation, Honey's two front paws clasped a brown felt pot embroidered with the word *Honey*. He had a flattened nose, a tiny smile, pink stitches parted in adorable idiocy. His sentimentality was a perfect match for Sylvie's.

Sylvie knew her fate would be linked forever to Jerome's unhappiness, and so she longed to simply make it disappear. If she could make it go away through will, or empathy—some act of magical transference. But to think that was as grandiose and futile as believing she could travel back in time and stop the Nazi troops from marching into Austria or invading Paris. There were women, then, who'd tried to do this—women who'd thrown themselves from windows when the French police arrived, so they would not betray their Resistance comrades under torture. Now no one remembered. People walked past these places every day. There were no plaques or markers.

The grief of the War will always hang over me, she thought, and Jerome, and Laura, and maybe even Ginny. The War affects everyone it touches. Long after the events themselves, the effects will linger. And these effects live on by breeding other causes.

Photo Gallery — Arad 1991

Spic 'n Span—Sylvie Green, 4x6 color snapshot

With washed-out hues, this tourist snap depicts a storefront typical of Romanian commerce during the post-Ceausescu era. The "storefront" seems to be a gated bedroom window on the ground floor of a pre-war residential building. By building out the interior windowsill and draping it with a bedsheet, the storekeeper has created a vitrine displaying articles for sale. These articles consist exclusively of cleaning implements and products.

More Cornell box than Brillo box, the work achieves a haunting power through its recontextualization of generic metal dustpans, shoe polishes and scrub brushes as if these objects had a value.

A single plastic bottle of green dishwashing detergent stands alone on the top shelf, flanked by a box of Dacia laundry powder, a box of Rex-brand soap pads and a single roll of toilet paper. (NB: The brand names "Dacia" and "Rex" evoke the tribal names of Romania's First People, who, according to Romanian popular legend, were descended from a conquering band of rogue soldiers who colonized the region during the declining years of the Roman Empire.) These consumables are flanked by a wallpaper brush, a plastic whisk-broom and two wire scrub-brushes, hanging from the shelf on cup hooks.

The bottom shelf presents a universe of brushes. These brushes mostly come in pairs: evocative, perhaps of Judeao-Christianity's creation myth, in which *pairs* of animals were rounded up before of the Flood, by Noah. There are bottle brushes, replacement broomheads, paint brushes, shoe brushes. A lone hairbrush stands upright against the sill, and in its shadow three nail-brushes rest like Jason's golden eggs atop of a nest of plastic pot-scrub brushes.

A single toilet brush festooned with pale blue ribbon hangs above it all, attached by hook and string to the vitrine's plywood faux-ceiling. Apparently curled once too many times, the ribbon dangles limply.

CHAPTER 3: WELTSCHMERZ

WELTSCHMERZ

May 30, 1991: US Department of State Advisory Notice 51341

The US Department of State advises US citizens to exercise extreme caution when traveling in Romania. American visitors may encounter large street demonstrations in urban areas which could involve significant unrest. They should avoid areas where such demonstrations are in progress, and in particular, refrain from attempts to photograph demonstrations.

Americans contemplating adopting a child in Romania should be aware that the Romanian government has announced that all adoption proceedings will be suspended as of June 1, 1991. Prospective parents are urged to defer travel to Romania. If already there, Americans should contact the US embassy in Bucharest immediately.

NADIAC—AUGUST, 1991: Jerome and Sylvie pulled up at the end of a short line of cars waiting to drive from Hungary across the Romanian border. They took this as a happy sign. No problem, now, to drive on to Arad and find a cheap hotel that evening. There was a longer and more guarded line trying to leave Romania into Hungary. Guards waved them into a special line for foreigners. Sylvie felt a little thrill when she saw how many packs of Kents were being passed to border guards from the domestic line. First the gypsies, now the Kents. They'd reached the entrance to the end of civilization as she knew it. They'd get up early, and their search for a Romanian orphan would begin.

After buying entrance visas at some outrageous price, they were directed to a line where soldiers searched the car for contraband. The only thing they really had to hide was the empty nylon zipper bag. Coyly, Sylvie offered three Kent cigarettes to a soldier, but he shrugged and simply waved them in.

The first thing they noticed in the Romanian border town of Nadiac were the money-changers, waving wads of worthless, black market currency in full view of the soldiers. One dollar bought two hundred Romanian lei. Eagerly, Jerome bartered the best change but no one here spoke French or English and he soon gave up, bewildered.

Beside the road, a clutch of dirty geese and chickens pecked the dust surrounded by the diesel fumes of ancient trucks.

The Hungarian town of Mako, just two hundred yards away, had already turned into a distant memory. Mako was a pretty town, with bright and tidy cottages adorned with pink geraniums in flower boxes. Its chickens were a smug, contented bunch, foraging green lawns behind the picket fences of their yards. Here, the chickens seemed half-dead, and there were no geraniums, no snug cottages: just a dusty road, lined by half-built concrete towers. Men and women hung around outside these buildings, as if they couldn't bear to do anything but sleep in their apartments. In Mako, old peasant couples drove brightly-painted horse carts on the tree-lined streets. But in Nadiac, the carts were drawn by mules and there was nothing quaint about them. Instead, they seemed inevitable: a throwback to another century. Grim, scythe-wielding peasants stood at the back of open wagons, returning from their Sunday labor.

Just twenty miles outside the City of Arad, Jerome and Sylvie sensed a creepy atmosphere of fear unlike anything they'd known. "I shall never forget the utter hopelessness that overtook me," wrote the English traveler William Kingston, "when I realized how unsuited I was to a country whose manners, costumes and customs ranged downwards from the 14th century to 200 BC..." (*Romanian Rambles*, 1888)

Jerome is an experienced traveler. He's traveled throughout Africa, around the Ecuadorian highlands, he's met members of the Shining Path while traveling in Peru. Still, he knows little about the backward Eastern European countries like Albania, Bulgaria, Romania. Drawn to places in the world where time stands still, Jerome and Sylvie see their travel to Romania as an intellectual adventure. There is a growing sense that certain nations will be exiled from the changing New World Order. They want to know what this particular kind of dereliction looks like, to experience their own personal dereliction writ large across a culture. Will their special knowledge of unhappiness enable them to do some good?

Three months after Jerome and Sylvie leave Romania, the Romanian correspondent for the *LA Times* reports:

In a 108-year-old building lacking hot water, flush toilets and a telephone, 234 young girls with shorn heads and ragged clothing spend their days embroidering napkins to sell to tourists. Food allowances have been doubled since the revolution, but store shelves in impoverished Romania are as empty for orphans as for everyone else, so the children still subsist on bread and fatty sausage. They spend aimless hours in the fenced dirt yard, or roaming the peeling corridors of a dormitory that reeks of sewage and mold. Most are clad in slippers and thin sweaters, although piles of warm winter clothing arrived weeks ago from Austria. The donations remain unsorted for lack of matron's interest, time, or both.

"It's very difficult to get people who are morally suited to this line of work," said orphanage director Dorel Ritivoi, noting his own salary of 2,600 lei, or $74 per month. Much of the aid this year was stolen by desperate villagers wanting shoes and coats for their own children. In the dormitory, a bank of shiny new sinks stands in the center of a mildewed bathroom. Two West German handymen with the Roman Catholic Church's Caritas Aid Society began work on the plumbing in early fall, but left hurriedly when one fell ill. The children still wash in ice-cold water. "There is no one here to finish the job," explained Ritivoi.

Sylvie holds the little dog up to the window to observe conditions in the homeland of her future sibling. If Lily understands the gravity of the Romanian situation, perhaps she'll be less jealous of the baby? Coming from the Dog Pound, perhaps she'll be empathic with the orphan?

Sylvie and Jerome don't know where they'll stay or who to talk to. They haven't read the US State Department's Advisory Notice. They don't even know who is president of Romania. They are completely unaware that there is an English couple, awaiting trial for "baby theft" in prison in this very town, after trying to cross the border into Hungary with a helpless orphan.

But even if they knew these things, mere facts would not affect them.

YEARS LATER, after Sylvie left Jerome, she finds a photo of them rolling on the grass beside a pond. They're in the Poconos for a weekend, so it must be 1986 or so, before they bought the houses. Jerome is stretching out his arm to take the photo. His aim is slightly off, and so they're barely in the frame—just two faces pressed together in the bottom right hand of the picture. The meadow grass around them's dying out—it must be early in November, when everything is tawny blue and golden. Their eyes are closed. Sylvie's face is flushed against the cold. But smiling... you can tell they're kissing even though the photo ends around the middle of their noses.

Sylvie wears a thrift store jacket with a black fur collar. Her dark brown hair is thickening like a horse's for the winter. Jerome's hair has started growing back—he no longer shaves his head, and now his hair is long and curly. His eyes are closed, like Sylvie's—eyelids heavy. The sky behind a hill is that vapory bird's egg blue that happens sometimes in the autumn when cold air suddenly gets warmer. The photo is a kind of rapture: two heads pressed together like a heart, as close as they will go. It was the time when she still trusted him.

Eighteen months before Jerome took this picture, Sylvie had her first abortion. The first one didn't really count. She and Jerome had just been going out for several weeks, if you could call it that—having lunchtime sex one afternoon a week at his apartment. But even though the pregnancy was technically her fault and they were not officially 'involved,' Jerome turned out to be a gentleman. He took her to the clinic, paid for the abortion, and didn't try and talk her out of paying extra for the general anesthesia. Jerome was cool, and she was smart enough to not freak out—although, she noted, the experience of being pregnant with him was not entirely unpleasant. When their lunch-time dates resumed, they both implicitly agreed to act as if the pregnancy had never happened.

At that time, Jerome was living in a room carved out of his friend Martin's loft near the South Street Seaport. His room's a sheet-rocked rectangle lined with books: a platform futon on the floor, an Indian curtain in the doorway. The only permanent feature is an enormous worktable pushed up against a bare brick wall. On this wall, Jerome displays the artifacts that he's collected from his trips to Africa and Turkey. There is a buffalo-hide water bag, necklaces of amber beads, a money bag adorned with feathers and a bull-whip.

Three framed photos on the desk provide Jerome with continuity. There is a snapshot of his mother standing outside their apartment during the first weeks of the German Occupation. There is one of Ginny's headshots from her modeling career, and finally a color snapshot of Jerome at 35, naked above the waist and brandishing the newborn Laura. Jerome's obligations to these women guide his actions and their photos sound a warning to his many female guests: *Do not expect anything beyond what happens in this room.* The windowless north wall of Jerome's room is lined entirely with books on death: *Death: A Social History*, *Death on the Installment Plan*, *The American Way of Death*, *Death-Rites of the Pygmies*, *Death Within the Camps*. He also has a large collection of textbooks on mortuary science. Underneath the platform bed, he's stashed a cardboard box of gay male S/m zines.

Except for all these books and papers, Jerome's room could easily be dismantled and evacuated within an hour.

Sylvie's visits to this room are scary, challenging and unsettling. They fuck, and then they talk. Their sex is totally disconnected. It's like a therapy appointment. She never knows for sure if Jerome actually likes her? Sometimes, he lets her hang around and watch him underline whole passages of books after they've put their clothes on. He uses color-coded magic markers and a ruler to be sure his lines are straight. These passages are what he'll talk about in class tomorrow.

At these times she's less afraid of him, because Jerome seems like a schoolboy with a book-bag. His fastidiousness comes as a surprise because she'd always seen him as a person constantly in motion. Jerome was as thin as a single brush-stroke in a Dadaist collage, rushing lines bisecting out and overlapping back onto each other.

A year before she met Jerome, Sylvie had been hospitalized at Bellevue for an unknown catastrophic ailment. Because she had no medical insurance, they put her on the Public Welfare ward. Rats scuttled underneath the radiators of the twelve-bed dormitory. All around her, women moaned and screamed throughout the night, and Sylvie watched her blood flow upwards through the IV tube because there were no nurses on the ward to change it. It was curious, she thought, a kind of 18th century bedlam hell, in the middle of the world's greatest and most powerful financial city. The windows of the Public Ward looked out above the highway spanning the East River. Everything outside was speed and light, but inside, shit and blood. At night, she played a tape of Alban Berg, his jagged range of screech composed symphonically, and she felt like she was understanding something then, about the century. When she met Jerome, she knew he understood it, too.

Sylvie sees Jerome as someone who has traveled monumental distances. Her lunch-time dates with him are the first sex she's had with someone she imagines as a "man." She feels this thing about him, and the stories that he tells about his life confirm it. That he is someone who has consciously been drawn through larger currents. She sees him moving from the Polish slums of Paris to being student president of the Sorbonne. She sees him traveling the Turkish steppes, and then progressing largely through chance within the academic hierarchy of American universities. Married to a shy woman who he'd worked with in the French Communist Party, he was studying French medieval texts as he moved numbly from Fairfield, Iowa, to Swarthmore College, to Ohio, and finally to Columbia University.

A friend of some of France's boldest thinkers, Jerome's intellectual ambitions were enormous, but he had no ambition of his own.

Sylvie feels she's also traveled monumental distances. As a child in Bridgeport, very little was expected of her but when her family moved to Wellington, New Zealand, she found it possible to just explode. Precociously, she'd been a critic and a journalist but when she moved back to New York City at age 21 she was suddenly a lost and gauche New Zealander.

Since that time, she's known a lot of people who just don't care, and a lot of other people driven only by ambition. She's never yet met anybody like Jerome. Someone pursuing their own interests, oblivious to questions of career. Propelled by chance and circumstance, Jerome still manages to leave traces everywhere he goes.

Before they'd met, she'd been a fan of Jerome's cultural events and publications. Secretly, she has the arrogance to think that she can do this, too: construct a life in which she issues intermittent bulletins on her experience, and find enough people interested to matter. She has no taste for building up an art career. From what she's seen of this, it's way beneath her. Auditioning for an experimental theater play, the director asks if she has any special skills? *I walk and think and talk*, Sylvie replies, relishing her own Zen wit, but still she's devastated when she doesn't get the role.

Among the Ivy-educated trustfundarians of New York's underground, Sylvie's often been dismissed as scatterbrained and stupid, but she feels much more intelligent since she met Jerome. She believes that he and he alone can recognize her certain—talent—for abstraction. She thinks his recognition is enough to draw it out and make it true.

Sometimes Sylvie sneaks a look at the S/m zines when Jerome is in the kitchen. She wonders if the sex they have could accurately be called S/m? She's a little bit ashamed by how much all this absorbs and then derails her. She's had rough sex before with guys who didn't like her. Guys who thought that fucking was enough to take her energy away and make her powerless. In the world she moved in, sex was what you did. What these partners wanted from her was transparent, so it was hurtful sometimes, but not troubling.

But when Jerome touches her, he becomes impossible to locate. His absence turns her on: it's like he is an instrument of something far outside himself. When he makes her come, all this fucked-up gender stuff dissolves and she feels her body spinning backwards towards itself at different ages, 14, 11, once, she went back as far as 5. But this is something that they never speak of. When it's over, Jerome becomes as talky-chummy as an older cousin. They talk about poetics, politics, Sylvie's plays and films, his projects.

Within the small world they move in, Jerome is well-known as a sexual player. He cultivates a tough, mean leather look with his shaved head and motorcycle jacket. He has many other girlfriends, and meeting him makes Sylvie question everything she wants and needs. Does sex have to be exclusive? Does it even have to be part of a relationship? Sitting on the bed, she is acutely conscious of all the other women who have been there, who will soon be coming back. She wonders how they handle it… is sex with him the way it is for her, a psychotropic drug? And yet she knows that Mean Jerome is not the true Jerome—she sees him as he might have been at age 19, shy and reading poetry.

Eighteen months after Sylvie's first abortion, Jerome's stopped seeing all his other girlfriends. He's let his hair grow back. The biker jacket's been replaced with a heavy wool knit sweater. When Martin finally gets married and wants the loft back for himself, Jerome resignedly moves in with Sylvie. Sylvie rightly sees her conquest of

Jerome as her greatest triumph, but through his transformation, she's changed too: her tough androgynous persona has just collapsed into a state of happy openness. Having lived for years off topless dancing, she's always been quite cynical about the signs of female heterosexuality, but with Jerome she feels protected, small. Everything is a little bit erotic, and she feels like a contented animal.

So when Sylvie became pregnant for the second time that very afternoon—the afternoon Jerome took the photo of them in the Poconos—she knew it was the time, for her, that really counted. They'd already found the Thurman house and were waiting on their loan approval. In six weeks they'd move into the house, and their baby could be born there.

Two days after they took the photo at the reservoir, while she and Jerome are driving back to New York, Sylvie senses she is pregnant. The consciousness of this spreads across her body like a flush and rests implacably within her heart. For the first two weeks, Jerome's not overly concerned. After all, he knows she has a wild imagination. But when she comes back from the clinic with a positive test result, he is indignant. "But I already *have* a child!" Jerome protests. Surely men like him are only required to have one?

Because having *one* has forced him to participate, however superficially, in the toxic triviality of life in the United States: the clothes, the toys, the friends, the stupid TV programs. And this compounded, in his case, by the accoutrements of affluence Ginny must insist on. The camps, the therapists, the parent-teacher meetings at the outrageously expensive private school, where his daughter's academic progress counts for less than her low, they told him, social standing in her "peer group." Laura cried and cried the day she learned that he was moving in with Sylvie. When he finally calmed her down, she told him, "Daddy, I will kill myself if you have another child," with the sang-froid of a 12-year-old. But who's to say she wouldn't? And then what would he do? It's already bad enough that Laura doesn't live with him, but Ginny.

Jerome never knows when he'll see his daughter. He has no visitation rights. Since he and Ginny never married, they'd never been divorced, and he didn't have the heart to see a lawyer. When Ginny has a boyfriend he gets to 'baby-sit' his daughter for entire weeks, but presently his only scheduled contact is to walk her to the school-bus several times a week. To the extent Jerome knows anything about his daughter, he knows that she's unhappy, and her unhappiness is probably his fault. But could things be any different? He pities Ginny's idleness. Raising Laura is the only thing that gets her out of bed, her only work.

As Laura enters puberty, each day she becomes more like her mother. Ginny teaches her to be a woman by seeing him as the enemy. They sit together on the bed teasing him about his hair, his clothes, his work, until he slinks away, defeated by their gales of girlish laughter. The only time he feels a sense of kinship with his daughter is when she totally breaks down, becomes a mirror of his anguish, and while he knows that this is hopeless and perhaps despicable, he cannot resist.

Pregnancy, Jerome knows well, is like anthrax: the secret weapon at the bottom of the arsenal of every female terrorist. He never would have married his Communist Party comrade if she hadn't feigned a pregnancy. He was 23 years old. By the time the pregnancy was deemed hysterical, he and Bebe were already married and it took him ten years to escape from that. Ginny's attack on him has turned out nearly fatal.

So when Sylvie tells him her exciting news, Jerome asks: "How fast can you get rid of it?" She's deeply shocked. (There's not a maternal bone in Sylvie's body; he knows she must be faking this Madonna shit for some effect.) "It's not an It, Jerome. It is our baby." "Ahhh, sweetie," Jerome laughs. "I thought you were a feminist."

For weeks, her breasts, which in the past she'd mostly managed to ignore, are swollen, highly sensitive. She feels a swirling kind of gravity, as if her cells are thickening to protect the baby. Since none of Sylvie's East Village artist friends have ever wanted houses, husbands, babies, Jerome's the only person she can think to share her feeling with. She talks about the soft spot on the baby's head, her little cheeks, the way she looks when she is smiling. Jerome chides her for extracting emotional blackmail. Sometimes after reciting dreams of mobiles, wooly sheepskin mats and baby sweaters, she stops short and looks him in the eye: "Jerome, don't you *want* to have a child with me?" And this reminds him of one of his favorite lines from Shakespeare: "No, but *making one is such great sport!*" King Lear shivering on the heath, betrayed... his thoughts exactly.

Forced to endure another several weeks of Sylvie's pleading, Jerome searches for another channel. "Do you really think you have accomplished enough to have a child?" She sobs. *What is it* about her life that forces her to become an art star in order to do what every other Bridgeport girl could do at age 16: just breed? Already she's written and produced three plays and two experimental movies. She teaches English Comp at a community college. She's gotten several artist grants and residencies. Just *how much* accomplishment would be enough? Does she have to get a MacArthur fellowship? A Guggenheim? Or just an NEA?

"Look at Kathy, Lizzie, Betty, Pat," Jerome insists. "They have international careers, and you don't see them getting pregnant."

"Do not expect any help from us if you get pregnant," her parents warned when she left home at age 16. Why did the people closest to her find the thought of Sylvie having children so impossibly grotesque? The baby, Sylvie realizes, is a symbol for what deep down she's always known. Her life will never have a value of its own, apart from her achievements.

For the next few weeks, Sylvie lies beside Jerome in bed imagining their baby. The baby is the first thing she's ever had that was completely hers. The baby is her secret. She likes picturing its tiny fingers, toes. It's like the room's a boat, and she is traveling somewhere. "Jerome," she reaches for his arm and whispers, "I bet the baby's gonna have your eyes." Like his mother, Jerome has the ice-blue eyes of an Alaskan husky. They're very proud of those blue eyes in Jerome's family. Blue eyes were what got his mother through the War, sauntering past the Nazi guards on Blvd. Montparnasse to barter rations. He remains unmoved.

Beyond these efforts, Sylvie remains clueless about how she might seduce him. She'd always been an independent girl, but now she's not so sure. Because while Jerome finds Sylvie interesting, he has a reservoir of love for Ginny. There's very little *interesting* about Ginny. Whenever Jerome thinks of her, his eyes mist up with pity. Idle, aimless, Ginny is the tragic heiress. "She is so helpless," Jerome sighs.

Sylvie wonders if her independence really serves her well. Ginny, in her helplessness, is completely lovable and she is not. When Jerome speaks to her about their baby, his voice gets very hard. "I am responsible for Laura. If you refuse to terminate this pregnancy, do not expect my help or my support."

So really, what to do? Twice a month she gets sad letters from her parents in New Zealand. Her father's unemployment benefits are running out, they're two months behind on payments on their ten-year-old used car. At 31 she has no education, contacts, special skills that will enable her to do anything but what she does: scrape by. She could always go to law school—but how would she find the money? She doesn't even have an undergraduate degree. Who would watch the baby while she went to class? Does she really want to be a lawyer?

After seven weeks of wallowing in these thoughts, Sylvie has a first trimester abortion. Right through the night before, she refuses alcohol and cigarettes with the involuted smile of an ascetic because, she says, "I'm pregnant."

No one at the clinic asks her if she wants to change her mind. Her eyes are teary as the nurse-anesthetist puts the needle in her arm. Like a survivor, Sylvie remains engrossed in holding the operating system of her mind together. She will refuse all loss of consciousness or control. She has delivered herself to this and vows to stay awake to better contemplate her shame, but the anesthetic does its work and she's out before the count of five.

Awake in the recovery room, she immediately knows her body's different. Her breasts, she thinks, have already reverted to their normal non-existent size. She feels herself again as who she was before the pregnancy: empty, raw and jagged. She thinks: *This loss is permanent.* Someone offers her a cup of tea, a biscuit. She holds the cotton blanket in her fists and cries.

Twenty minutes later, Sylvie is officially recovered. Jerome walks her from the clinic to the elevator down the hall. It's lunch hour, and knots of female workers crowd the elevator in their cheap Joyce Leslie power-suits and nylons. All these women, Sylvie thinks, have children.

When they leave the building Jerome gives Sylvie money for a cab. He has a class to teach, it's Thursday afternoon. Ginny has a date tonight, so after school he'll go to her apartment. Laura can't be left alone and Ginny probably won't come home. With luck, he'll get to spend the whole night with his daughter.

BUT WHEN Jerome and Sylvie cross the border into Nadiac, Romania, their expectations of adventure tourism are immediately derailed. The massive clumps of individuals idling along the road look like escapees from a 19th century debtor's prison or Corot's asylum. Soldiers, starving oxen, worker-convoys. They stop to ask directions at a bar. In the courtyard, 30 bedraggled men sit on folding chairs watching a Bulgarian soccer match on black and white TV. Romania was once the "Paris of the East" but here no one speaks anything except Romanian, a language that apparently consists of joining Turkish suffixes to ancient Latin roots.

In Arad, one grand boulevard traverses the entire city. A tram track, surrounded by a median of uncut grass, divides the boulevard in two. Inspired by the Belle Epoque, Arad's buildings were once stolidly ornate but now, in 1991, their cornices have fallen off, their balustrades are worn away. Made of grimy soot-stained stone, the buildings clearly haven't been maintained for a least a half a century. It's as if the entire city went to sleep a hundred years ago, but slumber hasn't stopped a century of aging. Desperate now to find a normal place to stay, Jerome stops the car and asks the hobbled passersby, in perfect French, *Madame, Monsieur, can you recommend a nice hotel?* The men and women gape. They haven't understood a word. They aren't giving anything away.

Ten years later, the Romanian correspondent for the *New York Times* will write:

ROMANIANS DEMAND A BETTER LIFE

Bucharest, Romania—About 10,000 workers marched through this capital city Thursday to protest poverty, low wages and corruption in national politics. Some of the demonstrators claimed that times were better under communism.

The protesters stopped in front of the government headquarters in downtown Bucharest to call for the government to resign.

They chanted, "Thieves, Down with Corruption," and "Ceausescu, Where Are You?" in reference to the communist dictator Nicolae Ceausescu, who was overthrown and executed in 1989.

The government raised utility prices last month as part of a plan to bring them up to international levels. Monthly utilities now can cost up to $50 a month, a drain on budgets in a country where the average monthly salary is about $100.

Since the 1997–2000 recession, about 35% of the population lives just below the poverty line, defined as a monthly wage of $40.

It could be that the situation in Romania is a correlative of Jerome's personal unhappiness, writ larger than he'd ever dreamed. An *entire nation* is selected—not by Nazis, but by global economic flows—to rot in ignorance and poverty. While some East European countries join the international economy, others like Romania are marked. A downward spiral starts, in which entropy is reached and then exceeds itself, becoming negative. There is nowhere things can go from here but further down.

But that first evening in Arad, Sylvie isn't thinking much about the long-term prospects for this backward nation. It's curious, of course. The people in the few Third-World vacation spots she's visited—Oaxaca, Goa Beach, Negril—have a certain energy, although they're obviously poor. But here the people seem like Troglodytes or dwarves. She's reminded of a story her friend David Rattray liked to tell about a 19th century European merchant ship forced to winter in an unmapped Greenland cove. Upon landing, the Danish sailors were amazed to find that they were not alone. A stunted tribe of primitives emerged from sodden huts, babbling in an unknown language. This odd race, they later learned, were descended from the survivors of a wrecked Copenhagen tourist ship that beached there fifty years ago. A millennium of regression occurred in just two generations.

Sylvie wonders if reaching this strange end that is Romania will be what it takes for her to finally have a baby. Will the baby—or Romania itself—shock her husband out of his peculiar slumber? Perhaps he'll finally write *The Anthropology of Unhappiness*. Jerome is like the Tin Man, and she is Dorothy, searching for the ruby slippers. But at first glance, Romania is nothing like the Land of Oz.

SYLVIE'S THIRD aborted pregnancy occurred three years ago, nearly one year to the day of her last conception. By then, she'd quit her part-time teaching job in Harlem so she could live upstate in Thurman with Jerome. Adjunct teaching barely paid the round-trip bus fare, and so instead, Jerome found her a little job working freelance for a New Age publisher. Consistent with her life, the job turns out to be a scam. Her boss, Ginny's ex-boyfriend Chuck, pays her inflated fees to write reports on unsolicited rants by flying saucer lunatics. The entire company turns out to be a money-laundering front for Sun Yun Moon. Meanwhile Jerome leaves Thurman every Tuesday morning to teach his classes at Columbia. On Thursday night, he rides the last bus back to Glens Falls, which is 30 miles away.

They only have one car, so each week Sylvie meets him at the bus station. She brings Lily along to meet him with her, bundled in her red plaid doggy sweater. The nights up here are very cold. *What kind of life is this?* Sylvie sometimes wonders. This is not exactly *Uncle Wiggly in Connecticut*. This isn't Ridgefield, the affluent suburban haven of her dreams. Instead of a commuter train, her husband rides the Greyhound bus, and their "station wagon" is a rusting Ford Granada. She longs to be the waiting, pretty wife, but the baby that she's holding is actually a dog.

The sad and dying town of Glens Falls is a metropolis to their Thurman neighbors, who only go as far as Albany once a year. The local paper eagerly reports on Evie Baker's visit to the Glens Falls podiatrist. There's no TV reception in the Thurman hills, no touch-tone dialing on the phone. In fact, it isn't possible to get a private phone line. Jerome and Sylvie share a party line with four hick neighbors who live miles apart on Dartmouth Road. Born and raised in Thurman, these neighbors had never met a Jew or seen a black person. Laid off from the local mill, these locals made a living cutting wood, tapping maple syrup, raising pigs, when they weren't selling used cars to each other.

Glens Falls is deserted by the time the bus arrives at 10. A few derelicts sip their coffee at the Ideal Diner, next door to the terminal. Shivering underneath a streetlight, Sylvie looks up and down the avenue at Ellis' Cocktail Bar, Shabat Import/Exports and an independent record store. Bongs, Guns 'n Roses and Metallica. Cheap apartments up above the downtown stores; several boarded up brick factories. Sylvie wonders who the people are that live here. Have they chosen Glens Falls as the destination of their dreams? Like her, have they come from other places?

Sylvie checks her breath under the yellow light. It's only late September, but the air's already cold enough to see it. It's the second time she's fallen back in time like this. The first was in New Zealand, traveling to towns like this as a young reporter. Staying overnight in cheap hotels in Timaru and Dunedin, she used to like to make believe that she was John Dos Passos. *The young man walks fast, but not fast enough—One town is not enough, one life is not enough*—but then the bus pulls up, and there's Jerome! She clutches

Lily's paw to wave and they drive home, Jerome telling her who he saw, and all about his classes.

Twice a month she rides the bus to New York City, though mostly New York scares her now. She and her friend Fran Myers are collaborating on a screenplay. Sylvie's old East Village block has turned into a yuppie feeding trough of trendy bars and bistros. Her old friends are either doing so well in their careers that they avoid her, or so badly that they've disappeared. New clubs have replaced the ones they used to go to. Her apartment's rented out, she doesn't really have a place here.

Speculation bristles in the air. The poor, about to be displaced, have launched a huge attack on hubcaps and car stereos in every street-parked vehicle.

Once, on St. Mark's Place, Sylvie passes one of her old boyfriends selling his belongings on a blanket. Will Holloway was a poet who she'd known from around the neighborhood. More socially adept than the average St. Mark's poet, Will had quit his bookstore job and built a successful business, selling heroin to Soho artists, rock stars. After they broke up, Sylvie's heart had leapt when she saw him walking hand-in-hand with his new girlfriend, who was reportedly an advertising exec, on East 12th Street. Now he has Karposi scars from AIDS around his face and neck. She buys one of his old records.

It's only rarely that the overwhelming sadness of the city galvanizes into anything like rage. And when it does, this rage is quickly channeled into new career-paths in the art world. The Whitney Program teaches rich kids to mount institutional critiques. Karen Finlay dresses up in bustiers and garters to preach feminism, and everyone applauds her triumph over Jerry Falwell.

During these trips, Sylvie sees a movement therapist in the West Village. Lately, the sessions have revolved around the brutal deaths of Sylvie's two pet ducks who were eaten by a neighbor's German Shepherd. By breathing deep into the empty space around the sockets of her thighs, she finds it's easier to visualize the carnage that was Jack and Margaret.

The screenplay she and Fran are working on is about another kind of end. Set in the early 1960s, the script's about the end of Europe, the end of ideology, when Pop Art ruled and New York became the new world culture capital. The therapist tells her, *It's alright to mourn.* Sylvie wonders if it's possible to be saved by history.

By the end of her first year in Thurman, Sylvie's pregnant, but this time it doesn't feel as sexual as before. This pregnancy is graver, more maternal. By now her baby-lust has turned into a running joke between her and Jerome. He sees her girlish urge for nesting as a further proof of Sylvie's flightiness, her total lack of seriousness.

Ambivalent, she browses lots of books on pregnancy and childbirth. The stuff about breeched babies, spinal anesthetics and lactation pumps make it easier to agree each time Jerome insists that motherhood would mean she's "given up" on her "career."

Sylvie knows that she still wants one. She just doesn't know what it will be. She knows there's something deeply wrong about the way she's living with Jerome. She no longer pictures she and Jerome together with their baby. But her awareness of conception is as instant as it was last time. Before she even takes the urine test, she dreams about the child. He is a boy, his name is Lewis. In this dream, she no longer struggles with Jerome, but just sneaks out alone to buy the baby stuff.

When the test result confirms her dream, the termination of her pregnancy seems so inevitable she and Jerome hardly bother to discuss it.

Still, she hates herself for having the abortion, and she hates herself for becoming someone who's mourning two dead ducks. This time, there isn't anyone she can talk to, and certainly not Jerome. As he sees it, he's held up his end of the bargain: he's married her, he's moved with her to Thurman.

Instead, she talks to Lewis, this third child who isn't theirs, but hers. She finds that she can talk to Lewis better than she's ever talked to anyone before. She tells him stories and he listens, eyes wide open. She imagines them planting tulip bulbs in the back yard. She tells him about the Shaker children, who prepared their flowerbeds so carefully, because they were giving each new plant a home. All her childlike stabs of happiness have been wasted with Jerome, but when Lewis sees a thing, he really sees it. She likes his voice. He tells her things she's never known. Together, they learn the names of all the plants and animals in Thurman.

Her attachment to this imaginary child becomes so passionately overwhelming that she knows she has to end it soon. The holidays are coming, and Jerome has plans to bring Laura to Paris with him for a family visit. Sylvie won't be coming: Jerome and Laura need to spend some father-daughter time alone.

She schedules the abortion for the 16th of December, the day before Jerome and Laura leave on their vacation.

Everything at the clinic happens more or less routinely, but five days later when she's back in Thurman all alone she starts to feel a little strange. Runs a fever. Catches the bus back to New York for an emergency appointment at the clinic. They do an ultrasound and find there is a residue of fetal—is it, tissue? The residue of Lewis. The abortion's been performed too soon. She'll be alright, she just needs to come back in two weeks so they can finish.

She remembers, back upstate, she took a crazy drive around Lake George. She stopped the car above an icy bank at Deer Leap Point. But then she didn't.

PARATAXIS IS a strange literary form, born at the beginning of the Middle Ages. Old epic stories that had once been handed down by tribal elders pass into the hands of storytellers. Flashing back and sideways, holding back the outcome of events, these tellers fracture old familiar and heroic tales into contradictory, multiple perspectives. It becomes impossible to move the story forward without returning to the past, and so the past both predicates the future and withholds it.

SIX MONTHS LATER, Sylvie and Jerome go out for a drive around Lake George one Sunday afternoon. Fat robins poke around green lawns. It's early June—the tourists won't be coming for another month. Heading north from Lake George Village, they pass the kitschy bungalows with funny names built in the 1950s. Gentleman Johnny's, Oooooo Sullivan's, Halcyon Lodge, The Hill of Happiness—that's Sylvie's favorite. The kitsch thins out at Sabbath Peak. They gaze at symbols of real wealth, the kind of wealth they really envy: discreet, traditional. The old slate roofs, the gabled porches, perennial gardens made a century ago, the rough stone fences. To see these things is almost to possess them and they are satiated, happy.

Sylvie hasn't been here since the night she took her crazy drive. When they stop at Deer Leap Point to look across the cliff-banked lake, they see a pair of nesting hawks above the alder. Six months later, everything is different. The bottom of the air is warm, and you can feel the vapor of white puffy clouds against the sky. This spring, Sylvie has turned 35—a fact that normally depresses her. But now she wonders if the laws of seasonal renewal might apply to humans, too.

After that awful winter night at Deer Leap Point, she knows another pregnancy with Jerome is out of the question. It's much too late for them to have a child. They know too much about each other. Too much has happened. The anthropology of unhappiness wedged between them is not a mystery any more. But couldn't it be possible to build something from this knowledge? To work with it and not let it defeat them? If it was too late to have a baby of their own, why not adopt one?

The elegance of this construction gave her goose-bumps. Her heart leapt to her throat. Were they both not orphans, in a certain sense? She'd wept when Marx's application of Hegelian dialectics onto human history had been first explained to her. Everything made sense. The orphan would be her and Jerome's child correlative. It might be possible to save another human life through this single metaphoric act, despite (in fact, because) they'd never have the psychic means to save their own lives.

Clearly this child could not be American. Abortion was so readily available, the only unwanted US fetuses to reach term were the careless spawn of Pro-Life trailer-park Republicans. Better if their orphan was (like them!) a person born of tragic circumstance, beyond anyone's control. There was civil war, there was stunting poverty, there was brutality and torture.

Sylvie cheered right up as she explained this notion to Jerome. Why, at this moment there were some 72 wars being fought around the globe! Hutus were massacring Tutsis, Georgians were killing Chechens, Russians were suppressing the Uzbeki rebels—not to mention all the Latin American civil wars.

Stunning in its Zen perfection, the Orphan Notion was an act through which all the pieces of Bad History could be symbolically redeemed within a single (happy!) act of synthesis. Jerome agreed with this in theory, though he failed to see how a Hutu or Uzbeki child would fit in with their routines. She saw his point: in order for the metaphor to work, the child would have to look as if it could have been their own baby.

Then... what about Romania? They'd read the tragic tabloid stories, seen the photos taken in the orphanages. Romania was a *European* country, with a French tradition. Despite the fact they'd killed a quarter-million Jews, this happened mostly in the eastern provinces—the urban Jews had gotten off the hook, and in fact attained great prominence in the Communist Party. Why, some of these Romanian orphans could conceivably be Jewish! They knew American adoption agencies were importing Romanian orphans to the States... but the cheesy culture of these agencies, with their workshops, focus groups and 'candlelight commitment ceremonies' was a turn-off. Besides, they charged upwards of $10,000.

Jerome was a seasoned traveler. Unlike the suburban moms and pops that used these agencies, he didn't need anyone to smooth his passage. Wasn't French practically Romania's second language? They'd go straight to the source, they'd deal directly with the baby's desperate parents. Why, $3000 (for them, a bargain) could be enough to save a whole extended family.

It was a fairy tale that suited both of them, for different reasons. And so Romania became the nation of their dreams.

Photo Gallery—Arad 1991
Pentru A Participa in Siguranta Sante Publikada—
Sylvie Green, 4x6 color snapshot

This appropriated image repictures one of the large, multi-colored posters displayed on outdoor kiosks and municipal buildings in the City of Arad throughout the post-Ceausescu era. Evoking Sherrie Levine's bold appropriation of Walker Evan's humanist Depression-era photos, Green crops the poster slightly in the upper left-hand corner. Produced by the Romanian Department of Public Health, *Sante Publikada* features a brightly colored cartoon drawing of a large black dog with a red line slashed diagonally across its body. At first glance, the poster seems to be an injunction against household pets. But a strip of cartoon images beneath the dog depicting toxic foreign matter passing through a human esophagus, stomach and intestine indicate that *Sante Publika* was made to warn an illiterate populace against the health risks entailed in eating dog meat.

JUST TEN WEEKS after this epiphany, Sylvie and Jerome are actually *in* Romania.

Arad's International Astoria is the only building on the boulevard that looks like a hotel, so they pull into the parking lot. Taller than any other building on the boulevard, the 11-floor hotel is an impressive structure built in the 'international modern' cookie-cutter style favored throughout the 1970s in Eastern Europe.

Outside, 20 cabs await an absent clientele. Jerome squeezes their indignant dog into the nylon zipper bag, while Sylvie goes inside to rent a room.

Unlit, the hotel lobby appears strange and cavernous. The local staff have tried, apparently, to turn the hotel's sleek and easy modernism into something much more homey. Kitsch tapestries adorn the walls. Shabby Turkish rugs have been thrown down over the marble.

At one end of the room, an elevator operator dozes on a folding chair. The woman behind the Lucite check-in desk wears a black bra and lacy see-through blouse, topped by a kind of flight attendant's jacket. Behind the desk, a row of broken clocks display the wrong time in Moscow, Beijing and Havana.

The room-rate at the International Astoria is $175 p/night, payable in cash US dollars only. The hotel does not take credit cards. They have a single phone line, no computers.

Sylvie panics. Not only can she and Jerome not afford to stay here, they've already changed their US money into Deutschmarks, Czech crowns, and the pile of worthless local currency Jerome bartered for at the border.

They're stuck, and she is overwhelmed by the absurdity of Jerome's non-existent plan. Why didn't they take a plane to Bucharest, like normal people?

Outside in the parking lot, they pursue this argument. Lily thrashes around inside the nylon zipper bag while Sylvie berates Jerome for his cheapness. Jerome is incredibly relieved when one of the waiting taxi drivers approaches them. Travel is an adventure into chance: finally, it's working. The man looks, maybe 50, but who knows? He's dark and stocky, with gold caps over several molars.

By now Jerome has little confidence that anyone in Romania will understand him, so he half-mimes, half-speaks in pidgin French. *Dormir*? He rests his head against two outstretched hands. Hotel? The driver looks them up and down, then says quite clearly: "You are American."

Eagerly, Jerome and Sylvie nod. For once, they are not going to try and qualify their nationality or dispute it.

"But you have not come here on vacation."

Well no, who would? The absurdity of this is obvious.

The driver waits for them to speak, and Sylvie imagines that the man is trying, incrementally, to gauge whether he can trust them. Suddenly it's all very John Le Carré. Just how far does the driver think it's safe to go? She arranges her face into something earnest and expectant. She is Sally Field in *Not Without My Child*. Jerome seems, as usual, oblivious. He guesses that the driver is a tout for some (thank god!) cheap, unregistered hotel.

And this is true, though not entirely.

"If you like, I can bring you to stay *at my own house*," the driver says appraisingly. "It will be safe. And it is comfortable. My daughter, you see, she speaks good English, and she is a friend of many people. You will stay with us awhile, and eat with us, and sleep. And then, for what you want? My daughter, I think, can help you."

Sylvie and Jerome look at their feet. They hardly dare steal glances at each other. The man smiles at them broadly, and gestures slightly towards their little dog's front paws and head escaping from the zipper bag. "Oh, I think I understand why you are here. What you are looking for... it will be difficult. But with my daughter's help, it will be possible."

In the weeks before they traveled to Romania, Sylvie read a story in the *New York Times* about a gypsy man who gave up his daughter for adoption. Before bringing her to the orphanage, he bought a tiny pair of gold stud earrings, and her mother pierced the baby's ears. "In gypsy culture, gold earrings are the symbol of a loved child," the correspondent noted. Still, Sylvie wondered, if the man could buy the earrings, why couldn't he afford to keep his daughter?

Jerome and Sylvie thank the driver and get back into their car. He leads them to another section of the city.

CHAPTER 4: THE REVOLUTION WILL BE TELEVISED

THE REVOLUTION WILL BE TELEVISED

THE PAVEMENT on the roads gets rough and worn, and then there is no pavement. They haven't traveled very far. The driver stops his cab outside a tidy little house behind a garden wall. His name, he tells them, is Rodescu.

The house has two white geese outside, a small brick patio.

Inside, a peasant woman in a housedress is fixing something in the kitchen. Rodescu's wife. She is all smiles and rolls of flesh. Rodescu speaks to her. She welcomes them and pats their little dog. Rodescu's wife does not speak any English.

Rodescu takes them through the house. There is a TV set, a small new white refrigerator. His daughter, Alina, isn't home but he shows them around her room. She has framed portraits of herself, a single bed, a sewing machine. Alina, the man tells them, is a dressmaker. Finally he takes them to a tiny room done up for guests and helps them put their things down. Jerome takes his Toshiba laptop out, and Sylvie wonders if this is where he'll finally start to write *The Anthropology of Unhappiness*?

They want to take a walk, but Rodescu warns them not to go too far. Their dinner will be ready soon. Besides, he tells them, there are many gypsies.

Even though it's taken them a full week's driving to arrive here,

Jerome and Sylvie have that queasy feeling that comes when you get off the plane after crossing several time zones. A yellow tram car passes by outside the house. There are no vehicles, no power lines. They listen to the sound of horse's hooves on the dirt road, the rumble of the tram. Clearly the Rodescus are much richer than their neighbors. How did they become so? Their fridge and the TV are powered by a battery-operated generator. Had they lived like this throughout the Ceausescu years? Had the revolution in Romania changed anything?

LESS THAN TWO YEARS before, Jerome and Sylvie had intermittently observed Romania's revolution unfold on wide-screen quadraphonic television. They were in Jerome's old friend Félix's Paris loft. In France to spend the holidays with Jerome's mother, their goal was to spend as little time with her in her apartment as was possible.

Jerome's mom still lived in the fourth-floor tenement near the Bourse they'd taken when they returned, defeated, from the Promised Land. Like so many other immigrants who'd survived the War, they'd left France for Israel only to find that there were no jobs there. Jerome's uncle Adam, who'd survived in Poland, returned with them to open up a tiny grocery store on rue Richer. Once the home of many Polish Jews just like them, the neighborhood was now almost entirely North African. The apartment had a toilet in the hallway, and the same brown ceiling water stains Jerome had stared at in his youth, looking up from reading.

Compared to this, Félix's loft was much more glamorous. A famed psychiatrist and philosopher, Félix Guattari was also a relentless host and entertainer. So when the Revolution started being broadcast live on CNN, Félix welcomed Jerome and about a dozen other friends to camp out in his living room to witness and discuss it.

In terms of market-share positioning, Romania's "media revolution" timed out perfectly. The show began on December 22—in Europe, a short work-day—when the studios of Romanian National TV were seized by a broad spectrum of insurgents. Dictators Nicolae and Elena Ceausescu fled, only to be captured one day later and tried on Christmas Eve by an impromptu "People's Court." The three-day live feed ended with a bloody denouement on Christmas day, when the pair was duly executed (off-screen, with several bullets through their heads). Photos of the corpses beamed around the world, symbolic of the Fall of Dictatorial Communism.

This spectacle was vastly more compelling to French audiences than Frank Capra movies and the Vienna Boy's Choir. Christmas Week, December 1989 was the second to last week of the second to last decade of the century and millennium. There was this feeling that the 20th century should just hurry up and end. Could this be it? The *fin* is coming early this *siecle*, the writer Angela Carter noted wryly.

Félix welcomed the Romanian Revolution as a chance to open up his loft and reignite the communitarian spirit that reigned before the Winter Years set in, the mean-spirited backlash against his generation that was the 1980s. He'd been depressed for most of it. Two years before, he'd taken one more shot at life by marrying a bird-like waif he'd met on the street named Josephine.

Once off the street, Josephine turned out to be supremely bourgeois. She convinced him to resign from his directorship of La Borde, the experimental psychiatric hospital he'd founded, famously, two hours south of Paris. There was nothing at La Borde for her to do. At 28, Josephine preferred for them to live in Paris. Throughout the 1970s, La Borde had been a haven for

French intellectuals and movie stars experiencing nervous break-downs. At its height, La Borde had rivaled R.D. Laing's avant-asylum, Knightsbridge Hall, in intellectual prestige and tabloid notoriety. Félix demanded absolute equality between doctors, psychiatric staff and inmates. Shared tasks and Quaker-esque group meetings took the place of psychotropic drugs. Still, once these treatment models were established, there was still the dreary task of running it.

So maybe Josephine was right when she'd talked him into using most of his inheritance to buy and renovate two floors of a building on rue Sentiers in Paris? While on one hand, the loft was a concession to the acquisitive zeitgeist, it might also be a place where Félix's many friends could re-convene in style. When the bills piled up, he'd gone back to private practice.

Still, the loft had not shaped up as he'd imagined it. Josephine disliked his snobby friends, and they spent many evenings there alone, slumped before their wide-screen tri-system quadraphonic television. But when the Romanian events erupted on December 22, they were joined by many of Félix's friends: artists, journalists, psychoanalysts.

Within moments of the seizure of Romanian State TV by an odd band of insurgents—led, on that afternoon, by a poet—CNN picked up the satellite signal and beamed it round the world. Until then, Romania had been closed to foreign journalists. While the international media boarded planes to Bucharest, the whole world watched the poet Mircea Dinescu take the microphone and exclaim "Brothers! Thanks be to God! We've Won!" on what had just been re-named Romanian Free Television.

But time was getting all mixed up between live broadcast from the studio and documentary re-play. In between triumphant speeches, the rebel anchors replayed tape broadcast yesterday on Romanian State TV just before they'd seized the station.

The documentary tape itself was ambiguous and confusing. In it, Nicolae Ceausescu stood out on the balcony of the Great Hall of the People addressing an unruly mob that appeared to number in ten thousands. Flanked by his wife Elena and several high officials of his Security Police, Ceausescu bleated to the crowd about treason sown by enemies of the people. His voice cracking to be heard, he pledged a New Year's pay raise to the loyal working class of Socialist Romania. But then a high-pitched scream erupted somewhere out of frame behind a curtain, and the screen went dead. Cut to: stock footage of the Romanian National Choir singing patriotic anthems. And then the picture came back on in time for everyone to see the Ceausescus turn to flee the balcony, stumbling off behind the curtain.

Back in the studio of Romanian Free TV, the stand-in anchor reported that the Ceausescus had then "fled the roof of the Great Hall by helicopter." Where the dictators actually *were* remained uncertain but they were likely on their way to Libya, protected by elite members of the Security Police. These officers, according to the anchor, were meta-human killers who'd been culled at infancy from the orphanages and trained at special camps to become kamikaze Ceausescu guard dogs.

And then again—Romanian Free TV reported—*at the same time* that Ceausescu fled the balcony, "patriots" on the Romanian police force had discovered some 4000 corpses in Arad Province dumped in a cemetery outside of Timisoara. Presumably, these were victims of a massacre conducted jointly, *on that very day*, by the Ceausescu Security Police force and the Army.

Could this be true? On December 22, Romania's borders were still closed to foreign journalists. That afternoon, the nation's out-ward-information flow was controlled entirely by the insurgents. And now *the whole world was watching...* the same TV show.

Outside Félix's loft, it was another monochrome-gray December afternoon, office workers scurrying around for their last-minute Christmas shopping. But, shades of *Naked Lunch*— they were storming the reality studios in Bucharest! Was this the world's first totally McLuhanesque, Burroughsian revolution?

Jerome had no illusions about the transformational power of the media. He had very little interest in Romania. But he found himself conflicted about the scene in Félix's loft. Félix was one of Jerome's oldest friends. He was Félix's US publisher, but their relationship had never been primarily professional. He and Ginny had hung out with Félix during those first years at La Borde. He'd known Félix's first and second wives, he'd helped Félix's eldest daughter get settled in New York, he'd introduced Félix's work in America. He'd just assumed that he and Félix would spend some time together getting stoned and talking about the old days, and philosophy. But as friends arrived to witness the revolution on TV, Félix drifted further out of Jerome's radar. He was at once the bourgeois host and the countercultural savant, presiding over an ideological slumber party.

Jerome fidgeted on the couch while Félix's acolytes, analysands and former students swapped platitudes about the end of politics, the global village. Félix's Spanish translator, Ricardo Gallo-Pena, a sleek and 35-ish well-fed rat, was there. And Juliette LeBrec, unfortunately. LeBrec had done her residency at La Borde. Now she had an upscale private practice and wrote occasionally on female sexuality for *Le Figaro*. Plump and tiny as an apple, she felt obliged to interject the 'woman's point of view' on everything. Because she'd never fucked Félix, she mothered him.

As the Romanian Revolution unfolded on TV, Sylvie practiced her invisibility. She didn't speak a word of French, and Jerome was too impatient with the conversation in the loft to translate. François Cusset, an anarchist from the École Normale, was taking a hard line about the myth of Eastern Europe's "struggle for democracy." Didn't the dissolution of the Soviet Bloc just reinforce the triumph of American Empire? Félix responded with an approving nod. Because of course, McLuhan's pulsating rhapsody of images could never be entirely divorced from power.

Joints were being passed, but Ricardo Gallo-Pena tried hard to memorize Félix's utterances. He could not believe his luck. Originally, Félix had agreed to *have a coffee with him* during his trip from Buenos Aires. The Romanian Revolution changed their casual meeting into a close encounter, which could easily become the subject for a feature article in the Ideas section of *La Prensa*.

On the TV screen, the poet Mircea Dinescu, who was a bulky man, stood behind a folding table. Except for the odd cognate (dialectic, flux, image) Sylvie couldn't follow the discussion in the loft. What interested her most about the TV broadcast was the poet's sweater. Dinescu wore a loose and dirty garment made of nubby homespun wool. There was nothing international about this sweater. Unblocked, uncarded, sagging down around his knees, it was most likely knitted for him by his wife or his mother. The poet's sweater was a very distant cousin to the rustic, hand-knit items she'd seen folded on the shelves at Benetton. It was as gray and greasy as a sheep transported from a Flemish landscape painting to Chernobyl.

The Berlin Wall had fallen thirty days ago. Staged to happen on the 51st anniversary of Crystallnacht (the night when Nazi Party members renounced Germany's rule of law and rampaged through Berlin's Jewish neighborhoods), the event was real, but more importantly it symbolized the ending of Bad History.

Not everyone at Félix's loft was completely skeptical about the fall of communism or the revolutionary potential of the media. Two of Félix's former followers from La Borde sat on beanbags on the floor. Brigitte and Etienne were looking forward to the New Berlin. In their mid-30s with no professional commitments, they moved around a lot, making independent videos which they financed mostly through the sale of drugs. Unlike the others in the loft, they watched a *lot* of television. They'd never thought the spectacle of government had anything to do with them.

As a dozen badly-dressed Romanians bumbled around the studio, Etienne expounded his and Brigitte's stoner logic about how TV comprised a system that could not be analyzed outside itself. Transparent in its own opacity, TV was truth, it was the collective memory of an expanded tribe. If you kept the cameras running all the time then anything could be replayed at any time and everyone would be accountable.

Ha, said Félix. There is no such thing as chaos. Chaos is always engineered, and when it isn't, it is quickly commandeered by someone.

Sylvie flipped through one of Josephine's *Elle* magazines. Josephine wasn't here, or was she? Words like *fin*, *histoire* and *idéologie* circled around the loft like dead air in a sick building.

Meanwhile on Romanian Free TV, philosophers, poets and former members of the Ceausescu government crowded behind Studio One's lone microphone to address the nation. Instant subtitling hadn't been invented yet. A French journalist with CNN made a live voice-over free translation. The effect of this was as thrilling as a horse race: a sense that these events might be unfolding faster than analysis.

Sylvie remembers attending the first New York screening of a Godard video-film at the Bleecker Street Cinema. (She hadn't met Jerome; was still a member of the East Village's punk masses.) Two hundred people lined up outside the theater door to see the movie, but the subtitled English print was being held at JFK by customs. Thinking on her feet, the curator Jackie Raynal plugged a hand-held mike into a borrowed amp and stood in the center of the auditorium, translating. Raynal had been magnificent: squinting, stumbling over words, finding them and losing them. There was this feeling, then; of being part of a small group located at the center of the world; of receiving a direct transmission that would be carried farther by these chosen people. This impression had turned out to be faulty. And now, Romanian Free TV was broadcasting to the *entire world*, not 200 art-lovers. And wasn't it a paradox that Romania, the most backward of all European nations, could over-turn its history overnight on global, live TV? Information was immediate: there was no longer any need for the apostles.

No one in Félix's loft—or in any of the western media—had a clue about who these Romanians might be. There was a general sense the situation there was humorously medieval.

Imports halted when Romania withdrew from the World Bank in the late 1970s. There was no fuel, no food, no cars, no running water. In his New Year's message to the nation at the dawn of 1984, Ceausescu extolled the horse-drawn cart as a mod-ern, fuel-efficient means of transportation. He was arguably the only left-wing paranoiac in charge of an entire country. While an entire population starved, Nicolae and his wife Elena—who also served as the Minister of Science—sought to double it by banning birth control. Just as Chairman Mao responded to NATO's sanc-tions against the sale of pesticides to China by issuing every citizen with a flyswatter, the Ceausescus believed that with enough people, Romania could exist in isolation. As a European country, Romania's special brand of misery lacked the gravitas of third world poverty in Africa or Asia. Like Maoist China, Romania was a 20th century nation ruled by parable.

Everyone at Félix's loft knew one or two Romanians. They were the sinewy pockmarked men and women, utterly devoid of sex, who, once in Paris, managed to recreate their native squalor in tiny deux-pieces apartments. They mostly lived around the Blvd. Montmarte, and sat around cafés all day because the plumbing in their rooms was perpetually faulty. The men had greasy tufts of thinning hair, the women wore cheap handbags. Both sexes spoke atrocious French. A great number of them called themselves philosophers, working long into the night producing strange impenetrable tracts on topics no one in Paris cared about.

One of these creatures had given Félix his philosophic masterpiece to read, something about *The Crystal Matrix Space of the Romanian Unconscious.* There was a world of difference between these people and other Eastern European immigrants, like, for example, the Bulgarians. The Bulgarians were also foreign, but in a good way, because they've been trained in French traditions. Take, for example, the philosopher Julia Kristeva. While Félix found the implications of Kristeva's work reactionary, she was intelligent and also married to Phillipe Sollers. Kristeva, you could talk to her.

Sitting at Félix's side, Jerome began to feel increasingly more Jewish. Strange that he would feel any sympathy at all for these Romanians. Hadn't the Romanians turned out to be the most zealous of all the European anti-Semites?

During the War, they'd avenged the death of each Romanian soldier by rounding up and executing 100 random Jewish citizens.

Goebbels himself had been disturbed by how eagerly Romania sought to implement the Final Solution. He'd urged Romania's president, General Ion Antonescu, to slow things down a little bit… it was difficult, logistically, to dispose of all these corpses. Rebuffed, Antonescu appealed directly to the Fuhrer. Why not kill two birds and dispose of the Ukrainians while they were cleaning up Romania? Practically the only neighbors who hadn't once colonized Romania, the Ukrainians were a "numerous primitive mass of Slavs" whose presence posed "a serious biological problem" with respect to European birth-rates.

As the TV droned on in Félix's loft, the Romanian Revolution's actual content remained elusive. Were the poets still in charge? By the end of the first day, George Bush I was on TV, applauding the demise of Communist Eastern Europe's final 'domino.'

THERE WAS a pervasive feeling among Félix and all his friends that change would always happen for the worst. Born before the triumph of the spectacle, his was the last generation to whom things would really *matter*. In his heart, Félix still felt personally betrayed by the victory of consumerism over communality.

Jerome also believed that things would always happen for the worst, but his 'worst' was different than Félix's. While Félix and all his friends waxed nostalgic over friendships and romances forged on the barricades of May '68, Jerome scorned this cheery, false utopia. For him, the worst had already taken place, at Auschwitz. "It could be worse," Jerome liked to say, in the face of everyday unpleasantness. Unlike the others, he knew how much worse the worst could be. In fact, he eagerly awaited it.

Jerome used this slogan as his secret means of asserting his own Jewishness among gatherings of gentiles (and nearly every intellectual gathering in France was one). "It could be worse," he liked sighing, with a helpless shrug. Hadn't this motto saved him and his sister from the Warsaw Ghetto? When the Germans entered Poland, Jerome's parents had the foresight to imagine just how much worse the worst could be. Unlike their parents, siblings, cousins, they'd immediately packed their bags and fled. And then the worst had followed them to Paris. Jerome felt supremely pleased each time he caught a gentile's eye and muttered it. "It could be worse." Of course the French had no idea what he was talking about.

Unlike Jerome, Brigitte and Etienne remained convinced that things were actually getting better. They loved watching the Romanian Revolution on TV. The slapstick chaos of it reminded them of their own videos. For them, the media was an electric current cresting on the surface of the ocean. Maybe there was an actual wave behind it, maybe not, but if there was, nobody knew what it was or how to read it. In this sense, they were now Félix's equals. And did interpretation matter? The fact they'd never read Félix's work had not prevented them from making videotapes about his influence. Félix was a celebrity.

Watching Félix hold court in his enormous loft, Jerome thinks bitterly about his own childhood. When he was 12, they'd come back broke from Israel and bought a one-room grocery store on credit. He remembers Uncle Adam wheeling a cart of vegetables down rue Richer from the market at Les Halles market at 6 each morning. He'd never thought about Félix's wealth—almost every-one he knows has money. But still. He remembers working behind the counter after school, selling tins of mackerel.

When Félix throws back his head and laughs, which is some-thing that he does quite often, his wire-rimmed John Lennon glasses slide down off his nose. He is so comfortable within his tubby skin, with nothing but contempt for the young solipsistic strivers who work out in gyms. He goes to cocktail parties with the president, has recently been enlisted to advise the French Minister of Culture. No one expects Félix to be anything but what he is: a great philosopher and clinician; a 1960s guy with lots of influence and money.

Sylvie isn't bothered by the conversation in the loft. She knows that she's invisible to Jerome's French friends. She knows that even if she spoke the language perfectly, they wouldn't speak to her because she isn't anyone to them. Her opinions wouldn't matter.

Félix's young wife, Josephine, also finds the conversation in the loft extremely boring. She stays up in their bedroom smoking cigarettes and watching MTV, tuned to another channel. Unlike her anarchistic husband, Josephine has no fixed sense of who she is. Mostly it doesn't really matter. But still, she keeps on making tiny stabs at trying to discover it, or something.

The week she bought her JVC Hi-8 camera, she'd tried to make a video with him. They were being driven to an airport, and she turned the camera on and asked Félix to tell her, *What is philosophy?* Félix thought she was being cute. He grunted: *What do you want to explain?* For every question that she asked, he asked another, but really she was wanting him to tell her how to live. The video was a document of her helplessness, his arrogance. He told her that she wasted too much time talking on the phone. She should write things down, because *when language isn't written down, it's nothing.*

Two afternoons a week she goes out and meets a boyfriend closer to her age. She can't stand to be around the loft, can't stand to listen to Félix's friends. The loft is, after all, half hers. Why can't Félix respect her privacy? She sees them look at her and think about his children, who are *practically her age.* But this does not concern her.

Jerome resents the fact that even though he'll be in Paris for two weeks, Félix still has not invited him to dinner. Jerome is a *contemporary* of Félix's, but here he sits with all the other hangers-on and leeches. Jerome is not a former student or an acolyte, much less a fucking *translator*. He is a tenured full professor at one of America's top universities. Yet when he speaks, it's impossible to get Félix to listen. Sylvie observes Jerome's anger and frustration growing like an object in the foreground of the Romanian Revolution.

The cold and cloudy afternoon seeps into dusk outside the loft's enormous windows. An announcer—this time, not a poet but a bureaucrat—on Romanian TV takes the microphone and begs for "Comrade Ion Iliescu" to come down and address the nation from the studio. Change, it seems, will always happen for the worst.

On Félix's couch, Jerome jabs the air to make another point. He thinks about how much of his career he's spent advancing Félix's work. Not for money or credentials. He did it purely out of friendship. And yet—the more he's helped Félix, the less Félix has recognized him.

Upstairs, Josephine shuts off her TV and stuffs a wad of cash into her pocket. Some friends of hers were going to swing by this afternoon, but apparently they never made it. She descends the spiral staircase like a Kabuki ghost, scrutinized by Juliette LeBrec, who finds her marriage to Félix inappropriate. In the hallway, Josephine puts on her leather military coat and slips out to buy more heroin. Thank god she's out the door before any of them notice.

AT THIS VERY MOMENT, Nicolae and Elena Ceausescu are cowering in some bushes at the Tiregetsu Nature Preserve, just 45 miles from Bucharest.

The helicopter that mysteriously appeared to whisk them and their two bodyguards off the roof of the Great Hall of the People wasn't bound for Libya after all. Within minutes of alighting, the pilot received a radio message instructing him to land immediately. They were hovering above a field in suburban Bolentini-Vale when he dropped the 'copter down and commanded everybody out.

The helicopter disappeared, and from that moment everything went blurry. Nicolae, Elena and their bodyguards ran across the field and flagged down the first car that they saw, a Dacia sedan. Elena broke a heel, she wasn't wearing the right shoes. The four of them got in and ordered the bewildered driver to take them to Bulgaria. No one in the Ceausescu party had a gun. The hijacked driver—realizing that Bucharest had fallen—thought he'd go to the police, but he wasn't sure if this was safe. Had the police seceded to the rebels? Meanwhile, Elena wondered if they shouldn't go to the Ukraine instead, so when they passed the entrance gates at Tiregetsu the driver pulled into the parking lot, refused to go another mile. Nicolae grabbed Elena's hand and ran off into the park but the bodyguards refused to move. Were they in collusion with the pilot? What about the driver?

Looking for a sheltered spot to hide in Tiregetsu Park, Elena wishes she could go back to Petresti, the village of her birth. There, she knows, the people love her.

Meanwhile gunshots ricochet around the streets of Bucharest, bodies falling everywhere, against the building walls and curbs. No one knows, will ever know, just who these shooters are. In the makeshift studio of Romanian Free TV, a man named Ion Iliescu mounts the podium. The poets are no longer there. Iliescu—a former Cabinet minister for Ceausescu, raises up his arms as if embracing god and announces: "Friends, the army is now with us." Wild applause and cheers erupt throughout the studio. Who is Ion Iliescu? After his demotion from the Ceausescu cabinet, he managed a state printing plant. Why would he have inside knowledge of the army? "Citizens," he says, "a National Salvation Front has just been formed in order to restore democracy, law and order."

AS THESE EVENTS unfold, Jerome thinks guiltily about his mother. He and Sylvie left her place as soon as they woke up and missed the enormous lunch she'd been preparing, just for him, all morning. His mom is 82 years old. He sees her climbing up four flights of stairs on rue Richer with her arthritic leg and heavy shopping bags. In three more days he'll leave and she will weep the night before he goes. And now it's after 8 o'clock, they're late for dinner.

HE AND SYLVIE leave Félix's loft into the freezing rain on rue Sentiers. It's five blocks to the nearest Metro, then three more to the rue Richer. Sylvie steps into the street to hail a taxi. Just who does Sylvie think she is? Enraged, Jerome yanks her back onto the sidewalk.

She looks at him like he's from outer space. "What?" she stutters. "It's late, I'm cold. Let's take a taxi."

But the money that they're spending here in Paris isn't hers. It was given to him by his mother.

Sylvie thinks about the dinner that will inevitably be waiting for them on the table: the fat-drenched breaded cutlets warmed up on the double boiler, the lumpy rice, the over-boiled beans. She thinks about his mother hobbling back and forth between her tiny kitchen and the dining room. "Jerome, it's rude. We're already late enough. It's wrong to keep your mother waiting."

But what does Sylvie know about his mother? In all her 80-something years, she's never wasted money eating out or riding cabs. She carried those fucking cutlets all the way back from the market at rue Mercadet. This trip she's given him $3000, but she won't blow six bucks on a cab. "Taxi, taxi," Sylvie simpers, like the American brat she is, not understanding that there's nothing left to show for your six dollars once you've paid the driver.

"Jerome, I think you're fucking crazy."

But money is abstracted time and it is hemorrhaging everywhere, on garbage bags and oil heat and paper towels and restaurant meals and all the other wasteful transitory things that she insists on. Jerome thinks constantly of dying. If he can stop this slippage, he can maybe halt the process.

Most days Sylvie wakes up feeling like there's a boulder on her chest. Her greatest challenge is to see if she can roll it off by evening. She has mostly given up on happiness. The vision of an ideal future where unhappiness will be replaced by something else has gotten so remote she can't begin to see a path to it. Everywhere she looks she sees a wall. Her life has turned into a maze that she's too stunned to figure a way out of.

The only elegant means of escaping from the torpor of their lives would have been to have a baby. A baby would have forced them into some momentum. But they'll never have a child for exactly the same reasons that Jerome won't let her take a taxi. And these are the *same reasons* why Jerome allows himself to be insulted and ignored by Félix Guattari and all the other famous people whose careers he spends his life advancing.

"Why," she asks, as they walk closer to the Metro, "don't you have any ambitions of your own?" The therapeutic impulse quickly turns into a taste for blood. "I think you hate yourself," she says, as if this is the first time it's occurred to her. "We come to France, and it's as if we're not together. We don't make any plans. You spend all your time running back and forth between Félix and all the others and you don't even seem to notice that they treat you like a graduate student. You're 51 years old, don't you have any self-respect? They never ask about your work. It's like, you are their servant."

"If you don't like my friends in Paris, you can just go back to the East Village and find another secretary job," Jerome answered prissily. They were waiting for the subway now. "Look at your so-called friends, they're all still living in their rat-holes, waitressing and topless dancing." And he was right. None of Sylvie's friends had lofts or art careers or babies. "Why do you have such unrealistic expectations? It's useless to compare. Félix was born into a world of privilege and money." This stopped Sylvie short. But still, she wondered why who you are at 6 years old is who you'll always have to be?

FOUR THOUSAND residents of Bucharest were killed by snipers in an unofficial civil war during the next two days. The violence climaxed when the Ceausescus, after being captured in the Tiregetsu bushes, were escorted back to Bucharest, tried and executed. No one to this day knows who the snipers were or who commissioned them. The Ceausescus were tried on-camera, live, on Romanian Free TV on Christmas Eve, in a hastily arranged half-hour pageant. On Christmas afternoon, photos of their bullet-fractured corpses were given by the army to the media.

"A terrible burden appears to have been lifted from Romania," announced the US State Department. (Note the circumspection of the word 'appears.') "The United States shares the rejoicing of the Romanian people." The *New York Times* declared a triumph for democracy. Sugar, coffee, meat and fruit flooded onto empty shelves in barren stores throughout Romania

Three months later, an independent coroner's investigation proved that many of the Timisoara corpses that sparked the Revolu - tion had in fact been dead for decades. They were not the bodies of heroic dissidents killed by Ceausescu's goons. They were skeletons exhumed by bulldozers from pauper's graves the day before and laid in ceremonial piles to simulate a massacre. The bulldozer-operators vanished, it remains uncertain where they came from. The Revolution was, in fact, a civil war. Its only *actual* victims were the 4000 killed in Bucharest, during a civil chaos quelled by Ion Iliescu. Later still it was alleged that these unknown gunmen were in Iliescu's employ. Documents were lost, the investigation halted without any final proof. And even if the proof were there, would any of it matter? So yes, in terms of the instant mass diffusion of a panoply of lies and violence, cynically arranged through gross manipulation, Romania *did* achieve the world's first Media Revolution.

Nine years later, Félix and Josephine are dead: he of heart failure, she of a heroin overdose six months later. The Romanian regime changed hands a dozen times. Each new government was marked by its own forms of engineered incompetence and corruption. The IMF withdrew the third installment of its World Bank loan. Romania's poverty—now greater than before—was no longer the work of an isolated madman; it was internationally negotiated and constructed. Subject of ten thousand articles and books during the early 1990s, the Romanian 'revolution' is now dispensed with in two words. It was a 'palace coup.'

Is it possible to describe the orphaning of an entire nation?

DEAR SIRS, wrote D. P. Scholtz in a letter to the *New York Times* in April, 1991, I don't know who makes me sicker—the baby brokers, the fathers who quote prices on their unborn children, the orphanage directors, the Romanian Government or the adopting couples. These people who come to adopt say they want to help, they pat themselves on the back for bringing medical supplies, and in the same sentence, talk of picking out a child or two, as if an orphanage were a supermarket. If they really cared about these children, wouldn't they want to keep the families intact and improve the children's standard of living? Their behavior is appalling. My heart goes out to the children.

SYLVIE GREEN was looking for something to believe in, and guess what she found?

... The field scattered with wild white daisies, buttercups and Queen Anne's Lace... the wainscotted porch ceilings, painted celestial blue to make the porch-sitters think of heaven... the diners, the motels, the tall banks of pine along the secondary roads... the clap-board houses with real shutters decorated with the cut-out signs of crescent moons..., she wrote in a notebook she kept intermittently in Thurman.

She and Jerome both knew each other's deep capacity for sentiment, and for years they observed the Adirondack countryside as if it were an artifact left only for their pleasure. As if the world outside their car had been displayed within a great vitrine. They saw rows of pachysandra planted in neat rings around the fruit trees. Apple blossoms on the road to Harrisburg quivered frailty in the April breeze, and it was at times like these their torpid state would escalate to the allegoric splendor of a medieval painting. Objects shone with meaning, and they understood these signs.

And yet ultimately just gazing didn't satisfy them. They needed to possess things. They needed evidence that the symbols of the life that passed them by could be cared for and protected. They foraged and they bought. They scavenged fifty lilac branches from the road-side, wrapped them in wet paper towels and put them into mason jars as vases. They salvaged armchairs from the dump, shopped for fabric, re-upholstered. In Thurman, each new day held boundless possibilities, and Sylvie would exhaust herself in finding them 'til they stumbled into night. She became the interior decorator of their deeply sublimated fantasies. Still, eventually this was not enough. *Habitation gives a landscape shape...* but alone, with just their little dog for company, she and Jerome moved through it like ghosts. They needed an infusion of fresh blood, someone to tell stories to besides each other. Without a child, it was difficult to maintain this artificial paradise, and so Sylvie's enthusiasm became increasingly passionate and manic: White impatiens planted beside a garden path of flagstone from a nearby quarry! Strawberries and rhubarb! The month of June! Animal gut dried and threaded into snowshoes!

Jerome withdrew. He never did entirely believe in Sylvie's fabulations. He'd given up his life in New York City, thinking Thurman would do quite nicely for an early funeral. Though Sylvie didn't realize it at the time, her enthusiasms were absorbing all the air in their shared tomb. The suffocation only hit her later, when she flew to Berlin to meet Jerome. When they were getting ready for their great adventure in Romania.

CHAPTER 5: BERLIN DEATH TRIP #1

BERLIN DEATH TRIP #1

UNLIKE THE COUPLES in the foreign adoption brochures Sylvie
collected, Jerome and Sylvie didn't simply leave their home and
travel to Romania together. Summer 1991 found Jerome in Berlin,
with a generous academic fellowship from the DAAD. Sylvie had
no plans of her own that summer. Except for a 10 day video workshop she'd arranged in mid-July with the Town of Thurman
Youth Group, she was at a loss for where to be or what to do. Earlier that year, she'd decided that, on principle, she'd no longer
accompany Jerome on any of his trips unless she was invited, too.

The DAAD had told Jerome they'd pay for Sylvie's ticket,
but Sylvie refused to count this courtesy to her husband as a *professional invitation*. Cash was cash, Jerome couldn't see the
difference. "Ahh cherie," he'd said, when she laboriously defined
her meaning of *professional invitation*, "you always have to pay for
the symbolic."

But when some friends from Paris offered him $1000 to rent
their Thurman house in August, Sylvie made a deal with him. She'd
vacate the house and join him in Berlin if he agreed that they could
travel to Romania together. Since the DAAD was already paying his
expenses, Jerome anticipated a net profit of $1000, which would
come in handy. Traveling from Berlin, he'd get to see the former

Soviet Bloc Eastern European countries one more time before they changed forever. They might even put the orphan thing to rest! Who knows, maybe some deserving local family would let them metaphorically "adopt" a son or daughter. They'd send a small check every month, pay for food and books. The kid would be profoundly grateful, and Sylvie could carry around the orphan's picture.

SYLVIE HATED flying overnight to Europe because it was cramped and sleepless. About the only thing she trusted now was sleep. She hated that the only flights available from JFK to Europe were the red-eyes that discharged you in a foreign dawn, jetlagged and exhausted, having to stagger through an entire day before you could pass out. She hated the airline dinners she invariably ate, thinking the starchy food might help her sleep. All night long the airplane movies flickered just above her eyelids, which weren't thick enough to shut them out. Sometimes she'd manage to drift off for forty minutes over Iceland, but then the rush of overlapping interrupted dreams just left her even more exhausted. Sylvie looked to dreams as a means of figuring something out.

Still, she felt a cautious optimism. Jerome had actually agreed to join her on this quest to find a Romanian orphan. Lily, stoned on doggy-tranqs, was sleeping in the nylon zipper bag underneath the seat. Sylvie realized if they actually *found* a Romanian orphan, they'd probably have to buy a second nylon zipper bag. Though she'd been so busy fighting with Jerome before he left she hadn't really had a chance to think this through.

It's summer 1991, and Nirvana's on the radio everywhere you go. She'd heard Nirvana for the first time in April, when *Nevermind* had first come out. Jerome's ex-students John and Jennifer had driven out to visit her in East Hampton. Jerome was in LA that spring as a Senior Mellon Visiting Critic, and she'd stayed behind to build a second-floor addition to their East Hampton house. She'd figured they could use the Mellon's $30,000 to build an extra bath and bedroom, and thus squeeze another $4,000 each year from the summer rental. Besides, Jerome could use the beautiful, sky-lit upstairs room as his office during the nine months each year they actually *used* the house. In these luxurious surroundings, he'd finally have the confidence to start in earnest on *The Anthropology of Unhappiness*, and then everything would change, they'd no longer be unhappy.

Sylvie had the whole place to herself the day that John and Jennifer came out. The Thurman carpenters she'd hired (at a cheaper day-rate than East Hampton contractors) had gone home to see their families, and she was touched that even without Jerome around, John and Jennifer had still come out to see her. John was a music video director. Jennifer wrote essays about sexual politics and gender and danced three nights a week at Billy's Topless Lounge. Though their fathers were a Washington DC lobbyist and a shopping mall developer, both of them were highly critical of the house. *They* lived in low-rent Williamsburg. Didn't Sylvie find East Hampton bourgeois and elitist?

It had been so long since Sylvie'd had any friends, she was overwhelmed by how to fill their day-long visit. What do people do? Mostly they sat around the sparsely furnished living-room, smoking cigarettes and playing John's new *Nevermind* cassette repeatedly. John said that everybody said Nirvana was important, and Jennifer talked about her job at Billy's Topless Lounge as if she were the first girl with a Columbia BA to ever do this.

Jennifer was a babe, with dreadlocks, nose rings and tattoos. Her transparent nylon baby-t ended just above the piercing on her naval, and Sylvie reflected on how much the world had changed since she herself had topless danced a dozen years before. In Sylvie's time, the girls wore paramilitary camouflage when they weren't whoring. Still, she thought, maybe Jennifer's generation had the right idea? Better, perhaps, to dress like a whore around the clock and thus achieve a fully integrated personality.

After listening to John's *Nevermind* cassette about six times, Sylvie went out to do an errand. She came back with a bag of groceries and a new blue sweater for her little dog, who was still recovering from surgery on her benign tumor. Jennifer picked up the sweater, still in its plastic bag and laughed: "Is that how people spend their time out here in the Hamptons? Buying sweaters for their dogs?" And John, of course, laughed too.

WHEN SYLVIE isn't trying to catch some airplane sleep, she holds on tight to the armrests of her seat. She's terrified of flying, she hates to think her life will end before it has begun. Throughout the eight hours that it takes to get to Berlin-Tegel, Sylvie snaps to alert each time the plane hits turbulence, wondering *at which moment* of the crash her heart will stop. She hopes to be relieved of consciousness before she hits the ground.

During the past year, she'd become gnawingly aware of her own unhappiness. Disgusted by it. Still, she did not know what to do. Jerome's career had taken off phenomenally. The French theorists he'd been promoting for a decade had finally been embraced within the art world, and as their impresario and cultural interpreter, he was suddenly in great demand. But her own films? Hardly anyone had seen them. Moreover, they were in total opposition to the things that people liked about Jerome. Her movies were unfashionable: messy, inchoate, intensely private spirals of association. Too punk to be a formalist, too intellectual to be underground... she'd been a fool to think she could be some kind of female Guy Debord.

Sometimes when they went out with Jerome's successful artist friends, he'd ask for tips on how his wife could manage to improve her floundering career. And she was mortified. The friends would offer non-committal meaningless advice about mailing lists and seeking "well placed mentions" in the press.

Having been around the art world now for 15 years, Sylvie knew exactly how the system worked. She knew that to make the system work for her, she'd have to change her work, but what would be the point of that? She'd never wanted to be known for being known. All she wanted was to talk about the things that interested her and be listened to by someone other than Jerome. Why couldn't she have that?

Sylvie doesn't see the point of travel. She doesn't see the point of anything anymore. "What's the point?" has recently become her mantra, followed by "I'll never be happy again." She talks romantically about her own death. Sometimes Jerome tries to cheer her up by turning her despair into a routine. Taking out the same Pro-Walkman he's used to interview Félix and Paul and Jean, he "interviews" his wife about her suicidal thoughts.

Leaning back against her feather pillows, Sylvie drones on about the nature of despair. Life, she claims, acquires value only through its meaning. Since she isn't often making films, she has a lot of time to read.

She likes to organize her reading jags associatively, in big digressive clumps. She thinks if she reads backwards far enough, all the things she's drawn to might connect. Lately, her reading of the philosopher Simone Weil led her to *Gilgamesh*, *Tristan and*

Iseult, and then across the world to ancient Bali. Within the Balinese folk tradition, kings were ceremonially cremated with all of their possessions so they wouldn't suffer from a break in continuity when they crossed over into spirit-life. The Balinese kings had many wives, and at the climax of the ceremony each wife ascended a high plank and threw herself into the flames, where she was burned alive.

Sylvie finds this practice very beautiful. Because, as she so earnestly tells Jerome, it's an enactment of the principle that human life acquires value *only when it has a meaning*. If these women's lives have been defined exclusively through their relation to the king, upon his death their lives no longer have symbolic meaning. Their ability to invest themselves completely within this symbolic order creates a meaning. Does it matter how this meaning is derived?

At the beginning of the summer, Sylvie had rented their East Hampton house to Gayle Robertson, a voice-over actress who'd recently become the voice of a new sports and spa-type beverage, Crystal Lite. Gayle's radio ads for Crystal Lite, The Healthy Choice had broken out on stations nationwide, and she was now weighing up her options between LA and New York.

Gayle was four months pregnant. She, her husband Dean and their blonde toddler Sean lived in a Tribeca loft on Reade Street, just four doors down from a place where Sylvie'd lived with her friend Liza Martin about a million years ago. She and Liza whored together out of the then semi-finished loft, to finance their experimental theater plays about whoring.

"Kids," gushed Gayle as Sylvie walked her through the house, "aren't they the *most*?" Gayle and Dean were powerful reminders of what might have been if Sylvie had done things right.

Between the time she banked Gayle's check ($8000) and drove upstate to Thurman, Sylvie found the time to shoot three scenes of what she hopes will be a pilot for the script that she and Fran are working on. Everybody said the only way to sell an independent script these days is to send it out together with a pilot as a "calling card." She'd used half Gayle's money to shoot three 16mm scenes, although if the film was ever made, it would have to be blown up to 35mm film. And then the Nagra broke, and so the soundtrack hadn't been in sync, and she'd had to pay the lab to have the whole mess transferred onto video again. It was mid-June when she finally had the film. Jerome called from LA and told her to come out and edit at the art school he was teaching at, but when she got there the semester had already ended and the editing bays were closed.

Time stretched out forever in LA. With nothing much to do, Sylvie spent her mornings taking Lily out in Echo Park. Jerome was already two months late with *Death: The Unfinished Life*, the essay that he'd promised for a large New York museum show, so Sylvie went out afternoons as well so he could have the apartment to himself. Eventually Jerome would tearfully accept her help, and this would bring them closer, and the cloud of the unfinished text would lift, but that month she took long drives and shopped the 99 Cent Stores of Echo Park.

On these trips, she liked to visit Benjamin, who ran the Sunset Blvd. Ultra-Discount Store with his mom. Benjamin called Sylvie *senorita*. He was about her age, and had a withered arm, although he seemed quite cheerful, stacking boxes on tall shelves with his prosthetic hook. His mother, he had told her once, took thalidomide during her pregnancy, so he'd been deformed since birth. Still, there they sat together, ringing discount items up behind the register. Sylvie felt a little humbled by his lack of bitterness. She can't help comparing his situation to Jerome's. Living with this terrible deformity, Benjamin has a good word for everyone, while Jerome hates almost everyone with no good cause.

THE FEW TIMES they go out together, Sylvie is amazed by how deferentially Jerome is treated by people in the LA art world. In New York where everything is shit, it's enough to more or less exist, but here people want Jerome to be the Great Man. They see him as their link to the French theorists whose names are strewn throughout the pages of *Flashart* and *Artforum*. Jerome finds it all a little compromising and embarrassing. As if to justify his presence on their coast, he tells everyone he meets about his plans to "make a special LA issue" of his magazine. He'll call it *LA It's A Riot*, in honor of the racial violence that erupted earlier this year throughout the city. "Awesome," everyone replies. Sylvie wonders how he'll do this. The only LA people who he's met are in the art world, and all of them are upper class and white.

Jerome leaves for Berlin at the end of June to start his DAAD fellowship. Sylvie takes their little dog back with her to Thurman. There, she has a fellowship of her own: a $1500 Regional Arts Decentralization Grant, to help the Thurman youth make videotapes about the history of their town.

She spends the first days of July touring Myron Cameron's sawmill with a group of junior highschoolers. The Camerons are a major Thurman family, and all the kids in Sylvie's group are Camerons by either blood or marriage. In this sense, Thurman is a little like the art world: everyone's related in some way.

They drive out to Bowen Hill and pay a visit to George Mosher, who, at 82, still has a hand pump in his kitchen to draw water from a well. George demonstrates the tricks he's taught to

Tippy, the amazing talking dog who's been his sole companion since his wife died several years ago. The little wire-haired white mutt dances on his legs and yips with pleasure at the sound of George's voice. During the Depression, George could no longer make a living as a trapper, so he walked six miles down to Stony Creek each day for relief work rolling logs into the Hudson River. He tells them all about his route, the ancient logging roads behind Round Pound and Number Nine Mountain. George shows the kids the stump that used to be a finger before he lost it trapping foxes. They visit Fanny Harris, who ran the general store on High Street, and Lila Wallace, who came from Albany many years ago to teach at the one-room schoolhouse out on Dartmouth Road. None of these buildings are preserved. The history of the town lives only through these people, who will soon die. On the one hand, Sylvie wants to be a powerful advocate for this culture, but she can't, because their dereliction is too close to hers.

After finishing the video, Sylvie packed and left for Germany. Hiding Lily in the nylon zipper bag, she caught the Trailways bus to Albany and then a cab, and then a shuttle flight to JFK. All of Sylvie's transportation was paid for by the Germans, a fact Jerome finds deeply moving. Not only did it signal his importance, it was a form of reparation, too.

"I have good news for you!" Jerome exclaimed when he received the DAAD invitation. "They're going to pay your ticket, too!"

Remembering the four times she'd applied for the same grant in her own name and been turned down, she howled: "Why do you tell me it's good news? It's good news for you, Jerome. But not for me."

And Jerome, who was normally so oblivious to these things, was deeply moved. The hopelessness of Sylvie's sadness made him dimly conscious of his own. Romania, he thought, was not so very far from Germany. They'd been talking about adopting a Romanian child for months now. Why not give in, and actually travel to Romania, and put the thing to rest?

This concession quickly cheered her up. It was a tiny seed, but still enough for her to turn into a pearl of total fabulation. She imagined she and Jerome entering the orphanage, soberly dressed. She was in a navy suit, and Jerome looked like François, in an expensive cardigan and slacks. Unlike the peasants who wrote outraged letters to the *New York Times*, she and Jerome were sophisticated travelers. They understood that in a country gripped by poverty, American ideas about cleanliness and the sanctity of childhood don't apply. The orphanage director—kindly, female, middle-aged—spoke perfect French as she led them to the open dormitory. Walking past the metal cribs, a certain child would catch her eye. Before Sylvie made a move, he'd hold out his tiny arms to her. He would be their child.

Jerome would insist on tracking down the birth parents of the child. No mere First World baby-grabbers, they would volunteer to be the child's American "aunt and uncle." A long relationship between East Hampton and some backward Transylvanian village would begin.

But the airplane ride was endless. Last night when Sylvie called Jerome, he was so excited about being in Berlin he didn't want to talk about the orphanage at all. What, she wondered, is the nature of this mission? She felt all of her belief in continuity slipping as they passed through several time zones.

This morning when she'd popped the doggy tranq in Lily's mouth, she'd felt a lump between two nipples on her chest. Was the tumor coming back? The lump had re-appeared around the same place Dr. Silverstein, who was Thurman's only vet and only other Jew, had taken out the tumor, and he had sworn to them the tumor was benign. Did Silverstein habitually lie out of misguided social conscience, to spare his hard-up clientele the agony of declining chemotherapy for their household pets? She wouldn't put it past him. But why had she and Jerome been perceived as child-like hicks by him, and not as fellow Jews?

Her neighbor, Mr. Putnam had been driving the Trailways bus from Warrensburg that morning. Dogs were strictly not allowed, and he'd been nice enough to pretend he didn't see Lily's whitened muzzle protruding from the nylon zipper bag. George Putnam, 58 years old, still lives with his aging mother in a trailer home they've set up beside what was once the family farm. The road they live on bears their name—Putnam Crossing. The Putnams are another famous Thurman family, with a history that goes back nearly 200 years.

THIRTY YEARS AGO, the Putnam farmhouse was destroyed by fire. The structure was, by then, as sprawling as a boarding house, with room for several Putnam generations, although all its rooms branched out from a simple cabin built by George's great-great-grandfather, Reverend Enos Putnam, in 1828—or was it 1842? Ordained as a Wesleyan Methodist minister in Albany—or was it New York City?—Putnam came to lead the local converts of this new reformist sect. Passionately opposed to slavery, Enos and Sybil Putnam transformed their humble parsonage into an important station on the Underground Railroad that relayed fugitives from Georgia—or was it Mississippi?—to freedom, into Canada. The Putnam parsonage lay some 15 miles from the commercial wagon line in Warrensburg, halfway up Crane Mountain. Enos built a secret room down in its cellar… although who, you'd have to wonder, would bother pursuing anyone over 15 miles of icy rutted trails to this remote locale?

None of these facts were ever written down, but Mabel Tucker and the other women at the Thurman Historical Society talked about the Reverend Enos as if they'd known him personally. In Mabel's stories, it was always dark (like Negro skin) outside, and very cold. According to Miss Tucker (who, at 78, was the Official Town Historian because she remembered more than anyone), Enos regularly loaded up his horse-drawn wagon down in Warrensburg with "Negro slaves." Had these people come from Albany, from Saratoga? She wasn't really sure, but Enos covered them with hay and drove his horses back to Thurman. Mabel wasn't certain where the fugitives would go when they left Thurman, but she knew that Sibyl had a home-cooked supper waiting. The Putnam children carried lanterns, quilts and candles down the basement stairs.

One hundred forty nine years later, Reverend Enos' great-great-grandson, George, drives the air-conditioned Trailways Bus from Warrensburg to New York City. The bus is like a metal snake, traveling down Thruway 87. George pulls into the Port Authority Bus Terminal at 1:15 p.m., spends an hour in the cafeteria, and then gets back behind the wheel to drive to Warrensburg again. During the eight years he's done this trip four times a week, George has never left the Port Authority terminal. New York does not exist, not really. Real time for George is time that happened over a century ago in Thurman.

The only things worth fighting for, Sylvie thinks that morning as she drives along the River Road to catch the bus in Warrensburg, *are intangible*. Because she felt this very passionately, she believed it must be true. It's early August, and mornings are already getting cold. Streaks of clouds are wrapped around the base of Jimmy's Peak, she sees a large gray heron in the water. Two months before, the ancient nations of Croatia and Slovenia had seceded from what would soon become the former Yugoslavia. *The only things worth fighting for are intangible*, the Slovenian freedom fighters said. They needed to retain the language and the stories, the holidays and myths, that defined them as Slovenians. Their secession triggered off a chain of Balkan civil wars which were the final chance, the freedom fighters said, to reclaim history. They felt this very passionately; therefore, they believed, it must be true.

The man who'd sat beside her on the shuttle flight to JFK that morning asked Sylvie what had drawn her to the Adirondacks. She couldn't quite explain.

"Your footsteps have more weight," she'd said. "You move through space a different way." How could she explain this so he'd understand? "There is this—viscous sense of continuity, like everything is being held in place. People live there all their lives, and they remember everything that happens. None of it is written down, but nothing happens in the present that outweighs the past. It will probably be gone within a decade. It's like I'm witnessing the end of something."

Once, after staying up all night in New York City, she'd felt an urge to go to Canada. A truck-driver she'd met at Munson's Diner near the West Side Highway took her all the way up to Lake George. It was early November, she tried to hitch a ride but no one stopped, so she'd walked across the village to the beach. There, she'd seen a black man in a cowboy hat and a white woman in a fringed suede jacket locked in an embrace. Everything combined into this image, and it was the most beautiful thing she'd ever seen. At that moment it seemed possible to both *be* them, and to be *outside* them, all the loneliness in the world, the mountains and the lake. It was around that time that she'd decided to make movies.

Funny she could say all this to a stranger. He'd been so kind. These days her eyes tear up when anybody shows the slightest kindness, recognition, willingness to listen. She's so overwhelmed she forgets the book she's saved to read en route to Germany, but by the time she navigates the terminal and finds the Lufthansa check-in line, the omnipotence that carried her from Thurman vanishes. She's Sylvie Green again, on her way to meet Jerome.

The plane arrives at Berlin-Tegel 40 minutes late. She hasn't slept or had a cup of coffee. Moving through the regulated airport traffic flow, it occurs to her that plane rides are not unlike the Nazi transports. In both cases, passengers are ordered to surrender documents and belongings to be crowd-controlled like cattle, and then removed from time. The German customs officer threatens quarantine if she can't find proof of Lily's rabies vaccination, but the health certificate stamped by Dr. Silverstein is still in Sylvie's unclaimed bag. *Once the individuation of the human subject is destroyed*, Sylvie muses, after Hannah Arendt, *atrocity becomes banal and all forms of horror are allowed.* But look, there's Jerome behind the International Arrivals rope, waving!

Sylvie tries to share this new epiphany about the fascist roots of late 20th century transportation, but Jerome hurries her along. They'll go back to his Charlottenburg apartment, she can have a nap. At 6, they're meeting his friends Heidi and Peter for a drink, maybe they'll go on to dinner. Later on, they'll join some friends of his in Schöneberg at the Jungle, which is now the club where everybody goes.

"The Jungle is the new Area!" Jerome excitedly intones. Area was a New York club that closed three years ago in 1988, to be replaced by one called Quick, a name that Sylvie had interpreted as an arcane referencing to death, *The Quick and the Dead*, 'quick' the antonym of death in medieval English, wasn't 1988 the year that everybody died of AIDS?

Jerome loves being in Berlin because it reminds him of the "old days," the early 1980s in New York, when artists squatted in unfinished lofts and gave their work away for free. Berlin is much more lively than Los Angeles. In the past three weeks, he hasn't had a second! He's busy juggling his old projects, and has already started several new ones with his Berlin friends. Next week there'll be a party in his honor—they've already made the flyer—and they're calling it, get this, *The American Friend*—you know, Wim Wenders?

Sylvie experiences a fresh wave of exhaustion as Jerome leads her, her luggage and the little dog to the bus stop. They pass the taxi ranks, of course. She'd been *hoping* he'd spring for a cab, maybe bill it to the Germans? But Jerome has thoroughly researched this and has other plans. They'll catch a free shuttle to the U-Bahn, take the subway to the Kudamm. From there they only have to cross the street to catch a tram-car to Charlotten-burg, and walk four blocks to the apartment. Sylvie has no doubt her summer tenants Gayle and Dean would already be *in* a taxi, no matter how annoying they might be.

Two days before she left LA, she'd finally had a chance to see the three scenes she shot for her movie pilot back in New York. The footage made her cringe. There was this awful gap between the movie that appeared on film and the one that lived inside her head.

The movie, called *Sadness at Leaving*, was a kind of espionage romance. There was all this goofy spy stuff in it, but really, it was about witnessing an end. Carl Halman leaves East Germany in 1959 to become a "sleeping agent" in New York. He's Turkish, an idealist and a communist. The East Germans give him an apartment, money, friends. He will build up a new identity. He will call himself a writer. "But when will you contact me?" Carl implores. "A year, a month... maybe never."

"You'll travel to New York," says anti-fascist General Shevchenko, his control. "You'll meet people who can help you there. But you won't know yet who they are."

And wasn't that how things happen, more or less, in everybody's life? You assume some kind of identity, quite arbitrarily. What happens next depends on chance. Once in New York, things spin out of Carl's control when he is caught in the détente between the East and West. In the script, she and Fran had used an Orhan Veli poem as voiceover. The poem gave Sylvie goose-bumps:

> *I wonder if it is lustful*
> *A tank in its dreams*
> *What do airplanes think when left alone?*
> *We did not seek happiness*
> *We invented sadness*
> *Were we not of this world?*

But what's ended up on film—the chase scenes and the dialogue—doesn't feel like poetry at all.

Sylvie drags most of their luggage from the shuttle to the U-Bahn. Jerome can't carry much—he has arthritis in his hip. Sylvie wonders: *why am I alive at all?* At the Berlin Zoo, they relay the luggage to the tram across the Kudamm, where Jerome has a special treat in store. He's discovered how to beat the fare! You simply slip into the stream of passengers exiting the rear door.

"You are so fucking cheap," says Sylvie. Jerome doesn't understand her sourness. Didn't the DAAD just pay her trip? Why is she so critical? Why isn't she more excited about being in Berlin? They'll be visiting a real Romanian orphanage soon.

The nightmare of history weighs down on the brains of the living... Jerome is so excited about getting a free tram ride to the free Charlottenburg apartment, he barely registers her resentment. It's as if each pfennig he extracts in Germany bolsters the credit side of a ledger he's been keeping all his life.

Yes, he thinks, Berlin has been incredible. Everyone is making films and putting concerts and events together. The artists actually support each other. But these impressions of mere *individuals* haven't changed his hatred of the German race.

CHAPTER 6: THE NIGHTMARE OF HISTORY

THE NIGHTMARE OF HISTORY

CHARLOTTENBURG WAS BEAUTIFUL in a leafy, Brooklyn Heights kind of way. It was the sort of neighborhood Sylvie longed to live in, with its quiet streets, limestone buildings and absence of striving. Charlottenburg still belonged to sensitive, oval-faced elderly women with long gray hair neatly fastened in buns. Piano music drifting out in the street... if she wasn't dragging their luggage along it, this street would be where Sylvie wanted to be. Jerome looked at these women with their little dogs and imagined them knitting scarves for their boys at the Front. *There is no such thing as innocence*, he thought bitterly.

Upstairs in Jerome's third-floor apartment, Sylvie sprawled on the living room couch while he made them a salad. The apartment was perfect, with its white corniced boxes of rooms, smooth plaster walls, and Workbench-style laminate furniture. Catching her breath, she feels a strange déjà vu.

In fact she *has* been here before—at least, she's seen it on film. Two years ago, her friend, the experimental filmmaker Ken Kobland, had stayed here on a DAAD fellowship and made a whole film in this apartment. The film, as Sylvie recalled, was about a table—birch legs, white laminate, yes!—it was the same table that now serves as Jerome's desk. Ken was the Busby Berkeley of structuralism. In his film, blotters and papers and pens had danced all over the table. For the grand finale, the table was deluged with white paper snow.

But now, Jerome's laptop and the framed black and white photo of his mother, taken during the War, occupy Ken's famous desk. Jerome still brings this photo with him wherever he goes. Six years ago, when Sylvie first saw it at his friend Martin's loft, she'd made some polite passing remark about his mother. *What a good-looking woman*, she'd said. Seeing just a 32-year-old blonde woman in a shearling fur jacket and a dreamy expression, Sylvie had failed Jerome's secret test. She hadn't noticed the Star of David partly hidden by the jacket's large lapel. At the time, Sylvie barely knew what the Yellow Star was. The War was something she'd seen on a sit-com called *Hogan's Heroes*, and later on, as numbers tattooed on the arms of old men and women who prowled the Lower East Side like transplanted lizards. "Huh," Sylvie'd remarked. "Are you Jewish?" She would never have guessed it. He didn't look or act Jewish. All her friends were American Jews.

Jerome says he carries this photo because it makes him think of History. Like most of his generation in Europe, he still uses the word with a capital "H": as if this abstract noun was a god or a person.

Recalling his years as a child in France during the War, the novelist Georges Perec says, "what marks this period is the absence of any landmarks." Like Jerome, Georges remained safely hidden outside of Paris while his parents fled. Both his and Jerome's parents had left Warsaw for France when Poland fell to the Nazis. Both families resided on rue Poisionnieres; both boy's fathers were arrested in Paris. Sent first to the French transit camp at Drancy, both boy's fathers eventually perished at Auschwitz. During their student years, Perec and Jerome founded a magazine called *Le Ligne General* with some other crazily bright young Jewish guys. They hated French humanism, loved American movies. The War shaped their sensibilities. It was too obvious to ever mention.

"There was no past," Perec finally wrote of his hidden childhood, "and for very many years there was no future, either; things just went on... You didn't ask for anything, you really didn't know what you should ask for."

Jerome's Yellow Star photograph is a strange talisman. Like Perec's sense of his childhood, it's both remote and compelling. The photograph is emotion, *brut*. In this sense, Jerome's "History" is as potent and vague as the "history" preserved by Mabel Tucker, George Putnam, and the Thurman Historical Society women. All of these people powerfully know that *something* happened *somewhere*, but they don't want to dilute the sensation of knowledge with too many details.

Still. Since his mother turned 70 three years ago, Jerome has interviewed her about the War each time he visits in Paris. Though they've already filled a dozen cassettes, the stories remain fragmented, inconclusive. Jerome can lecture for hours about the socio-economic factors that triggered the War, but he's still uncertain what happened and, when, in his own family. Perhaps like him, his mother senses that once a story has been fully told, it's over. "The crisis in language," Perec once quipped, "is not in words." To organize events sequentially is to take away their power. Emotion's not at all like that. Better to hold on to memories in fragments, better to stop and circle back each time you feel the lump rise in your throat—

Jerome remembers being in the same room when the Germans arrested his father. He was five, so it must have been early in '43—he remembers this very clearly. He and his sister Yvette were already living outside of Paris, in Carmen's house. But was it before his father's arrest, or later on, that Carmen told him and Yvette that their parents *had to go away*? Had he known *on that day* that his parents were hidden in the concrete potting shed behind Carmen's house?

Just before the French Vichy government passed the German Seizure of Jewish-Owned Businesses Act, his parents had sold all the stock in their small furrier's shop. As always, they'd been prepared for the worst. The proceeds allowed them to pay Carmen for board—at least, at first. Her house was in the town of Valvay, not far from Paris—a place that's long been subsumed by the larger city. But when did this happen? In 1940, when France fell to the Germans, or later? Had his parents been hiding with Carmen for two or three years? His mother remembers that "at first," "for awhile," they moved around Carmen's house very freely. Was it like an extended vacation?

Jerome and Yvette were playing in Carmen's living room when the officers came. He remembers seeing a big, shiny black car pull up, outside through the window. Full of chrome and wide running-boards, the car just looked like the gangster-mobiles he'd seen in the movies. Pretending to be a detective, he'd run into the kitchen, announcing: "Bad Men!"

And then a real French detective knocked on the door beside a Nazi SS officer. They were looking only for Jerome's father—they had no problems with Carmen, his mother, the children. So it must have been early in '43, before the general round-ups began. Jerome remembers the SS man's hat, with its gleaming eagles. He'd liked the eagles, remembers wanting that hat. Was his mother with Carmen back in the kitchen? No, maybe not— she'd gone out to barter some ration cards. He remembers his father walking out from the shed, but not leaving. His memory stops there.

Soon after that, Carmen found a new place for his mother to hide—a disused public wash house on the outskirts of the village. Why did Carmen take so many risks? Was she part of the French Resistance? Jerome doubts this was so. He remembers Carmen as a simple, unmarried woman who longed for children of her own. At age 35, she expected no more from life than once-a-week overnight visits from "Uncle Phillipe," a married shoe store proprietor who paid her rent.

After his father's arrest, Jerome's mother stayed in the wash-house, did not come back to Carmen's. Still, she was able to pay part of her children's board by traveling back to her old Paris apartment each week and picking up ration cards, which she promptly sold on the black market. Why did the family still receive ration-cards, once their apartment was seized? She has no answers, the War was full of anomalies. She remembers herself as a blonde, blue-eyed young woman striding past Nazi guards with a pile of *Marie-France* magazines clutched over her chest to hide the yellow star.

Sometimes his mother abandons this light mood of espionage romance and tells the story of their neighbor Martin. At these times, her eyes narrow, her voice becomes very hard.

By the mid-'43, round-ups of Jews had become an intermittent routine. Rumors of round-ups passed, perhaps twice a month, through the Paris Jewish community. She was relatively safe in Valvay, but Martin and his family had stayed at rue Poisionnieres.

One Friday, a rumor passed around town that the Germans would round up all Jewish men in their neighborhood the following day. Martin—and here Jerome's mother's shrewd eyes always glistened with tears—was *un bel homme*. He and his sons hid upstairs in the attic. Although she was French, the concierge there could (for the most part) be trusted. But nobody knew that the order had changed. While Martin and his sons hid behind boxes, the Nazis arrested his wife and young daughter, who, his mother intones triumphantly—and somewhat redundantly—*were never seen again*.

Jerome has no idea what happened to Martin, if he and his sons survived the War. He knows his own mother barely survived. On the day of massive Velodome round-up, when most of Paris' remaining Jews were deported, his mother traveled from Valvay to pick up her ration cards, as was her habit.

This time, no rumors preceded the round-up. It was June, one year later, and by then she'd nearly run out of things to sell. After claiming her cards at the Town Hall, she stopped back to pick up a couple of rabbit-fur coats she'd left at the rue Poisionnieres apartment. It was already summer, she wouldn't get much of a price. But still.

After finding the coats, she realized she had a long wait before the next train. Not wanting to risk the streets more than she had to, she stopped by a neighbor's apartment. Madame Krasinov, also from Poland, had stayed at rue Poisionnieres.

It was hot, Jerome's mother took off her jacket. She wore the horrible star not on her dress but her jacket, because, she reasoned, she could always turn down the lapel. The two women swapped news. Madame Krasinov showed her a card she'd received from her son who'd been deported two months ago. *You see?* the old woman said. *It's not really that bad.* Jerome's mother remembers holding her tongue.

They were drinking cold tea when two French policemen and a Nazi SS officer appeared at the door with a list. *Could you please help us?* they asked. *We need to know whose apartment is this.* The neighbor only spoke Polish, Jerome's mother repeated in French what they said. *This is my apartment,* the old woman insisted. Then they asked to see some ID. When they saw Madame Krasinov's name, they checked her name off the list and asked her to leave with them. *And who,* the SS officer asked Jerome's mother, *are you?* Smiling, she looked up at him and said, *Oh me? I'm just a neighbor.*

That night she hid under an old wooden rabbit hutch out in the courtyard. Forty thousand immigrant Jews were arrested in Paris that evening before 9 p.m. Just after midnight, a second wave of French and SS officers swept through the building, looking for stragglers, sealing all the apartments of Jews. Jerome's mother caught the first daylight train to Valvay. She would not go back to Paris again.

Jerome remembers the rabbits his parents kept in those cages. Trained as a pharmacist, Jerome's mother made a living in Paris sewing fur coats. "Fur," in their working class neighborhood, really meant "rabbit." They farmed their own rabbits for pelts, though later also for food. Jerome remembers keeping one as his pet, the one with the smoothest dark fur and pink eyes he called "Blackie." He remembers the day his pet disappeared and no one could say where he was, but that evening they ate rabbit stew. Jerome would not eat a bite. He remembers the Day of the Rabbit more than the day of his father. But when did it happen? Was this before the War started, or after? What did his mother do for the rest of the War, when she could no longer go back to Paris? What did she live on? Did she keep rabbits out in Valvay? And why were her ration cards waiting that day, if all Jews were being deported?

Jerome cannot remember. There was a chaos at the heart of things. Sometimes, he thinks he actually enjoyed the War. There were so many things to do: finding sharp bits of metal after the air raids, scavenging turnips out in the field, the constant feeling of danger. Dread made him feel more alive. Giddy and alert, he and the other kids watched German planes swoop overhead while they played in the field. Certain events remained fixed in his mind but the links were all inconsistent.

JEROME FINISHES making their salad in the DAAD's Charlottenburg kitchen. It's a nice green salade verte, with vinaigrette dressing. Outside in the hall, the photographer Nan Goldin was dragging boxes and cartons down the stairs.

It was August, 1991—the summer of the Year of Nan in New York, Berlin and Paris. The Kodachrome portraits Nan took of her friends, and showed throughout the 80s in dive bars and clubs, had just been collected in a large, glossy Aperture artist's book. Now Nan had a 57th Street gallery. She was showing all over the world. That fall, she'd been invited to Tokyo, where she took pictures of Shinjuko kids. That summer, she'd been personally invited to stay in Berlin by Joachim Sartorius, who headed the artists program of the DAAD.

In Berlin, Nan quickly decided to spend her time making portraits of the city's outrageous glamour-drag queens. (The queens in New York had by now all disappeared.) Within two weeks, Nan was a permanent fixture at all the transvestite bars, and Berlin's best after-hours. Returning each morning at dawn, Nan found Charlottenburg too bourgeois, too remote and too stuffy. When she complained to Sartorius, he found her a spot in another DAAD building in much-hipper Kreuzberg.

As Nan dragged her boxes outside, Sylvie picked at her salad. *Why*, she whined to Jerome, *do we have to see Peter and Heidi this evening?* The last time she'd been in Berlin, these two friends had snubbed her. There was no reason to think that anything changed.

It's not my fault, Jerome protested, as he often did when Sylvie recited the social atrocities waged against her by his art world friends. As their voices were raising, Nan knocked on the door. She knew Jerome from New York. He was the only one here in Charlottenburg she could talk to. She was stopping to say goodbye.

From her seat on the couch, Sylvie watched Nan Goldin's outlines as she gestured behind Jerome in the hall. It was one of those vintage summer sun dresses: rose chintz, with a flared poofy skirt and impossibly snug bodice. Its low dropped cowl neckline circled Nan's round, creamy white shoulders.

Sylvie loved the dress. It was just like the dress in one of Nan's most famous photos. Shot from behind, the girl encased in the dress collapsed drunkenly onto her boyfriend's broad chest. She had matted black hair and bare shoulders. It was a dress that told you everything could be simultaneously fucked up and beautiful.

As Sylvie studied the dress, Nan caught her eye above Jerome's shoulder. Sylvie's heart beat faster as she wondered if she should get up from the couch and go say hello?

Though she and Nan had never officially *met*, for at least ten years they'd gone to the same openings, dive bars and screenings. Of course Nan was always surrounded by friends, while Sylvie circled the room hoping no one would notice her awkwardness.

Three years before, Sylvie called Nan to ask if Nan would be willing to blurb Sylvie's new underground movie. Though the 57th Street gallery only came later, downtown Nan was a major celebrity. Jerome, as a favor, had gotten Nan's number for her.

Sylvie remembers holding the last digit on the rotary phone on top of the dial ten seconds before releasing it. She always did this before making an important call. Her life flashed before her eyes as she summoned up the nerve to lift her finger, place the call. But then Nan had been very gracious. Just send her the videocassette.

Two weeks later, Nan called Sylvie back. "Ok," she said, "I've written it. I guess I'm not much of a writer. But then again, I'm not sure I understood much of your movie." Unhelpfully, Sylvie explained how she'd collapsed a 600 page Henry James novel and Bataille's *Blue of Noon* into one twelve-minute movie. "It's, like, you know," Sylvie had said, "a hallucination of unfolding consciousness." God, how could she be such a dork? "Oh, right," Nan had said. "I guess it's not much of a narrative."

"Sylvie—" Jerome interrupts. "Come and meet Nan." Sylvie gets up, blushing furiously. Should she say anything about the blurb? Thank her once again? Or congratulate Nan on her recent success? Should she ask her how she likes Berlin, or what she's working on?

"Hey Sylvie," Nan says, standing in the doorway. "What are you doing in Berlin?" Hours pass while Sylvie contemplates the existential implications of this question.

Finally she says: "I'm visiting Jerome."

Nan smiles and says 'bye, trundling downstairs on her cork platform shoes with her boxes.

But later that night at Peter and Heidi's, Sylvie still wondered: *Was that the right answer?*

CHAPTER 7: BERLIN DEATH TRIP #2

BERLIN DEATH TRIP #2

PETER AND HEIDI's large and airy Kleistpark loft easily contained their living space and the offices of Merve Verlag, Peter's independent publishing company. A mellow, frog-like man who'd trained as a philosopher, Peter was a few years older than Jerome. Heidi, now in her late 30s, had given up her indecisive art career to run the press full-time a dozen years ago when she moved in with Peter. Peter disliked speaking English, and Jerome did not speak German, so the three of them spoke French while Sylvie scanned the room and fiddled with her wine glass.

They were talking then, about the movie Jerome started in Berlin six years ago. Like nearly all of Jerome's projects, the movie's still not finished. Although they clearly idolize Jerome, his German friends have doubts about the movie. Jerome had used the Kleistpark loft as his rehearsal studio, and they still remember how the film had practically consumed them both, with its never-ending chaos.

Although no one asks her for her thoughts, Sylvie shares Peter and Heidi's doubts about the movie. She'd come to visit for a week that summer in Berlin, in 1985, while Jerome was making it.

The Berlin trip had been Sylvie's second-ever trip to Europe. She was 29. She and Jerome had been going out (if you could call it that—he slotted her visits to him at his loft into a complex roster that involved five other girlfriends, and she rarely spent the night) less than a year. But when he announced in April he'd be spending the whole summer in Berlin on his first DAAD summer fellowship, she knew she had to do something.

Sitting on Jerome's lap in front of his enormous desk, she'd tried to be direct and open with him about her feelings. "If—if we don't see each other for three months, what will happen to our relationship?" She'd looked adorably pathetic, sitting on his knee and pleading. "But sweetie," Jerome told her with a smile, "you know that I don't want to *be* in a relationship." And then he'd made her come by squeezing his thumbs and forefingers hard against her nipples.

Sylvie pondered this exchange for days. What if Jerome was right? What if the whole *concept* of "relationships" that tormented her was unnecessary? How much, how little, did she need? Was his lack of care for her a kind of freedom?

Two weeks later Sylvie casually announced she'd spend a week or two in Amsterdam that summer. While she'd mentally accepted Jerome's hippie ethos of 'free love,' her behavior became more devious and feminine. Sylvie's younger sister Carla was apparently in crisis—surely Sylvie should go over there and try and sort things out? Trained as a classical musician in New Zealand, Carla had blown off a music scholarship to the Berlin Conservatorium, and was now living in a squat with some Dutch lesbians who were also prostitutes and drug addicts. Sylvie would descend on Amsterdam, save her little sister. Berlin was, what, five hours from there on the train? If Jerome felt like it, maybe she could come over for a couple of days and visit.

WHAT SYLVIE didn't realize at the time was that four of Jerome's other girlfriends had independently adopted the same plan.

Susan was "stopping over" in Berlin on her way back from Milan. Kathy was coming over for a week to "see her German publisher." Kimiko was flying in from Tokyo. Even Ginny threatened to stop by since she was already spending several weeks in Paris.

For Jerome, the heat was closing in. He'd already started having sex with Gisela, his Berlin landlady. Between the shooting of his Berlin film and all the girlfriends' visits, he'd had to buy a wall-sized calendar. Still, he managed it.

The Berlin trip was a calculated risk for Sylvie. Traveling, itself, cost money. She barely paid her rent by working as a temporary night word-processor, and every night she couldn't work she lost $100. Sylvie knew she was the shyest, poorest, least attractive girlfriend on the roster. Clearly if she used just sex and art-world popularity, she'd already lost. Still, she sensed it might be possible to win *by other means*. Because—and here the fact of Jerome's Jewishness came into play—deep down, she knew that he was not the asshole he appeared to be. Jerome was actually much more than his reputation on the scene as Best Friend of the Famous. Like her (and unlike the bratty offspring of the ruling class who comprised most of the art world) Jerome was loyal to his family. Like her, he had identified with words like "ruling class." He had a sense of politics. Sylvie had been a follower of Chairman Mao throughout her teen years in New Zealand. She'd demonstrated, been arrested, written mobilizing pamphlets for trade unions. Jerome had joined a splinter group of the French Communist Party during his teens in France. He'd mobilized against colonialism in Algeria. There was a *missing link* between Jerome's past and his highly-social New York present, and Sylvie knew she'd win if she could identify it.

There was a nexus between history, politics and art that Sylvie knew they both could meet in. Deep down, Jerome didn't merely want to be a friend to all the artists: he longed to be one.

Sylvie could teach Jerome to be an artist! This was something she was qualified to do. Since arriving in New York eight years ago, she'd apprenticed herself to several older artists whose accomplishments and fame were indisputable. Though she didn't know *what* work to do, she knew a great deal about art and *how* to do it. By witnessing these artist's lives and work, she'd learned to sublimate, to cultivate an inner life. Meanwhile, Jerome could teach her something about history!

Despite the fact she has no art world reputation, Sylvie is extremely grandiose. More than a steady boyfriend, she wants to eat and fuck the dead. She wants to be extremely intimate with history. Still, between this insight and the shared reality she dreamt of with Jerome, there were *logistics*.

From Amsterdam, she called Jerome up from a payphone. He told her how to catch the train, and promised he would meet her at the station. The train ride is a great adventure. Sylvie has very little money, knows no one in Europe, and speaks no foreign languages. So when she arrives at the Berlin terminal and Jerome is nowhere to be found, she panics. The changes are all closed, and she has no German deutschmarks. She waits beside the platform with her backpack for an hour, then starts sobbing.

Finally a friendly, English-speaking German helps her place a call to what turns out to be the Merve Verlag phone number.

Sylvie is outraged by this abandonment, but when Heidi answers, she says "Sylvie Green? But my dear, Jerome has gone to meet you at the airport." Sylvie wails. She has no money for a cab, no address, and no idea how to catch the U-BAHN. Audibly annoyed, Heidi agrees to come and get her.

Thirty minutes later, a tall, well-dressed blonde steps out of a silver BMW. "Are you Sylvie Green?" Sylvie nods. "You have obviously made a great mistake about arrangements." This woman, Heidi, reminds her of a female cop, with her pleated slacks and well-cut jacket. As Heidi's BMW purrs through the Berlin streets, Sylvie's reminded even more of Anne-Marie, the female doctor in *The Story of O* who's charged with grooming new recruits for the Chateau. This impression proves to be not entirely unfounded.

Six years later in August 1991, not much has changed. Heidi looks a little older, maybe even somewhat sad, defeated. She's gained some weight, and her intelligent, clear face has lost most of its aggressive edginess. Peter's still a jolly jowly toad, sitting permanently on his chair as if it were a lily pad.

On the plus side, Sylvie is much better dressed. Heidi, in fact, with her gently tailored clothes, served as an early role model. Since Sylvie won her pyrrhic victory for Jerome's affections, he no longer shaves his head. His curly hair creeps down around the collar of the Sisley summer jacket she picked out for him at Bennetton.

Jerome will be busy in the coming days. Sylvie notices he says nothing about their Romanian travel plans to Peter and Heidi. There's the *American Friend* party coming up on Saturday. Tomorrow, Jerome meets with Mathias, the cameraman who shot his still-unfinished film. Six years later, Mathias has a full-time job, but maybe Jerome can talk him into shooting pick-ups. And then, of course, they'll show the rushes from the movie at the party. The film is a rock video about Adolf Hitler. Ridiculous, thinks Sylvie. Jerome is not a filmmaker. Six years later, he still has no idea how lame the whole thing is, dressing some kid up to goose-step down the Kudamm. Do the Germans need Jerome to remind them of their past? Why doesn't he just start working on *The Anthropology of Unhappiness*? This is what the DAAD is paying him to do. She knows all about his grant proposal, she co-wrote it.

It occurs to her she might be married to an idiot, and when they leave the loft, she shares these thoughts. She's been in Berlin less than a full day, but for the third time since he met her at the plane, they fight. Unrestrainedly.

Throughout their better days—the days when Sylvie still believed she might be able to seduce Jerome—she was drawn to him not for what he was, but for what *he could have been*. Only she could see this. Because he was so permanently numb, he was a blank screen on which she could project anything. Still, beneath the screen she sensed the possibility of boundless comprehension. This was how she learned to talk: trying to engage Jerome's attention, telling stories that would push against his distance to the point there might be feeling. To do this was like walking through the desert to an ocean. When it worked, her efforts were rewarded with an outpouring of grief that moved like thunderheads across an empty sky.

When Sylvie moved him, Jerome's voice, which was usually so contained, erupted from his body and he sobbed. She was there with him, she understood. These were the moments Sylvie knew he loved her. For Jerome, there was no middle. But if she could be utterly precise, find words to capture and expand her thoughts and feelings, she could pierce the screen and be rewarded with his grief, which she interpreted as perfect understanding.

And the spirit of love which surpasseth understanding. They lived for sentiment, until it overwhelmed them.

During all these torpid years, Sylvie behaved like someone permanently stoned. Pretending to be dumber than she was, she kept Jerome amused with brilliant, childish topics. Strolling hand in hand along rue Montorgeuil, Sylvie asks Jerome: "Have you ever really *thought* about the telephone? The way voices travel through the wires across the world, and come out the other side?" She was similarly transported by air travel. "Just think, Jerome: last night we were in New York, and here we are buying bread at a boulangerie in Paris!" Her love was singular and irrepeatable, because she loved an image of Jerome that no one else could see.

The first summer after they'd moved up to Thurman, there was an infestation of yellow butterflies along the road to Lake Minerva. It was like a butterfly's Spring Break: as if every butterfly from Albany to Canada had agreed to meet and mate on one long stretch of gravel road.

There were butterflies spread out across the length and width of Northwoods Road, encircling each other, pumping up their filmy wings 'til they became these new and trembling four-winged creatures. Ten thousand single butterflies hovered on the shady blackberry bushes waiting for their turn to mate in the middle of the sun-baked road. They flapped their wings, preparing for the mordant ecstacy of public ritual.

The first (a female?) lands and spreads its wings wide open, twitching slightly. A second butterfly approaches, hovering just above the body of the first until she lifts her wings and folds them up around the other. *Ensorcellement*, encircling. The suitor is enclosed. Both sets of wings are twitching faster than a hummingbird's, and this goes on for minutes until both are exhausted. A butterfly's span of life is short, and the Northwoods Road is strewn with corpses.

Look in my face—my name is Might Have Been, the Romanian Jewish writer Mikhail Sebastian writes across his war-time diary like a mantra. "It is a line," he says, "that sums up my whole life." He's 34, and the 1940 Racial Statutes now prohibit him from working. His studio apartment has just been requisitioned by the Germans. Once, he was a lawyer and a magazine editor, now he's broke and camped out on his parent's floor, counting off the days before he must report again for "snow work," a mandatory labor imposed on all the Jewish men of Bucharest. "Snow work" consists of moving snow from one pile to another in twelve-hour shifts. Pointless to write another play: the theaters have been barred to Jews, and now he doubts he'll ever find the time or will to finish his next novel.

The first time Sylvie glimpsed her private image of Jerome was during one of their lunchtime sex encounters in his room at Martin's loft. Getting dressed, she'd noticed several framed collections of exotic butterflies mounted on one wall. Iridescent blues and greens, mounted with tiny pins on gold-leaf paper. He'd gathered them on one of his adventure trips around the Uruguayan mountains with a Mestizo guide.

"They're incredible," she says. "But why do you collect them?"

Over lunch, he tells her how, in his childhood, he'd made a butterfly collection. He had all of the equipment: a butterfly net, a killing jar, a bottle of formaldehyde. And then his voice breaks up: "They were so beautiful." Embarrassed, she makes all of the expected female noises about animals and cruelty. "So why'd you kill them?"

"I was living in a woman's house. Her name was Madame Carmen. It was in the country with Yvette, my sister. During the War. I did not know where my parents were, or why I couldn't see them. But when they left, the woman told us she was giving us new names: We would be Marie and Serge Bonnard. We would not tell anyone. This would be our secret."

"Ohhhhh," said Sylvie, when Jerome finished telling her the story. Suddenly she understood that all of Jerome's books on death might be connected to his Jewishness. And that his Jewishness could not be separated from the War. She understood that History, for Jerome, was a code-word for the Holocaust.

Sylvie sees her marriage to Jerome as a love story that could be summed up in just three lines. *There was an emptiness. It frightened her. She tried to fill it.* She guesses it's no better or no worse than any other.

TENSES SITUATE events relative to their closeness or their distance from the speaker. Rules of grammar give the empty space of human speech some shape. The simple past: *We left.* In more complex tenses, "have" and "had," the helping verbs, help to separate the speaker from the immediacy of events. *We had left. Had* forms a little step between what happened and the moment when you're telling it.

There is a tense of longing and regret, in which every step you take becomes delayed, revised, held back a little bit. The past and future are hypothesized, an ideal world existing in the shadow of an *if. It would have been.*

Outdoors in Bucharest, Mikhail Sebastian notices *the mute despair that has become a kind of Jewish greeting.* In the eastern province Transinistra, 400,000 Jews have been deported from their villages to concentration camps along the Russian border. Mikhail and everybody knows this. Gypsy children singing in the streets of Bucharest: *The train is pulling out of Galatai/Full of hanged Jews*... Jews have been banned in Bucharest from public markets; Jews have been told to surrender any downhill skis to the authorities. "You wonder," Mikhail writes, "what they will think up next."

Trauma literature describes experiences that aren't fully registered at the time of the event. Because the "who" recalling the event is no longer who he was before, the direct object of the sentence falters: "who," exactly, is experiencing it? "To be traumatized is to be possessed by an image of an event," writes Cathy Caruth, a theorist of trauma. Yet trauma also is a numbness: "no trace of any kind is left," adds Dorie Laub. "Instead, a hole..." Emotion becomes blocked because emotion just leads back to what you think can overwhelm you. Within this state, all future life is predicated by the past; becomes conditional.

Jerome does not remember ever being lonely during the years he spent as Serge Bonnard. Serge was a simple name. It was easier to remember than his own. He remembers practicing the name. Sometimes he called it out, to see if it could conjure up this other boy named Serge who he was meant to be. He pretended to be a fighter plane, using just his voice to skywrite out a picture of Serge, the boy who he would be. When the War is over, he cannot find his voice. It's lost inside his throat. He whispers.

LOOK IN MY FACE; *My name is Might-Have Been*. Nights, Mikhail escapes by listening to classical music until April 1941, when all the radios owned by Jews are confiscated. "The war is like a drug," Mikhail writes later in his diary.

Nearly fifty years after his mother escapes the Paris Nazi round-up, Jerome is arrested in an upstate New York supermarket, caught shoplifting a dog bone and a roll of toilet paper. He's stolen all his life, careful to confine his thefts to things of little value. In this way, he can experience the rush but play the Absent Minded Professor if things go badly. Jerome gives his Columbia University Faculty ID to the sheriff, who handcuffs him and takes him to the county jail. Photographed and finger-printed, he's released that night on bail: $500.

CHAPTER 8: WHO'S PEAKED?

WHO'S PEAKED?

JEROME SPENDS the next few days running around to pick up the pieces of *Second Hand Hitler*. Mathias agrees to shoot some more scenes, but Reiner, the guy who played Hitler, was hospitalized for mental illness shortly after the first round of shooting and no one knows where he is. Jerome calls his acquaintance Rosa von Praunheim, a well-known independent filmmaker, to press him for 'contacts.' Rosa wonders what kind of contacts Jerome is seeking—for casting, for funding, for distribution? Jerome does not exactly know. He sees the amassing of contacts as a virtue in itself, a hedge against the future. But Rosa is shooting a movie—maybe Jerome would like to stop by the set to interview him? Jerome could publish the piece when the movie comes out. Since Jerome believes he might need Rosa later for contacts, he doesn't say no.

It's August, 1991. Except for in Charlottenburg, Nirvana's on the radio everywhere they go. *I like it I'm not gonna crack I miss you I'm not gonna crack I love you I'm not gonna crack I kill you I'm not gonna crack...* Jerome has coffee meetings in Kreuzberg, lunch at the Café Einstein. At night, he meets young artists at the Jungle, a club that cultivates an interesting fusion between German hip-hop music and international techno. There was a feeling everywhere Jerome went that since the Wall had come down, Berlin would no longer be isolated.

The scene was shifting now, there was no longer any notion of a 'center.' And anyway, New York was over. For the first time since the mid-century, Europe could be as important as New York again.

Sylvie excuses herself from most of these meetings. They do not concern her. She walks her little dog along the boulevard, buys a pair of Salamander shoes.

In the hallway on her third day in Berlin, Sylvie finally gets to meet a real Romanian. Florina Elescu is a poet. Like Jerome, she is on a Summer Fellowship from the DAAD. She lives two floors above, in an identical apartment. Florina's noticed Sylvie and the little dog entering and leaving Jerome's apartment. Is she Jerome's wife? Would she like to come upstairs and have a coffee?

It's the first time since arriving in Berlin that anyone's actually addressed themselves to Sylvie, and she agrees eagerly.

Florina's place was identical to Jerome's, except that her books and papers had strayed considerably from the birch and laminate white Workbench desk, her clothes were not confined to the white closet, and her coffee cups had strayed from the white kitchen cupboards. She was working on a project that would be an encyclopedic compendium of references to her nation in "the German literature" from Teutonic fables to the present. Unlike Jerome, she seems to take her work here very seriously.

Florina boils an old metal coffeepot on the immaculate electric range-top. Did she bring this coffeepot from home? She is very interested to meet with Sylvie. Actually, she's been trying to arrange a lunch or dinner with Jerome, but he appears to be so busy! Perhaps he spends long days at the State Library? She, herself, for the first month of her Fellowship, had hardly left the library.

Sylvie understands immediately how Jerome would have struggled to avoid Florina. Conscientious and intelligent, she is a good-girl academic: the kind of woman Jerome dislikes most. Shamelessly middle-aged, she has a husband and three sons. Jerome dislikes most of his female colleagues because they take their work so seriously, and he despises academe.

Florina is a thin, bird-like woman of about 43 with thinning, unstyled hair cut just below her chin. With her frumpy knee-length skirt and silky 1980s power-blouse, Sylvie found it difficult to believe that she was actually one of Romania's best-known poets. She'd received a DAAD Fellowship and edited Romania's leading literary magazine, but she looked more like a secretary from Wellington, New Zealand circa 1973.

Still, Sylvie wonders why Jerome avoided asking for some guidance from Florina. She is, after all, not just a Romanian, but a prominent, influential person in her country. They'll be leaving for Romania in several days and still they have no plans, no contacts with an orphanage, no lawyer. Surely Florina's contacts would be more useful to them now than Rosa's?

But then again, Sylvie isn't totally surprised by Jerome's avoidance of this woman. In just three weeks, he's replicated the same social life he'd established in Los Angeles two months ago. In fact, it was the *same* life Jerome created everywhere he goes. He's already three months late with his catalogue essay for the New Museum (an essay Sylvie will eventually ghost-write when he breaks down and tearfully admits he *just can't do it*, thus rewarding her with his grief); he spends all his time running between phone calls, lunches, drinks and dinners with famous people in Berlin who want to meet him because he is known to be a friend of other famous people who they hope to know.

It occurs to Sylvie that her husband's actual profession was as a *carrier* of fame. The famous didn't always have the time to network for themselves, they needed someone like Jerome. Respected, well credentialed, he was a courtier who, while bearing messages between cultural celebrities in Berlin, New York, London and Paris, appeared to have a mission of his own. The Florinas of this world were totally outside of Jerome's orbit. He knew the playwright Heiner Muller, the filmmaker Wim Wenders, the writer Natalie Sarraute and the Nobel-winning novelist Claude Simon. Did he have time for idle, unimportant friendships? And then, of course it was important for him to hang around the clubs, meet younger people on the scene.

Who's Peaked? was a favorite guessing game among Jerome's new Berlin friends. (They also played it in London, New York and Paris.) Just as the Inuit had 33 words to describe different qualities of snow, Jerome and his friends enjoyed infinitely parsing different categories of fame. Most of them agreed that fame was best arrived at through a slow and steady build. Global media-culture had produced an instant form of fame that was short-lived and arbitrary. Therefore, Jerome and all his friends agreed, it was much better for the artist to crossover from the underground to mainstream culture after his *third* independent movie, her *fourth* one-person show. In this way, once the initial round of hype played out, there would still be hidden aspects of the biography and work for critics to discover. Jerome's ex-girlfriend Kathy really hit the mark in that respect. After self-publishing her work for years, she'd been signed by a major publisher only after finishing her fourth novel, the one about her mother's suicide!—arguably, her best.

Who's Peaked? did not apply exclusively to people. It also worked for restaurants, clubs and bars—in fact, entire cities. Jerome made himself quite popular at the Dawn of Global Culture, circa 1991, going around the world proclaiming that New York was over. In Los Angeles, Paris, Auckland, New Zealand and Berlin, everybody listened, wondering if their city would be next. Or maybe London? Barcelona? Florina Elescu didn't have a clue.

At 35, Sylvie Green was nurturing a form of snobbery far more exacting than her husband's. Fiercely independent, Sylvie embraced an anti-cool aesthetic. Florina Elescu seemed to be a perfect specimen, in that respect. Still, it might be difficult for Florina to befriend her. Florina was so womanly and settled, with her profession, husband and three children, whereas Sylvie was an old punk girl.

As Florina poured the coffee, Sylvie couldn't help imagining how she might look through this Romanian woman's eyes. The idle, younger wife of an arrogant and distant colleague? Sylvie found the image quite detestable. She was an artist, like Florina... but could she tell this nationally respected poet about her experimental movies? Sylvie had stood outside in a blizzard in a black lace bra, black mini-skirt and wig screaming *Plastic is Leather, Fuck You* in a videotaped homage to Antonin Artaud while Florina garnered medals... The cover story she'd been using all these years of following Jerome around the world was becoming like a blanket that had shrunk too small to reach her toes. At that moment, Sylvie Green believed Florina Elescu must know more about her than she knew about herself. *Women, of course, know everything.* But Florina didn't want to talk to Sylvie about poetry or art. She wanted to talk about Jerome.

"Your husband, he is a leading intellectual."

Well yes, although at that moment he seemed like just another asshole.

"He has an interest in Romania?"

Sylvie saw this as a chance to talk about the Orphan Project.

"I think he does," she hedged. "I remember him discussing the Romanian situation with Félix Guattari."

Not exactly a great opening. But how to talk about Romanian orphans with Florina? She and Jerome had turned the Orphan Project into one of their routines, something so hilarious it might just be plausible. But only in the bubble of their couple. Because now, she realized, it was impossible to talk to *anyone* about it without tripping over the half-truths that lurked behind each premise.

People in the normal world assumed married women adopted children because of infertility. There was a whole routine about this in the adoption brochures: shunning mutual self-blame, escaping heartbreak, adoptive couples make a Brave and Life Affirming Choice by welcoming a stranger's baby into their own homes and families. But she and Jerome had already aborted three perfectly good children of their own! And then again, the adopted child would be something that the couple *wanted*, not just an extension of the Talking Dog routine, a metaphoric fantasy.

Sylvie groped for sentences she could even half believe in, but every word was just another tug for cover underneath the shrinking blanket. The more she watched Florina watching her, the more she loathed the cowardice and compromise that were the only aspects of herself that seemed authentic. Still: Florina's English wasn't all that good, so she tried to keep it simple.

"Jerome and I," she started, "have been wanting to adopt a child for a long time." (First lie: Jerome had no desire for a child of any kind. He'd often reminded Sylvie that none of the women in the *Who's Peaked?* crowd had kids, so why should she? And this was true, of course. The *men* had children with ex-wives who'd suicided into dreadful suburbs so that they could raise them.)

"And we have been following the Romanian situation very closely." (Lie 1.5: They read the *New York Times* most mornings.) "And so we felt instead of just adopting a white infant in America (Lie 2: At $15,000, the cost of this was absolutely prohibitive), we could do something else, something that would really... (and here, remembering a code-word from her own Red Diaper childhood)...

make a difference." As soon as Sylvie got this out she winced, realizing the drives towards charity and parenthood were probably not the same.

Sylvie watched Florina processing the language. If the Romanian woman found the conversation strange, she didn't say.

"I would be very careful," Florina replied. "The situation in Romania—it is—changing very rapidly."

Ahhh, thought Sylvie. Perhaps she'll recommend a lawyer.

"In Bucharest, my husband is a carpenter, but he no longer has a job. There are two rooms in our flat. In the morning, before I leave for the university, I must often go down to the street to carry water. Winters are very cold. We don't always have good heat."

Sylvie glanced around the room. Volumes of Florina's poetry were piled up on the coffee table, shelves. Florina was hoping some of them might soon be translated into German. Sylvie wondered to herself how such primitive, peasant-like conditions could be imposed on one of Romania's leading intellectuals? Or were they simply punitive? Was Florina on the wrong side of the regime?

Lowering her voice to a husky whisper, Florina advised, "You have to understand. There are the proper protocols and channels. There are the international agencies, there are lawyers. I would suggest you travel first to Bucharest. There, you can meet with someone who can professionally advise."

Why did Florina speak so ceremonially? Sylvie herself, of course, had considered all these normal, ordinary things. But every time she asked Jerome whether they really shouldn't seek an adoption agency or a lawyer, he launched into a rant about graft, corruption, the World Bank and Third World debt. Assuming that their Orphan Budget was $3000 (one third of Laura's private school tuition; three times the yearly salary of Romanian engineers and doctors), did Sylvie really want to bestow this fortune on a bunch of vampirish intermediaries?

Shouldn't the baby's desperate family get the funds instead? Jerome saw this as a supremely Jewish question, in which he might combine *an engagement towards the social* with the need to *save a buck*.

Sylvie reluctantly agreed. Still, there was the question of the passport. You couldn't simply toss a baby in a nylon zipper bag and smuggle it through US customs like a dog. What if the baby cried? No. She'd called the Immigration Service, and been told the child would need a US passport. To get this, they'd have to meet with social workers, be approved, and have their application channeled through a licensed agency. The cost of this exceeded their initial Orphan Budget by about 500 bucks.

But Jerome had a solution. Wasn't he a dual citizen of the US and France? He'd simply show his French passport to the US customs officers, and voilà—the child would be a citizen of France. Could these fascist lackey border guards prevent him, a citizen of France, from entering America with his own child? Jerome thought not.

"I would like," Florina said, "to meet your husband." Sylvie could not imagine why.

"I would like to discuss with him, about my project. Because my fellowship in Berlin will end in two more weeks. And I would hope that he could discuss its relevancy with Mr. Sartorius. Because I would need to stay here more."

Suddenly it dawned on Sylvie that this woman's *real* project was to not return to Bucharest, at any cost.

Who was Florina Elescu, really? Sylvie mentally reviewed the few facts Florina had disclosed. She'd said her husband was a carpenter. Did that mean that she'd been powerful enough (and at any early age) to pick a sexy worker for a husband instead of just another intellectual? But then again, her husband's lowly occupation could signal a demotion—perhaps even from a high-ranking government post—by the Romanian regime. And what about her books? Romania's 'new' government was barely two years old, but the volumes here spanned back more than a decade. For these books to have been published, Florina must have been on friendly terms with Ceausescu's cultural appointees. And then again—her children. With three, she was two short of the state-mandated five. Did her privilege during the Ceausescu era extend to using banned forms of contraception?

A soft wave of recognition brought Sylvie to the fact that Florina actually reminds her of a *particular* New Zealand secretary she'd known many years ago. The woman was an incest-victim who, at 19, continued living with the father who'd forced sex upon her since her early teens. The woman's vagueness signaled something wrong that couldn't be articulated. She was too soft: her body had the tenderness of one who's dropped their armor much too soon, knows she must regain it, but cannot.

During Sylvie's first years in New York, she'd gone back to Wellington, New Zealand to spend the summer with old friends. For two months she'd eaten well and rested. By the time the return-date on her ticket came, the malnutrition bruises on her skin had gone away. That night, she'd sat on Eunice Butler's steps and wept, feeling that her body wasn't ready for what her mind was telling her to do. Fear, anticipation. Sylvie sees the same thing in Florina. From the safety of Charlottenburg, her body isn't ready yet to brace itself against whatever horror it recalls.

DEAR SIR, wrote Nicolas Murphy in a letter to the *London Independent* in March, 1992: *Your leading article states that most "orphans" had been placed in orphanages by parents who might want to renew contact or take them back in better times. Our experience shows this is rare. With the new legislation imposed, thousands of children who have no hope of even a roof*

over their heads will have to continue to sleep in the street or in railway
stations because there is simply no room for them in the orphanages. The
view that Romanian families may wish to adopt when the economic cli-
mate improves may be true, but how long will the children have to wait?

LATER ON that week, Joachim Sartorius asked Jerome and Sylvie out
for drinks.

Why did Sartorius want to see them? Had he heard Jerome was
leaving for Romania? Cornered by the German bureaucrat's cordial
social manner, Jerome felt compelled to justify his presence in Berlin.

"I think it's time," he told Sartorius, "to do a special German
issue of the magazine. Since the Wall came down, the whole cultural axis within Berlin is changing. In what sense will Germany
respond to the influence of Eastern Europe? I think that Germany,
with its proximity to the east, will revitalize the European scene.
Instead of simply bowing to consumer culture, the former East
Berlin is uniquely able to form a bridge between the west and the
Soviet bloc countries. So what we'll try and do is link up some of
the East German writers with their counterparts in Hungary,
Poland, Romania, Lithuania. I'll be traveling through the former
East during the next two weeks. I already have a team."

Sartorius seemed unimpressed. Really, he'd wanted to talk
about Nan Goldin. "You know, the purpose of the Berlin Summer
Study grant is to invite interesting people here to visit. In Berlin."

Thinking fast, Sylvie told Sartorius about all the people in the
Who's Peaked? crowd Jerome has seen since his arrival in Berlin.
Walter, Rosa, Heiner. Peter, Heidi, Nan and Wim.

Safely back on track, Sylvie asks Sartorius if he knows Florina
Elescu. "I met her in Charlottenburg. Did you know that she is
one of the most prominent poets in Romania? I think her work is

fascinating, she's in the middle of this terrifically ambitious project, but her residency's running out next week. I wonder if you'd considered giving an extension? She needs another month or so to finish—"

Smiling tightly, Sartorius responds with an amused paternal gaze. "Ah, you want to help Florina." Clearly, Sartorius is struck more by Sylvie's naïve transparency than the content of her plea. Still, she nods back eagerly.

"In fact," he says, "the Romanian portion of our program will almost certainly be eliminated. And for just this reason. It seems that when we invite artists from these troubled countries, they cannot help but take advantage of our hospitality. Yes, of course—they all want to stay. But the DAAD is not an international aid organization. We exist to foster cultural exchange."

But when the waitress brought a second round Jerome steered the conversation towards more cheerful topics. Has the East Village really peaked? Kathy's moved to London, Dennis moved back to LA. Walter's still on 3rd Street, but he's oblivious, he spends the whole day shut up in his loft and writing. Nan apparently loves Kreuzberg. The DAAD owns a few prime buildings there. Now that *New York is over*, there's a good chance Kreuzberg might become the new downtown.

Listening to the two men talk, Sylvie couldn't shake her first impression of Florina Elescu. The woman seemed to be a vessel of something truly wrong. When Sylvie was a child, the popular crowd she'd nearly managed to be friends with turned against her. They'd gotten half the class to show up with picket signs outside her house. *Sylvie Green Has Cooties. Sylvie Sucks.* At that moment, she'd been devastated. After several days she'd started to believe them, and maybe she still did. Still, Sylvie had never met anyone like Florina Elescu. Someone who, by being part of the strange history of her country, had become a carrier of contamination.

CHAPTER 9: FUTURE ANTERIOR

FUTURE ANTERIOR

Photo Gallery—Arad 1998
Booze 'n Smokes—Sylvie Green, 4x6 color snapshot

This photograph, taken in a hotel gift shop nine years after the fall of Ceausescu, displays the range of sin-tax luxury merchandise available in Romania's new market-based economy: three cans of instant Nescafe, two bottles of Irish Towser whiskey, and a carton of Winchester brand cigarettes.

Locked and lined with mirrored shelves, the display case is virtually empty.

TWO DAYS BEFORE the *American Friend* party at Peter and Heidi's Kleistpark loft, Jerome gets a call from the new media producer Josef Peichl. He and Peichl met in Austria five years ago at a conference Peichl organized, while he was still an unknown experimental filmmaker. The conference, Jerome recalls, was something about *Literature and Contagion*... the same old semiotic shit tricked out to reference AIDS and therefore seem more *edgy*. Peichl saw a post for Jerome's party up on WebList—he's afraid he's going to miss it. In fact he's 600 miles away in Haugsborg, Austria in a sanatorium, recovering from triple by-pass surgery.

Peichl quickly brings Jerome up to speed on his career developments. His films have all been purchased by the Austrian National Archives, and he's since branched out to digital and electronic media. He produces interactive videos; he serves as an advisor to the Austrian Ministry of Cultural Affairs on web-based knowledge. Perhaps Jerome's already heard about his world-wide summit on *The Digital Dialectic*? To Jerome, who hasn't even heard of email yet, this sounds like some high-tech form of finger-fucking.

Peichl got Jerome's number in Charlottenburg from Sartorius. It's a coincidence Jerome's in Germany this summer, because Peichl has been wanting to involve him in a project. He's just back from Tokyo, where he organized a conference on *Romania—The World's First Media Revolution*. Arthur, the American-Japan guy, gave a great analysis and the Krokers came from Canada. He wants to turn the conference stuff into a book and he thinks Jerome can help... they won't let him out of bed in Haugsborg, but if Jerome feels like driving out he'll gladly reimburse his costs—about $500?

Five years ago, Peichl was best known as the former boyfriend of a world-class feminist—how, Jerome wonders, has he suddenly become so well funded? All the smartest rats, it seems, are fleeing the non-profit ship for the glamorous, highly-capitalized world of new media technology. It occurs to Jerome that Haugsborg might be on his and Sylvie's route from Berlin to Romania. No one has ever offered him consulting fees to simply sit around and talk. He's never thought to put a price on his ideas, much less his presence. Still—one of his former students in New York was hired by

Ogilvy & Mather as a *semiology consultant*... and it galls Jerome to imagine this guy being paid obscene amounts of money to paraphrase his classes over lunch at Indochine...

So far, Jerome's refused to set a date with Sylvie for their departure, but he tells Peichl he can be there in a week. After the *American Friend* event, he just has one more Berlin meeting.

AS SYLVIE WALKS around Berlin she's surprised how easy it still is to identify the former East and West sectors of the city. Even though the Wall's been down almost two years, the grass in parks throughout the former East is wilder and unkempt. She passes Body Shops on Karl-Marx-Allee, Gaps and Bennettons on Rosa Luxembourg Strasse. It's strange, she thinks, they haven't changed the street names yet. There's more graffiti in the former East, but none of it is wild-style. Post-literacy hasn't reached the Eastern sector yet: graffiti on the buildings, sidewalks, highway overpasses is spray-painted as groups of *words* that make up slogans, mottoes, aphorisms.

Everybody talks about 'Easties' as if they were a strange and stunted race. It isn't hard to spot them on the street. Men with beards and hand-knit sweaters walk to work with brown-bag lunches and leather satchels. Women ride bikes along the boulevards in skirts and dresses, as if cycling was not a low-impact aerobic exercise but an actual means of transportation. There are no lycra shorts, no protective helmets. Everybody says it will take the East at least a generation to recover. After all, they've been deprived of media images of themselves for almost thirty years.

JEROME REMEMBERS traveling in Berlin six months before the Wall went up. It was summer, 1961. As a leader of the Sorbonne nt movement, he'd been invited to attend a conference on the Future of the Left organized by the Warsaw Student Union.

Jerome was 23, and he did not particularly connect the "Warsaw" of the student left to the "Warsaw" of the War, or of his family. Neither his mother or his Uncle Adam had been back to Poland since the War. That summer, the Warsaw students had invited several hundred of their European counterparts to camp out with them in tents for several weeks. The Future of the European left would hopefully turn out to be a great and liberating party.

But how to get to Poland? Gerard, one of the guys Jerome knew from the Algerian War committee, had a car. Jerome could catch a ride with him and Paul, who was Gerard's best friend since high school. At 23, Jerome still lived above the grocery store with his mom and Uncle Adam. He'd never spent much time with people like Gerard and Paul, apart from politics and classes. Gerard—whose new car was a birthday present from his father—had his own apartment. Tall, thin, well-dressed, Gerard had his future figured out. With a master's in geography, he'd work in the French Civil Service. Paul, who was less studious, planned to be an architect. Jerome was majoring in literature: that is, he had no idea what he was doing. Unlike Gerard and Paul, Jerome didn't have a driver's license. He'd never even been behind the wheel: his Uncle Adam still dragged a cart back from Les Halles each morning.

Jerome packed carelessly for this important trip: one pair of jeans, two shirts, a pup tent and a sweater. He was surprised, when Gerard picked him up outside the grocery store, to see his friends so well equipped with sports jackets, scarves and shaving kits in leather duffels. They had an entire library of guidebooks to each region in the trunk, archeological textbooks, topo maps. Of course they planned to use the trip to meet some girls, but the girls had better realize sex, for them, was just a recreational diversion.

Jerome was permanently assigned to the back seat before the friends left Paris. He didn't really mind this. It was nice, gazing out the window of the car, moving further from the grocery store and his cramped family apartment. He felt a dreamy kind of freedom. While Gerard and Paul talked about the Visi-Goths and compared their current girlfriends, Jerome's mind was free to wander.

Jerome was stretched out in the back-seat of the Citröen, reading, when Gerard and Paul picked up two girls outside a Strausbourg coffee shop. Agnes and Lisette were both 18, bee-hived and bubbly. One worked in a shop, the other in a factory. All their lives they'd dreamed about Italian men, so on a whim they'd started hitch-hiking. Gerard, the geographer, explained the perils of the route and offered them a ride as far as Poland.

As soon as Paul put their rucksacks in the trunk, the seating arrangements in the Citroen suddenly became more complicated. Gerard, who'd already picked out Agnes, claimed the back seat for the two of them. This left Paul driving, but should Lisette sit next to him, or by the window? Jerome didn't know. Did Paul want Lisette to be his girlfriend? Did Lisette like Paul? Should he be competing for Lisette, or did Lisette and Paul expect the two of them to share her? Lisette jumped right in the middle. Unlike the others, Jerome had never had a girlfriend and he watched, amazed, as Paul draped his gear-stick hand around Lisette's shoulders. Meanwhile, Lisette allowed her right hand to acciden-tally rest on Jerome's thigh. Jerome found this utterly confusing.

His torment reached a climax later on that night when they were camping in a field near Dresden. The three boys had two tents: Gerard's large family tent, originally meant for him and Paul, and Jerome's small pup tent. Agnes, obviously, would sleep in Gerard's tent, but Paul couldn't commandeer Jerome's tent for just himself and Lisette.

The night Lisette shared Jerome's small tent, wrapped up in a blanket beside his sleeping bag, was the most ecstatic of his life. He didn't sleep a wink, abandoning himself to Lisette's gentle, sleep-wracked movements through the heavy fabric. It was as if they'd fucked a thousand times! Drunk with love, Jerome emerged from the small tent that morning to see Lisette sitting on Paul's lap in the front seat of the car, sharing a big mug of coffee. Agnes cracked a joke—Jerome had better sharpen up his moves! Even Gerard leapt to Jerome's defense and coached him. Jerome was miserable.

Throughout the rest of Germany and into Poland, Jerome watched Paul and Lisette flirt. What could he do to make Lisette like him? He was so busy strategizing that when Paul proposed their little group should take an educational trip to Auschwitz, Jerome didn't bat an eye. The former concentration camp had recently been opened to the public. As they approached the ticket desk, Jerome was more concerned with whether he or Paul would pay Lisette's admission than where they might be going. Auschwitz had no special meaning to Gerard or Paul. Their parents talked about the War. Since they only knew Jerome as president of the Sorbonne Student Union, they had no idea that he was Jewish.

The friends tried to keep a respectful, somber mood as they filed past the exhibits, but it was hot outside, and Agnes thought they ought to stop and have an ice cream. At the concession stand, Jerome saw that Paul was creeping closer to Lisette. She even took his hand.

Mournfully, Jerome left his friends behind and wandered off alone, past piles of confiscated items. Mounds of eyeglasses, funereal piles of worn-out leather shoes. Auschwitz was as abstract to him as Poland. His Uncle Adam hadn't been deported there until the end of 1944, a few months before the Liberation. By then, his brother, Jerome's father, had already disappeared.

No one in Jerome's family knew exactly when or how his father died. Except for Adam, the Polish relatives had all preceded him, and the exhibits didn't offer any clues.

Jerome walked past old photographs of burly Kapo butchers in a trance state. His father was a short, slight man. Had he been gassed? Or did he die of malnutrition? Walking around the corner, from a diorama of the camp and its environs, into the only gas chamber preserved in the museum, Jerome gasped: he saw Paul's back pressed up against the wall, and just behind it, Lisette's body. Paul's tongue was in the young woman's mouth. Elbows bent, palms flat, he was dry-humping her against the gas chamber's white tiled walls, underneath a shower head.

JEROME LEFT France for the United States when he was 26 years old, thinking he could leave the War behind him. Three thousand miles away from his mother, Uncle Adam and Yvette, it might be possible to escape the grocery store, the guilt, the dingy rue d'Enghien apartment with its bouquets of plastic flowers and perpetual smells of Polish cooking.

Safe in America, he was finally alone. He liked that there was nothing here that interested him. No one asked him any questions, no one noticed that he spoke the French of someone who's erased their origins. But as he moved numbly up the rungs of academe, the War insinuated itself in Jerome's body deeper than it ever had in France.

Attending French Department dinners at the midwestern college where he taught, staging half-hearted liaisons with safely married women, Jerome thought constantly about the camps. He understood the quality of discipline required to survive there. Against the blank generic backdrop of mid-century Americana, Jerome caressed his fantasies of Auschwitz the way that Humbert Humbert groped Lolita's pre-pubescent body.

As he moved to ever-more prestigious colleges around the American Midwest, Jerome invented games and rituals to keep himself in shape for survival. He knew that anything could be withdrawn at any time. There would be no reason and no warning. Need was weakness, so he kept himself alert, preparing for the worst.

So long as he remained within this state, very little bothered him. He chuckled to himself, *It could be worse*. His head was filled with images of starvation, suffocation, scenes of torture, medical experiments in which a human head is grafted onto someone else's body, like funny Mr. Potato Head, a stupid children's toy they advertised on TV... during these years, Jerome sustained himself with a delicious secret knowledge of just how much worse the "worst" could be.

Later on, in New York City, Ginny introduced Jerome to drugs. On drugs he found that it was possible to replicate the survivor game even more deliciously. Like an addict in the early stages of addiction, Jerome lived for the omnipotent enlightenment that swept through his body at the moment when he started getting off. Being stoned—especially at work—gave him possession of a special, secret knowledge. It occurred to him that smoking pot might be to the Holocaust what TV was to independent cinema: an infinitely repeatable reduction of something that was once essential, highly-charged. Survivor Knowledge was so much more exacting and select than stoned epiphanies and cosmic hippie babble.

Jerome knew deep inside himself that *anyone* at *any time* is capable of *anything*, and things will always be completely absent at the center. Given this special knowledge, Jerome saw little point in trying to advance beyond his tenured Associate Professor job after arriving at Columbia. He was in a French department, yet he hated all things French. Was there any point accumulating money, or possessions, or respect? He knew how quickly all these things could be eliminated. Better, then, to minimize his needs and plan ahead.

Jerome discovered fasting during his first stoned days in New York. Fasting offered him a marvelous, self-regulated pain and independence. During his many fasts, Jerome distantly observed the hunger pangs that, on the first and second days, transformed his solar plexus into an aching chasm. The difficulty of this stage, he knew, would pass, around days three and four, into a floating feeling of euphoria. Eventually this also leveled off. Days five through ten were easily the best. Before the weakening effects of hunger fully hit, the body's endorphine alert receded and he walked around the city like a desert nomad, at peace and fully self-contained.

While others attended boring academic conferences, Jerome experimented with extending this plateau of bliss deeper into the second week. These were the good times, when he knew he needed no one. He liked to visualize his stomach contracting into a taut, athletic vessel. The image of it gave him something close to pleasure. *People were dogs, driven only by their basest needs*. This fact had been well documented. If he could eliminate his need for food—*The transport's grueling purpose was to subdue, humiliate and disorient those about to be killed...* Jerome underlined this passage from a history book with a yellow marker and a ruler.

Through years of intermittent practice, Jerome learned to sustain himself for three weeks without any food. He waited for a time when his survival skills would be tested. Jerome waited for another Jewish Holocaust the way Christians waited for the Rapture. But nothing happened. Books in America were never burned; they were simply remaindered, pulped, discarded. There was no round-up at Columbia. The New York subway cars were never re-directed to Bergen-Belsen. Jerome knew his inner life, if verbalized, would seem ridiculous and so he didn't speak. He knew how to keep his distance.

"The crisis in language," quipped Georges Perec, "is not in words." It could be argued that an anoetic memory of the Holocaust hovers over the French mid-century discovery of formalism. Using words like concrete objects, the practitioners of the French New Novel preferred descriptions of the phenomenal world over humanistic arcs of character and plot. It was as if reality could no longer be contained within a single story, so they devised new methods of bisecting it. Sets and subsets, the invention of experimental narrative... a refracted algebraic distancing effect.

Math problem: If you load 2450 Jews from the Romanian village of Iasi into 33 freight cars and keep them without food or water for the six days it takes to travel 280 miles to a labor camp in Calarasi, how many live Jews will reach Calarasi? Answer? Less than half! *The pile of corpses filled some of the railway cars halfway to the roof... Some captives tried to get a drink by tying pieces of their shirts into a kind of rope, which they tossed through window-slats towards nearby puddles to soak up water... So densely packed into the freight cars that they could not move, people went mad in the sweltering heat and drank their own urine or the blood that streamed from their wounds. The socialist Carol Drimer and the capitalist Solomon Kahan, the technologist Ghetl Buchman and the Talmud-ist Haim Gheller—all shared one experience alike: they went mad and died raving...*

"The only good father is a dead father," Jerome liked joking with his students at Columbia. He was referencing Lacan, of course, and not his actual father, who'd been deported first to Drancy, then to Auschwitz.

Each fragment of reality contains a little bit of poison. You must be careful when ingesting it, never swallowing it whole. You must prevent yourself from reaching false proscriptions of causality. When there is no longer any *Why*, reality is best experienced in tiny poisoned morsels. In this way, toxicity insinuates itself into the body of the receiver-host, who then becomes a carrier.

JEROME'S LAST MEETING in Berlin was with the poets Sascha Anderson and Gerhard Falkner. Both in their early 30s, the two men made a winning and unlikely team. Falkner was one of (West) Germany's leading younger literary personalities. Anderson, a neo-dada anarchist, had grown up in the (former) East. When both of them were in the early teens, their lives were changed forever when they read a German hippie book called *AcidKulturLit*. They didn't know each other then, and neither of them had actually tried acid yet, but when they pored over the first translations into German of the American Beat writers, they knew the dated wall of guilt and culture that separated both Berlins from the real world was about to crumble. Being young was finally more significant than being German.

In August, 1991—almost two years since the physical demolition of the Berlin Wall—they figured it was time to do a sequel. They'd heard Jerome was in Berlin that summer. They'd read his magazine, and heard about the cultural events he'd organized among philosophers and terrorists and pedophiles and William Burroughs. Maybe Jerome could help them figure out who was hot within the American literary counterculture? They already had a (former Eastern) publisher. Jerome would be their third co-editor. The project was surprisingly well funded. They'd pay him several thousand dollars, he'd get to pick which writers to invite on a lavish German tour. Towards this end, an impromptu gathering is organized at Sascha Anderson's.

Sascha lives in a cavernous ground-floor apartment in Prenzlauer Berg. Though considerably less gentrified, Prenzlauer Berg has fast become the Kreuzberg of the former East. The apartment seems to be inhabited by many people—it's hard to tell how many of them actually live there. When Jerome arrives with Sylvie, six or eight young guys who seem like Sascha's friends or followers are already spread out on some thrift-store couches in the living room, excitedly discussing counter-cultural trends and drinking beers. There are also several women, but they stay in the kitchen with a handful of small children.

Though Sylvie's stayed away from most of Jerome's Berlin events, she insists on coming with him to this meeting. Unlike Jerome's other projects, this anthology concerns her. It is something she can *do*. Unlike Jerome, she reads a great deal of American poetry and fiction. Before she married him, she worked at a poetry center in New York. She knows the St. Marks Poets, she knows the Bhuddist poets exiled in Bolinas, she knows the language poets, too. In fact, since 1989 she'd edited a fiction series for Jerome's press, a kind of occupational therapy they've devised to fill the (thousands of) spare hours she has while waiting for her movies to be funded. The series features first-person fiction written by Sylvie's friends and former friends. Because most of them are women, Sylvie sees the series as a philosophical intervention. Though written in the first-person, the books are well-constructed rants, not introspective memoirs. Finally, she thinks, a female public *I* aimed outwards towards the world, more revolutionary than the 20th century male avant-gardes! This is the only countercultural trend worth mentioning.

Still, no one in Jerome's *Who's Peaked?* crowd recognizes these as Sylvie Green's ideas because his name appears before hers on the masthead. Though he hasn't had the time to read these women's books, the press, he reasons, is his art work. What's more, his name gives their work an added credibility. They fight about this question constantly, though most of Sylvie's friends and former friends agree with her husband.

Walking through Prenzlauer Berg from the Senefelder Platz U-Bahn, Sylvie shakes off the torpor that has gripped her since arriving in Berlin. Unlike Jerome's other Berlin contacts, Anderson and Falkner aren't aging hippie-types. They're Sylvie's age, so they must be her contemporaries. Though as soon as they set foot in Sascha's place, she starts to wonder. Why aren't there any women at the meeting? Why are all the other females speaking German in the kitchen? Since she does not speak German, the men don't mind her sitting with her husband in the living room. On one wall of the room, there are several neo-expressionist paintings inspired roughly by de Kooning's *Women*. Sylvie sits beneath the one of two enormous cunt-lips sprouting fangs.

The Germans grill Jerome about the literary scene in New York City. Has any special group replaced the Beats? Who's peaked? Why did Burroughs leave his Bunker on the Bowery for Lawrence, Kansas? What about the Poetry Wars of the mid-80s? The Language school, the neo-New York School? The neo-objectivists? Ferlinghetti, John Giorno, Carl Rakosi?

Jerome doesn't have a clue. He in fact avoids the poets, with their petty feuds and righteous poverty. Endlessly competitive and introspective, they live in dumpy slum apartments and would knife each other for $5. Jerome prefers the painters and the filmmakers who live in Soho and Tribeca. There's money there, at least the things they fight about are real.

Sylvie thinks about her poet friends who started bands and bravely sealed their own obscurity by adopting arcane names that reference things no one but other poets know or care about. As an inverse snob, she finds their willful amateurism magnificently punk and appealing. They'd grown up working class, dropped out of mediocre schools and learned everything themselves, by reading. The poets all sold speed and sat around the floor on mattresses discussing John Donne and Robert Herrick. She finds their self-taught erudition more sublime than Jerome's *Who's Peaked?* form of recognition.

Still, each time she argues with Jerome for her credit on the series, he insists that *credit doesn't really count*. After all, she's not a writer, she's a filmmaker. But as she watches Sascha Anderson and Gerhard Falkner eagerly solicit Jerome's thoughts about contemporary literature, she thinks: *I'm 35 years old. Everything I do now has to matter.*

Jerome is fascinated by the cultural differences between his two new German sponsors. Falkner, who's obviously "of the west," seems to be the front man of the operation although Sascha has the money, and quite a lot of it, it seems, despite the anarchistic mess of the apartment.

Instinctively, Jerome takes Sascha for a Jew. Unlike Falkner, with his movie-star good looks, Anderson is small and rumpled and alert. Though Anderson isn't really Jewish, ten months from now he'll be described as *debrouillard*, a word that's practically synonymous with Jew, in a long *New Yorker* article by Janet Kramer. *Debrouillard* in French means: *a small and shifty hustler.*

Sascha's poetry, it seems, is less accessible than Gerhard Falkner's. Delivered as a threat, his poems are clumps of words describing disparate things: as if non-sequiturs comprised a new form of anarchist polemic. Janet Kramer noted this later. But Anderson's modest neo-dadaist attempts only came under Kramer's scrutiny when he was denounced as a Staasi spy by Wolf Biermann, a well-known hippie folksinger.

The fact that Anderson could recite his driveling diatribes in bars and then phone in a list of names to his superiors *on the same evening* was deeply shocking to both Biermann and Kramer. As if half of the East German population had not been charged for thirty years with spying on the other. Soon after Jerome cashed his (as it turned out) Staasi-funded check, Kramer would meticulously describe his host's red beard, his darting, rat-like eyes, his ironic, arrogant demeanor.

As the afternoon wears on, Anderson and Falkner press Jerome to help them make a list of possible contributors. The three men reel off the names of other men. All white. Sylvie finds the reality of this unbearable. Finally she says: "You know, there aren't any women on this list," though no one in the room has asked her. Still, she's been around this world for 15 years and knows that there are *never* any women on the list, unless someone consciously decides to put them there. The names that spring to mind perennially as *edgy* but still *credible* are inevitably male. And yet, the writers she admires most are female.

"What about Bernadette and Gail, Alice and Eileen and Ann and Susie?" she offers. No one in the room has heard of any of these writers. Most of them are dykes. The rest look like they might be. The men just gape as Sylvie mounts a passionate defense of how *female lived experience can be channeled through poetic avant-gardist forms, but in the process, changes them.*

Thoroughly embarrassed, Jerome thinks fast for a compromise. "What about," he ventures, "Kathy Acker?"

Sylvie presses her thin lips tight and glares at him. At this moment, Acker is in London, at a peak of notoriety that only certain literary men enjoy. As famous as an actress or a female rock star, she's accomplished this by distancing herself from all the dowdy women Sylvie's mentioned. Acker understands that writing, without myth, is nothing and female myths don't run in groups. They're always singular.

The image she's invented for herself is every bit as radical and striking as her writing. With her shaved head, red ruby lips and muscles, she shows off her tattoos in vintage lingerie. At other times, she wears a muscle-shirt and boots and rides a Harley. Her photographs are everywhere: *The Face*, *ID*, and *Interview*. And—better still—one of her books has just been banned in Germany as child pornography.

Of course, thinks Sylvie, if there has to be a woman, Acker would be it. Her books seduce and challenge heterosexual men; her photos just seduce them. Sylvie once saw the anti-censorship crusader Karen Finlay play the Paramount. In a black satin corset and spike heels, Finlay raped herself with yams to cheers from frat boys in the audience. Was it a coincidence that she and Kathy Acker were the only female artists in their world to get anywhere near the mainstream? Why could the famous artist men be friends, the women just competitors? Was sex still the only passport to success if you were straight and female? Across the globe in 1991, in Yugoslavia, New York and Kreuzberg, wars were being fought for meanings which five years later would seem quaint, and five years later still, unfathomable.

Acker's name was added to the list. It was an excellent idea. She'd come on tour, she'd be the headliner.

OUTSIDE THE APARTMENT in Prenzlauer Berg, the evening dusk seems Kodachrome and magical. As they walk across the square, the bleeding mush of yellow headlights into dusk reminds her of an arty film she'd seen a million years ago. The linden trees along the boulevard are blossoming. Is this the same linden-smell the dada artist Hugo Ball described while sitting out the First World War in Switzerland?

Sylvie thinks: It's very ancient here. A shabby row of granite buildings slump together in a rectangle as if they're holding hands around the park. Lenin's dark bronzed body strides into the future from its granite base, now streaked with pigeon-shit and red graffiti.

During Sylvie's first trip to Berlin when she'd caught the train from Amsterdam, Jerome locked her up for an entire day in his Berlin girlfriend Gisela's apartment. Gisela was out of town and he'd arranged to use the place for Sylvie's visit, but he forgot that the apartment front door locked from the inside when leaving. He'd left, oblivious, while Sylvie slept, to do auditions for his Hitler video. When she woke up alone she figured she'd go out and get some coffee but found the door was locked. She couldn't leave. She had no idea where Jerome was, he hadn't left any phone numbers. The only Berlin number that she had was the one for Heidi and Peter. Panicked, Sylvie called the loft only to be told by Heidi: "Jerome is casting now. He cannot be disturbed. I cannot pass a message."

Jailed with an entire day before her, Sylvie wept. Eventually she bored herself and began exploring Gisela's apartment. Who, she wondered, was this woman Gisela? Jerome described her as a waitress-translator, and Sylvie wondered why the women always have these hyphenated jobs? The men are all philosophers, artists, filmmakers.

Gisela has the same books everybody has—J.G. Ballard, Jean Baudrillard, Walter Benjamin and William Burroughs—and most of the same records. Sylvie notices that Gisela's bought the new Lydia Lunch LP. The seal's already cracked, she takes it out and plays it. The second song on the first side of the record grabs her violently. It's a cover of an old pop radio song, smashed to pieces, re-inhabited.

> In the cool of the evening when everything is getting kind
> of groovy
> I call you up and ask you if you want to come with me and
> see a movie
> But you say No, you've got some plans for tonight
> And then you smile, and say, Alright.

Love is kind of crazy with a spooky little girl like you…

No question, everything in Sylvie's present life was fucked. But when she played the song that afternoon in the mid 1980s, she found it possible to move outside herself to something else. *Everything is in the voice*, thought Sylvie. Lydia's voice moved around the room from the record player like a searchlight. The voice tells you everything it has discovered. And then the voice gets hard enough to let you know that these discoveries don't really matter.

Sylvie remembered hearing Judy Nylon singing *Jailhouse Rock* at Max's Kansas City. The way she'd used her voice to turn that dopey Elvis song into a dirge for everything, and nothing in particular.

Sylvie picks the needle up and plays the *Spooky* song again. This time she starts dancing. She remembers how Birgit and Wilheim Hein had played the entire Spooky song in *Love Stinks*, their experimental film about Manhattan. The camera held for three whole minutes on a flashing light atop a fire truck on Greenwich Avenue. This light was the entire city.

You always keep me guessing I never seem to know
 what you are thinking
And if a fellow looks at you you can be sure your little eye
    will be a-winking
I get confused 'cause I don't know where I stand
But then you smile, and hold my hand.
Love is kind of crazy with a spooky little girl like you.

Sylvie plays the record 40 times. It is completely mystical. She keeps herself amused by tripping out and dancing to the record. For the moment she's transcended everything, feels strong: as if she'll always have resources of her own to guide her.

BUT NOW IT'S 1991 and Sylvie wonders if she's used them up?

Across the avenue beside the park, they pass a residential storefront window with a variety of puppet-parts. She sees the floating heads of dolls, the arms and legs of ancient marionettes. Sylvie imagines the old shopkeeper behind her ornate register, wrapping doll limbs in brown paper tied with string. A curtained-off back room; an electric jug; cigarette burns deep into the counter. A sign, hand-painted in blue script, hangs above the window. She'd seen a *David Letterman* show to this effect, about Shoe Repair Shops in Manhattan. The old Italian shoe men were ridiculous, of course, a dying breed. How preposterous for anyone to think a shoe would be repaired and not discarded.

A strange sense of connection stops her. What she is feeling is a surfeit of unescalated time, when buildings were receptacles for human stories. She thinks about the walks she took around New York when she arrived in the late 1970s. There was a store-front puppet show on near Avenue A on East 10th Street. The show—run by Jeff Weiss and his partner, Carlos Ricado Martinez—ran at odd times, and anyone could walk in off the street and buy a ticket. She remembers people sitting outside their buildings on East 10th Street in the summer, watching television. She remembers shooting pool some afternoons at a 3rd Street bar called the Kiwi, where people weren't artists, they were simply unemployed. It was the time before Sylvie questioned herself each time she turned a corner. She hardly thought about herself because there was always something just in front of her, mysterious and wonderful to discover.

All of New York's mystery has long since been depleted. But in the former-East, you felt it lingering and holding on. Does Jerome see this? Sylvie doubts it. In the old days of their couple, she would have coaxed and goaded, thrown herself into a rhapsody of emotion 'til her body wanted to explode with feeling, becoming pure sensation, so that Jerome could feel it too. She would have felt what she was feeling exponentially, because she was feeling everything for two.

But now she doesn't see the point. Jerome has betrayed her. He can't feel anything without her, but her dreaminess and all the old routines she's built with him have left her without anything. For years she thought she could amuse herself forever, having interesting thoughts so she could share them with her husband, but now it's not enough. Jerome might *care* for Sylvie, but he *admires* Kathy Acker. For years, she'd tried to stretch her thoughts and feelings out beyond herself to something more poetic, indirect and lateral but now through sheer frustration, her thoughts are hardening into principles. Normally Sylvie spoke in a well-tempered mid-Atlantic accent, but now she feels her mother's Bronx Jewish voice rise up behind her own, criticizing everything.

She can't stand the clothes Jerome is wearing. Why doesn't he ever pack more than one pair of pants? He looks like an old *clochard*, they're dirty. Jerome's unwillingness to dress is directly linked to his unwillingness to have a life, set boundaries. Why does he say *Yes* to everything that anybody asks him? He's such a hypocrite! He's already three months late with the New Museum essay, why add another deadline that he'll never meet? And what does he know about contemporary writing? He never has the time to read, he's so busy hunched over his computer painfully revising the same few pages of these essays that he doesn't even want to write, but can't say No to. Why can't he just do something for himself? Does he really want to spend the next nine months editing a book for Gerhard Falkner? *The*

Anthropology of Unhappiness has turned into a joke, he'll never write it.

Sylvie remembers something her old acting teacher said when she was 22 and fucking him. She'd asked him why he left his wife and he'd replied "When she was 35, she just became too bitter."

Because after all, why didn't Jerome tell Falkner *she* should be their American collaborator? She'll end up working on the project anyway. Lately she's been demanding gifts of clothes when she writes Jerome's texts and grades his student's papers. For the last essay that she'd 'helped' him with, he'd bought her a $200 pair of shoes. And they were beautiful, that expensive pungent smell of leather, but still she wonders what it might be like to write things under her own name and buy her own shoes? Once, she'd ghost-written a wealthy woman's doctoral thesis. The job gave her a library card and paid her bills all summer, but in the fall the client got a Phd and she went back to topless dancing. Though as Jerome often points out, it's not *what* Sylvie writes, but the presence of his name that really matters.

Jerome can't understand what's gotten into her. Since coming to Berlin, she's been so violent and so angry. Dark rings beneath her eyes, thin lips trembling, she never was a pretty girl, and now she's babbling about feminism in that ugly voice that she's inherited from her mother.

"Why don't you just come out, admit that you're a lesbian? You cannot like me if you do not like my friends."

This time, Jerome pays both their fares when they walk down to the Karl Marx U-Bahn. They're going to meet Heidi and Peter for one last drink in the lobby bar of the Berliner Ensemble Theatre before leaving for Romania. The Berlin Wall has been down now for two years, but still, it's a novelty for westerners like

Peter and Heidi to come over here so freely. The Ensemble still performs a repertoire of Brecht and new dramatists from South Africa and Ghana. Peter will compliment Jerome on the Heiner Mueller essay Sylvie 'helped' him with. They'll speak in French, assuming Sylvie won't be interested in Muller or the German theater anyway.

THE BALKAN WARS were wars of images, wars of language, fairy tales and history. Fought by tiny former feudal states, they were the 20th century's last call for holding onto singular and national identities. Already, these identities existed only in the past, based on memories of events that stretched back 500 years. Like Jerome, the Balkan nations were struggling to maintain the singular unhappiness of their own histories.

Years later, after Sylvie left and Jerome was on the verge of turning 60, he'd be driven, suddenly, to find out what happened to the other Jewish children who'd lived with him throughout the War at Madame Carmen's. Carmen was already dead, but he'd remember one boy's name. A quick check of the Paris phone book would find one Daniel Bloorstein living above a tailor shop on rue des Poissonniers. He and his sister Yvette call Daniel up, arrange to visit.

At 60, Bloorstein hasn't thought about the War for nearly 40 years. Both his parents were deported, died at Auschwitz. After the War, Carmen tried to legally adopt him but he was 'rescued' by a second cousin of his mother and went back to rue des Poissonniers. Like Jerome and Yvette, Daniel soon fell out of touch with Madame Carmen. Like them, he "regrets" having been too busy to attend her funeral.

Around the same time that Jerome and Yvette look up Daniel, their old rue des Poissonniers neighbor and acquaintance

Sarah Kofman publishes a slim, upsetting book that chronicles the two years she spent hidden by a Christian woman who she called Maman, on rue Le Bac. Kofman's father was deported, died at Auschwitz. Although they'd known each other at the Sorbonne, Jerome and Sarah Kofman never spoke about the War. Like Jerome, Yvette and Daniel, Kofman broke off contact with her protector following the War, and found herself 'unable' to attend Maman's funeral. A distinguished psychoanalyst and philosopher, Kofman waited until she was 59 to write explicitly about the events of her hidden childhood. She spent nine months working on this small book. Shortly after it was published, Kofman killed herself.

Sitting in a rue des Poissonniers café, Jerome finds it difficult to hear what Daniel was saying. The two men strain to hear each other's voices. A New York healer told Jerome once, *You don't allow yourself to breathe*, and he quickly sees that this is also true of Daniel. Daniel fights back tears when he talks about his parents, but he doesn't really speak. The words stay squeezed inside his throat, and come out barely louder than a whisper.

FOR THE FIRST TIME, in Berlin that summer, Sylvie realizes it may not be possible to continue living with Jerome. She's much too old to play the shy defenseless waif that their routines depend on. All these years, while she's giddily played the pert gamine Jerome could recast his guilty furtive youth with, she's noticed other people building actual lives they seemed to take quite seriously. The *things* she'd thought she loved so much in Thurman... the dark green shutters with their crescent moons... the wide-plank maple floorboards milled in Johnsburg... these things were not enough to give their life a substance while they moved around like ghosts.

You've got to keep your eyes moving. So long as you keep your eyes moving, you keep the shock of it, the horror of it, to a minimum. Clinging to the sentimental symbols of their own dereliction, she and Jerome have become both the victims and the perpetrators of a crime scene.

In Berlin that summer, Sylvie wonders for the first time if she's used her own small stock of history up in trying to cheer Jerome up, in trying to overcome the anthropology of unhappiness?

CHAPTER IO: PRAGUE DISASTER

PRAGUE DISASTER

Photo Gallery—Arad 1998

Bus Terminal—Sylvie Green, 4x6 black and white snapshot

This image of Arad's Central Bus Terminal is remarkable for its unity of production qualities and content. Developed with expired chemicals at an Arad photo shop, the black and white tonality of the print is lost within a wash of grays and magenta. The terminal itself seems to function as a kind of neighborhood drop-in center. A group of men, apparently unemployed, sit around a makeshift outdoor table playing cards. Two drunks sprawl in plastic chairs, serenaded by a barefoot peasant playing the accordion.

Bus Terminal brilliantly conveys an atmosphere of *waiting*, although its subjects do not appear to wait for busses. Only one "passenger," a kerchiefed woman purchasing a drink from an outdoor vendor, carries luggage. Behind the vendor's plywood kiosk, a large bare tree stands in silhouette. The foreground road is rutted. Reminiscent of Edward Steichen's shocking late 19th century photographs of primitive French villages, *Bus Terminal* uses a modern medium (photography) to depict an ancient world. In this sense, *Bus Terminal* can be simultaneously read as a conceptual photograph and a document.

"CLEARLY, ROMANIA is an ungovernable country," the activist Corneliu Vadim Tudor said in 1998, nine years after Ceausescu's fall. "The disaster is so awful that the only way to govern Romania is through the barrel of a machine gun."

Three years later, he'll be elected president on a far-right nationalist platform. In 2001, the *London Financial Times* will rank Romania last among 12 former-Soviet Eastern nations lobbying for EU membership. Food supplies will be even scarcer than in the Ceausescu years. The urban middle class will flee Romania's cities to grow vegetables on vacant lots in their ancestral villages.

Despite his country's three trillion dollar debt to the World Bank, President Tudor will reject a promising trade partnership with Hungary, citing ancient racial conflicts between Romania's native Dacians and the Hungarian Magyars.

"Why do foreigners slander the Romanians, spreading false versions of their origin and condition?" the historian Sorin Mitu will ask, in a 1997 textbook published by Romania's leading academic press. "Foreigners have intentionally forged a tendentious image of the Romanians in order to perpetuate Romania's state of oppression and backwardness." Still, Mitu concludes, *it could be worse*. The Romanian race, at least, is not as despicable or as despised as their enemies, the Jews and gypsies.

FINALLY, ON an August Saturday afternoon, two days after their meeting in Prenzlauer Berg, Jerome and Sylvie are ready to leave Berlin and travel to Romania. They walk into a Hertz Rent-A-Car office on the Berlin Kudamm. It's cool and empty here: most Berliners have already left on their vacations.

Jerome holds strong views about the rental car transaction. He has a corporate discount (10%) from Columbia University, and expects two further discounts from his Auto Club and AARP memberships. When the Hertz employee insists she can accept just *one* of these three discounts, he accuses her of fraud. And then, to make things worse, she won't accept his cash, and he's already cashed his DAAD Fellowship check to pay for it.

"We accept all major credit cards," the young woman behind the counter keeps repeating. Jerome thrusts his French passport within inches of her face. "I am a citizen of France," he protests, as if she were a Nazi asking for ID papers.

Jerome finds this business of the credit card utterly defeating. *It's not the same thing* to change the deutschmarks into dollars, take them home and pay his Visa card as usual. He wants to use the deutschmarks from his study grant symbolically. Since the DAAD demands that Fellowships be spent in Germany, it's imperative to use these funds to *leave*. Defiance of this simple rule was Jerome's special, secret form of reparation.

Sylvie stands beside him cradling their little dog. Dogs are not allowed inside the building, but the girl behind the counter's been very nice about this. She tries to catch her husband's eye and cool him down, but Jerome is off and running.

As Jerome says, more than just a multi-national corporation, Hertz is a supremely *German* business. Like Mercedes, Volkwagen, Krup and Braun, Hertz most probably enriched itself throughout the War on forced camp labor. Sylvie wonders if rental cars existed in the 1940s? Or were they, like motels, an invention of the transient, expansionist post-War culture? Powerless to change the situation, she strokes their little dog and observes a balding 53-year-old man in dirty sneakers screaming at a neatly uniformed young woman.

Unlike other wives of bullies, Sylvie had never quite succeeded in establishing a secret code, in which the bully quietly succumbs to his wife's covert signals in the interests of his own protection. She blinks at him. She waves, but Jerome continues to ignore her.

Sylvie wonders if the Hertz clerk ever feels defeated by her job. She speaks a barely accented English—in fact, it's better than Jerome's. Does she regret the years of foreign language study that led only to a counter job, processing car rental applications? Her hair was freshly styled, her uniform was pressed, which was more than anyone expected of Jerome. Jerome was rarely judged according to his efforts. His reputation and credentials were considered indisputable. Here in Berlin, he was being paid extremely well for a project he had no intention of beginning, let alone completing.

Lately, words from Sylvie's Marxist-feminist youth have been coming to haunt her. Words like "white male skin and gender privilege" were perhaps… not so far off the mark? She'd seen other people work so hard and make so little headway. The New York art and literary world was more conservative in that respect than corporate America. In the non-profit cultural elite, who you *were* mattered more than what you did. Identity was fixed, you could sleep walk through your life, with the right pedigree.

As they traveled between LA, New York, Berlin, East Hampton and the southern Adirondacks during 1991, Sylvie sometimes broached this observation to Jerome as a purely *philosophical* question. In his new post as the Senior Visiting Critic at an LA art school, Jerome was learning all that season's buzzwords. He'd look at her derisively and laugh, "Well, aren't you PC?" Within the *Who's Peaked?* crowd, the phrase "PC" (politically correct) was already being used as a synonym for "stupid." Steeped in the traditions of French theory, Jerome abhorred reductive formulations such as these because they binarized the rhizomatic *milles plateaus* of 'thought.' The point of thinking wasn't if a thought was *true*. The point was, where could 'thinking' take you? The fact that millions outside the (white, European male) tradition were now clamoring to be heard did not, in these terms, constitute a 'thought.' More like an aggravation.

Increasingly Sylvie found that she herself identified with these millions. Despite the wealth of philosophic-literary references she shared with Jerome, it occurred to Sylvie that she might have more in common with Benjamin, the LA discount shopkeeper with the withered arm, in terms of *opportunities*.

Still, Jerome had rescued her from her East Village hovel. It was only thanks to him that they were in Berlin. Without him, she'd still be teaching English in East Harlem, word-processing or topless dancing. There would be no country houses, foreign travel, let alone the promise of the orphan. She's hoping as they travel east, the Orphan Plan will start to seem more possible, if not exactly realistic.

Jerome reluctantly gives the girl his Visa card, and they leave the Berlin Kudamm with a subcompact Ford Festiva. It's too late to leave today. On Sunday morning they get up and pack the car. By that afternoon, they're already in the former East and passing Dresden. Jerome wants to talk about the Dresden bombings, a prelude to Hiroshima, that presaged the victory of the Allied forces four months later. Vaguely, Sylvie wonders if this is the same Dresden famous for it's china? Perhaps after they've found the baby, they'll stop back on the way home and buy some.

Crossing the border from Germany into the new Czech Republic (a country which, until last year, had been part of the former Czechoslovakia) it's already very late. The new country of Slovenska (once the other half of Czechoslovakia) lies to the south. Josef Peichl's Haugsborg sanitarium is west of Prague. Perhaps they'll cut across to Austria, and then back down? Tired, they check into the Terminus Hotel at the border town of Litmorice. A dreary place, and hardly worth the $20 a night. But they go to sleep excited because they'll be in Prague tomorrow before lunch time.

BY AUGUST 1991, Vaclev Havel's Velvet Revolution has made Prague safe for a Junior Year Abroad from America's best colleges and universities. Endorsed by poets, movie stars and rock bands, the Velvet Revolution is a miracle of liberal market-driven principles put into practice. When Jerome and Sylvie drive through Prague's well-restored medieval walls, they're amazed to see the city teeming with well-dressed attractive people. Brown University seems to be especially well represented. And they are everywhere, these family friends and offspring of the Kennedys, starting online magazines, exporting architectural salvage and developing new internet-based companies. Business is transacted mostly out of doors, on blankets in the park, and on the terraces of once-stodgy governmental buildings converted into trendy upscale bistro bars and restaurants.

It is the apex of a period when everyone unreasonably believes the internet will be the conduit for an enhanced and newly democratic information flow. No one, apparently, recalls the farcical outcome of the world's first Media Revolution, that occurred 500 miles away a year ago in Bucharest. Forgotten also is the outcome of the 'cable revolution' that raged across America during the mid-1980s. Within two or three short years, the mass democratization of TV that cable promised had been reduced to a few pathetic public access channels... and who would want to watch them anyway, when you could watch the Sundance Channel (owned by Gulf + Western), HBO or MTV?

In just two years, Havel's Velvet Revolution has transformed the city's failing 19th century industrial base into a cluster of boutiques. As a quaint historic stop along the information superhighway, Prague is going to change the world, and for the better. Perversely, in the former

Yugoslavia just 400 miles away, Slovenians and Croats are f
Serbs, and Serbs are bombing the shit out of Bosnians, in an eff   ᴕ
maintain their own identities against the bland trans-nationalism of this
same superhighway. Still, Prague is the Haight-Ashbury of the 90s. The
young Americans who flock here believe wholeheartedly in their lives,
and the future and the new economy, and who's to say they aren't right?

"These people have no knowledge about history," Jerome remarks
bitterly as he watches well-dressed culture tourists ogling Prague's
architecture. To the uninformed, Prague seems like a medieval European dreamland, with its turreted castles ringed by moats built into the
seven hills that hunch like hungry crows around Vlatava River. Don't
they realize that these castles weren't built for charm or fantasy, but for
defense against the mongrel hordes and armies that threatened, on a
daily basis, to storm the city walls and enslave Prague's urban populace? As bunker archeology, Prague's castles illustrate the principles of
modern architecture: form must follow function. It pains Jerome to
see these once-foreboding medieval structures lightened, brightened,
into something skylit, blanched and glassy. Isn't it like the Ameri-
canization of sex, with the hideous Ruth Wertheimer and Dr. Laura
yammering on about their G-spots? Why has everything become so
banal? If sex is everywhere, sex is no longer sexual.

The city's mobbed. Wenceslas Square looks like a theme park
mall, Jerome can't find anywhere to park. "We are the last generation to whom things really matter," the philosopher Gilles Deleuze
said recently. And yes, of course, without a history or a memory,
how can any fact be truer than another? Last year, the Croat
nationalist president Franjo Tudman purged Croatia's Serbs from
civil-service jobs and restored his country's medieval flag. One
month from now, the Serbian JNA will unsuccessfully invade
Croatia, and in retaliation, all Croatia's Serbs will be interned by

Tudman's government. Within three weeks, unable to contain the situation, the European Community peacekeepers will flee.

Jerome and Sylvie are pleased to find accommodation plentiful in Prague, despite the high demand. Thousands of residents have fled their rent-controlled apartments for less fashionable locales, so they can rent them out to tourists at a profit. Within an hour, they have keys to a one-bedroom place for $40 a night.

And there are many things in Prague that Jerome wants to see: Franz Kafka's house, and Josevov, the Jewish Quarter. They hit the streets with Lily, who cowers in the crowd. Sylvie picks her up and carries her. "Look at the people here," Jerome sneers. "They've all flown in from other capitals." Unlike he and Sylvie, they haven't battled bedbugs at the Litormice Terminus Hotel. Instead they're drinking gin and tonics on the terraces, and strolling through the cobbled streets admiring the sights: Hradcany Castle, the John Lennon Wall in Kampa, the somber gothic arches that support Charles Bridge. The gargoyles on the old cathedral have been power-washed to look like Disney trolls. Carved to protect the 10th century Christian populace from demons, the gargoyles could no longer frighten anyone. The medieval mind believed that images could undermine the abstract force of evil. At night, they're underlit with soft pink gels.

Jerome is utterly dismayed to find the Jewish quarter swamped with tourists. The four-story family home Franz Kafka spent a lifetime trying to escape is jammed with attractive hand-holding couples in their 20s.

This is not the Eastern Europe Jerome had been expecting. There are no villagers stomping elderberries to make alcoholic drinks; no Soviet-style factories run at minimal efficiency. Havel has delivered Prague from the Middle Ages by opening it to the world, and now the city is awash in the vast exchangeability of consumer goods and signs. Buskers playing music in the streets—Jerome found this unbearably degrading. Why hadn't he used his Berlin contacts to set up meetings with Prague intellectuals? Though then again, these are probably the same people he and Sylvie are displacing with their cheap apartment rental.

Sylvie finds the city totally enchanting. Prague was the city of her ancestors, and she loved the crooked streets, the funny gargoyles on the bridges and the pastel-colored houses. There were pretty little dogs, and some of them looked like Lily. Was Prague the city of her canine ancestors? There were beautiful displays of amber jewelry in every second tourist store, perhaps Jerome would like to buy some souveniers?

Defeated by her enthusiasm, Jerome no longer wants to see much of the city. What's the point of looking at Secession architecture when none of the tourist cows who clog the streets know anything about the period? Newsstands pumped out magazines with pictures of the president standing next to Allen Ginsberg, Lou Reed and Madonna. Lou Reed indeed. Jerome despised the fuzzy humanism of the Velvet Revolution. Bitterly, he wished they'd visited the transit camp in Ostowa instead, where Prague's Jews were held en route to concentration camps in Poland.

He and Sylvie boarded trams and rode them to the ends of lines around the outskirts of the city. But even in the suburbs, everything was fresh and thriving. There was hardly any misery at all. Prague had turned out a disaster.

YEARS LATER, after Sylvie left Jerome, she felt compelled to go back to Romania alone. Living in Los Angeles, she needed proof that something different still existed. She thought by doing this it might be possible to understand her marriage to Jerome. In April, 1998 she re-traced their journey to Arad through southern Hungary.

In November 2001, she went to Bucharest. This time, she flew to Paris, then to Belgrade, and caught the train to Bucharest carrying a half-pound bag of French-Roast coffee. Purchased by her Paris friend, the poet Nina Z., as a small gift for the writer Adrian Dinescu's widow Cipriana, French coffee was by then impossible to buy in Bucharest, and so it was a special treat. Sylvie was charged with delivering the package to Vlad Russo, who'd been Dinescu's editor at Humanitas, Romania's leading academic/literary press.

In 2001, commercial flights between Belgrade and Bucharest had been indefinitely suspended, so Sylvie caught the train from Belgrade overnight. Even in the first class cabins, there was no heat, no food or drinking water on the train, and the toilet was an open hole. There were no blankets on the sleeper. The temperature dipped down to 22 degrees.

Upon arriving in the capital, Sylvie is relayed from host to host, who insist that it's unsafe for foreign guests to travel anywhere alone. That fall, the former actress Brigitte Bardot emerges as the champion of the 200,000 feral dogs that roam the city streets.

On a Thursday afternoon, Sylvie meets Vlad Russo at his home. Since de-regulated gas and electric bills have soared, Humanitas can no longer afford to heat its offices. Vlad and the other editors work from home three days a week.

Luckily, the electricity in Russo's middle-class apartment building hasn't been suspended yet—although, as he points out, many city residents have dismantled their own power lines so they won't be charged for electricity. Since the World Bank ordered the new government (the nation's tenth, since Ceausescu) to suspend electric subsidies, domestic power bills cost more than half the average monthly wage. Still, Vlad, his wife Francesca and his Uncle Vlad live in three cozy rooms they heat with coal on a salvaged antique stove. Though the place has not been painted since the rise of Ceausescu, at least it's toasty warm.

Sylvie caught conjunctivitis on the train. Since foreigners can't see doctors and pharmacists can't sell drugs without prescriptions, it's impossible to shake. As Vlad questions her about Romanian émigrés in Paris, Sylvie rubs her eyes. He assumes that she's allergic to his shedding dog, an aging beagle he calls Freckles. Gallantly, he suggests they take a walk. In the hallway, Vlad is pleasantly surprised to find the elevator running. They ride downstairs, and Vlad drags Freckles by his leash along the boulevard. (The dog is blind.)

Sylvie notices how the neighboring high-rise residential towers bulge out horizontally from their balconies. Since no one can afford to move, the balconies are glassed in and expanded as new relatives arrive. Plastic buckets hang like flags from poles. Defensively, Vlad insists the buildings are equipped with running water. It's just that many residents can't afford to use it, with the new de-regulated water charge. Women fill their buckets from open hydrants on each corner.

In Belgrade, a director of the International Red Cross told Sylvie he no longer goes to Bucharest, though supervising Romanian children's charities is his job. "The people who were once my colleagues… they aren't colleagues any more. They beg for things, for anything—not for the organization, for themselves."

Vlad fastens Freckle's leash to a pole outside the new convenience market on the corner. A slight man in his forties, Vlad shuffles through the store and picks up a small container of Mazola oil from the shelf. That month, *Details* magazine will run a story about a girl who sells herself into sexual slavery with the Romanian mafia to pay her father's overdue electric bill. Vlad Russo earns $160 a month at Humanitas. He takes out a 10,000 lei note to pay the clerk. The cooking oil costs $1.29.

CHAPTER II: EDGE PLAY

EDGE PLAY

AS SOON AS they left Prague, Jerome and Sylvie began fighting about Austria. At first, they disagreed about where this tiny German-speaking country actually *was*. The lines denoting national boundaries on Jerome's Michelin map of Europe were spidery and shaky. No matter how often she consulted it, Sylvie couldn't shake her innate belief that the European nations were stacked vertically, from north to south, in descending order of post-industrial development.

In Sylvie's cosmologic scheme, Germany naturally sat on top. Austria would lie beneath it to the south, followed by the Czech Republic, Slovenska, Hungary, and Romania. Therefore, she'd imagined (wrongly) that when they reached the Czech Republic, they'd already passed the threat of stopping off to visit Josef Peichl at the Haugsborg Sanitarium.

Jerome, on the other hand, knew that Germany was both large and central, with several other countries grouped around it like the pieces of a puzzle. He knew that Austria wrapped around beneath Germany and the Czech Republic's southern borders, and that Haugsborg wasn't very far from Prague. They'd detour west to Austria, and it would be a short drive back to where the Czech Republic met Slovenska.

They'd cut their Prague vacation short. Sylvie hadn't minded. They'd had to keep Lily out with them all day because dogs were not allowed in the apartment and it was too hot to leave her in the car. Leashed and collared, she'd followed them around the ancient city until she was dehydrated and exhausted. Often they just gave up and carried her. Eyes half-closed, draped over Sylvie's shoulders, Lily looked like a fur stole worn out of season. What would Sylvie do when Lily died? She wondered if they'd have her taxidermied, stuffed, so she could be with them always? Back on the road, Lily was more comfortable, curled up in the little nest Jerome had carved for her in the back seat, between the jerry cans of gas and cartons of Kent cigarettes.

Sylvie wondered how much of Eastern Europe Lily actually was seeing? During the past year, her deep brown eyes had clouded up until they turned a filmy blue. She'd changed and weakened since the tumor operation, and had it really helped? Sylvie didn't dare to check the lump she'd felt two weeks ago when they were leaving Thurman. The dog was 12—the perfect age for touring Europe if she'd been a human child. But Lily wasn't. Her golden squirrel-chasing years were now a distant memory. Resting underneath the seat, with her gray snout supported by two graying paws, Lily lived in escalated, canine-time. In dog years, she was 84.

During their torpid years in Thurman, Sylvie liked reflecting on the experiential phenomenology of dog-time. Once, when visiting her friend Fran Myers in New Hampshire, they'd left Lily in the car when they went out for dinner. Throughout the meal, Sylvie contemplated how this separation must have *felt* from her beloved dog's perspective. If one dog-year equaled seven, how long did Lily wait for them to finish dinner? Having stopped attending school before her class tackled long division, Sylvie

found this problem overwhelming. Still, she knew it w
to leave her unattended.

Sylvie swore off meat when Lily had the tumor o
With heightened sensitivity, she refused to eat the creatures who
had once been Lily's cousins. The vet had promised to them the
tumor was benign, but was it? From Berlin to Litormice,
Litormice down to Prague, Sylvie held Lily on her lap, flipping
back her floppy ears and whispering the names of things that she
was seeing. Often, Lily shivered inexplicably in Sylvie's arms, and
Jerome would crack a joke to cheer her up: Lily was a Kierkegaar-
dian dog, get it? *Fur and Trembling*. One thing was certain: Lily
had a boundless range of comprehension.

Still, there wasn't much to see outside the car as they traveled
west along the Czech Republic National Highway. Meadows
spaced between the poplar trees, a few gently rolling hills behind
them in the distance. Occasionally, the monotony was interrupted
by a Soviet-style New Town, thrown up during the 1960s in hopes
of bringing Czechoslovakia into the 20th century. Invariably, these
towns consisted of apartment buildings, schools, and recreation
centers built around enormous factories. Of course their efforts
were misguided, but at least the Soviets had *tried* to create a higher
living standard in the country.

Since they left Berlin, Sylvie's noticed that Jerome has grown
much calmer. His Toshiba laptop remains buried underneath the
luggage. Nights, he doesn't even try to work in their hotel rooms.
So long as they stayed on the road, his unfinished text on Death was
temporarily forgotten. It was important for Jerome to be in the right
frame of mind when they finally reached Romania. Perhaps they'd
stop at one, or several, Eastern European spas? The trip could even
turn out to be therapeutic and relaxing. So Sylvie is completely

shocked when Jerome announces that they're heading west towards Haugsborg.

"Impossible," she protests. "We've already passed it."

Jerome stops the car, unfolds the map and points to Austria, a country slightly to the west, but Sylvie is confused. Hadn't they passed a sign to Brno, the Czech Republic's south-most city? She'd been certain Austria was somewhere farther north. But there on Jerome's map is a secondary road that leads from outside Brno west to Haugsborg, Austria. Jerome guessed that Haugsborg was no more than 100 miles away.

Looking at the circle on the map, Sylvie feels completely violated. Hadn't they decided *not* to go to Haugsborg? They'd fought about it in Berlin, in between their fights about Heidi, Peter, Florina Elescu, Joachim Sartorius and Gerhard Falkner. When Jerome dropped the subject, Sylvie just assumed he'd tacitly conceded.

How could he imperiously insist now that they go to Haugsborg? Wasn't Romania a trip that they had planned together? This was just further proof that they had never, really, been a couple. Real couples fought *constructively*. They used their fights as milestones towards a greater *intimacy*. The Haugsborg detour was Jerome's covert way of showing his contempt for her and for their marriage. Besides, that he'd even contemplate accepting Peichl's invitation just further proved his lack of self-esteem. Hadn't he said, five years ago, that he disliked the man intensely? They'd both laughed up their sleeves at Peichl's trendy academic conference on Literature and Contagion, they'd ridiculed his third-rate experimental films. How could they adopt a child, if Jerome had no convictions? Had he changed his mind, now that Josef Peichl was successful?

"That's not the point," Jerome protested. "Peichl is not a Jewish name."

"So what?" she asked, stumped by this non-sequiter.

"He is an Austrian. He has offered me good money... to do nothing. I think I should accept it."

Sylvie could not see why. Five hundred bucks was not *that* much. Why would he consider ruining their trip for this pathetic sum? Why would he even want to go to Austria?

Jerome is deep in other thoughts. "How old is Josef? About 50, 51 years old?" Perhaps—he was a little younger than Jerome, not much. To Jerome, that means that Peichl's birth occurred at the beginning of the War. "Did you know the Nazi troops were actually *welcomed* into Austria?" Jerome pictures Josef's mother cradling the infant with one arm, sig-heiling with the other. "The Austrians didn't lift one finger to resist the Nazis. On the contrary, they begged them to come in. Of course, Austria has always been a very Catholic country."

"Oh Jerome, don't start in on the Catholics."

"They've always hated Jews."

"That isn't true!" One of her poet friends had recently converted to Catholicism. Sylvie found this very admirable.

"Austria was like one big focus group for the Nazis! Did you know that when the Nazis came to power, Goebbels actually doubted that the mass extermination of the Jews would be accepted by a modern populace? They didn't want to risk dissent in Germany, so they tried it first in Austria. Guess what? No problem! The first deportations took place among the urban Jews in Vienna. Was there any outcry from your fucking Catholics? Not at all! The rest is history."

All over Europe, Sylvie thought, the present keeps getting mixed up with things that happened fifty years ago, or even centuries. The Albanians were seceding from Macedonia to protect their native language, while the Macedonians fought off the Serbs. Meanwhile the Thessalonians—a biblical race—were rising up as the "first" Macedonians against the Muslims, who'd only occupied their sacred ground during the past five centuries.

"Look," Jerome said. "We'll get a bite to eat in Brno, we can be in Haugsborg around 5. We'll see Josef for an hour, and we'll tell him that we have to go. We can still be in Hungary tomorrow."

This seemed completely unrealistic. Haugsborg was a 250 mile round trip on who knew what kind of roads? Why did Jerome insist on saying "we" when really all he ever meant is "me"? Jerome's "we" made Sylvie feel completely insignificant.

"Come on," he coaxed. "You've never been in Austria before."

He said it in a little voice, to indicate that he was quoting the first line from one of Sylvie's films. The one she shot in France, the one that started with her saying: *I'd never been in France before. For a while, I thought—this is incredibly exciting.* And it was, it had been. That same summer, after Jerome had locked her up in the apartment, she'd finally broken through with him. They were walking in the Turkish Quarter. For the first time since they'd met her tears had reached him and he understood just how alone she was. Pity flowing someplace close to love, he'd ditched his German girlfriend and taken Sylvie with him the next week when he had to be in Paris. France was the third European country she had ever been in. When their train finally rolled across the Belgian border, she'd stood up in the carriage, taken Jerome's hand and pointed out the window. "Look Jerome," she'd whispered, "a French cow." She'd never seen a thing so beautiful.

France had been the country Sylvie dreamt of as a child. Studying picture books of gothic architecture while the other kids played kickball, Sylvie's father comforted her by promising an

interesting life. She'd attend a great English university, the
a year in France and have adventures like the writer Henry
Eventually she'd come back to New York, begin a glam_ious
career... None of these things had happened, and until the day she
crossed the border with Jerome, she'd felt completely exiled from a
sense of possibility.

But in August 1991, remembering this movie made her cringe.
She was 35, remembering these childish dreams and their appease-
ment no longer gave her pleasure. Had she been so busy wallowing
in the distance between her inane dreams of happiness and her real
life, that she'd forgot to have one? It was time for her to *have* a
child, not be one! She should have focused more on her real life,
despite the fact that it was dumb and shitty.

She remembered hearing something that the writer Kenneth
Broomfield said about her films to June Goodman: "Oh June, you
know I can't *stand* Sylvie Green, don't even talk about her. The
way she spends her time making all those stupid little movies for
Jerome ..." June and Kenneth were two writers she admired, and
recalling this—although it happened several years ago—still made
her blush. She'd wanted to be *friends* with June and Kenneth, and
oh, there was nothing she could ever do to make them like her. If
she lived to be 70 and June was 83, in June's eyes she would still
be uncool and stupid. Which group had the longer memory—the
Serbs and Croats, or the writers in the New York art world—was
debatable. The only thing that stopped the art world feuds becoming inter-generational was the fact that hardly any of them bred. As
Jerome gleefully liked noting.

But wasn't this why they were going to Romania? The Haugsborg detour only underlined how fraudulent Jerome's commitment
was. But then again, the worst part of it was, it wasn't June who'd

told her what Kenneth said, it was her quote-unquote best friend, Fran Myers. Fran had spent the last two years bouncing back and forth between Sylvie and June Goodman. Because Fran had rightly judged that June would be the softest port of entry into Kenneth Broomfield's elite circle. Why did Fran think it was okay to transmit something awful June had said that Kenneth said about her back to Sylvie? But then again, it could be that she'd asked Fran point blank, *Do you think Kenneth Broomfield hates me?* one day over coffee. Still. Why didn't Fran think to exercise some tact, spare Sylvie's feelings? Had she become that insignificant?

"Look in my face—My name is Might Have Been," Mikhail Sebastian writes all across his war-time diary. It's August 1941 and he notices all the elements that once made up his life receding. His gentile literary friends continue cautiously to receive him, but for how much longer? Thugs and intellectuals alike parade through Jewish streets with bayonets and bags of native soil hung around their necks. To the east, 3000 Jewish men are rounded up and shot point-blank in the courtyard of the Bukovina Police Station. They leave behind a stagnant pool of blood that will later be mopped up by their female relatives, at gunpoint. "Powerless," Sebastian writes, "to speak or write. A kind of dull, muffled terror. You hardly dare look beyond the passing hour." He studies English, reads about the French revolts of 1848, thinking they might offer clues about the future.

Sylvie felt this insignificance every time Jerome used the word "we" to talk about himself... it was as if her own existence were annihilated. Alright, maybe Sylvie's needs could never be as important to Jerome as his daughter's—but did she have to come in second place to *Josef Peichl*? Factoring in the cost of gas, Josef's $500 shrank at least $100.

"That's not the point," Jerome spat out.

Driving south, Auschwitz hovered to the east of them.

FOR A LONG TIME, they'd stopped speaking. Jerome's body remained planted at the wheel, but he seemed to be someplace else entirely. Lines of argument ran through Sylvie's mind but none of them connected to the center. If she could just *explain* the nexus of her misery to Jerome maybe he could change it. But then again he'd become such a fundamental part of it. At what point had her life become so insignificant? She recalls the word as one her ex-girlfriend Liza Martin used in a videotape they'd made together. The one about Artaud, where Sylvie'd stood out in a blizzard in a black lace bra impersonating Liza. She'd re-created one of Liza's crazy rants while she built a snowman, about how Liza's horse-faced junkie husband, an Artaud fan, had made Liza feel completely *insignificant*, an ontologic state that linked her psychically to Antonin Artaud, the madman junkie poet who had been the patron saint of every junkie Liza'd ever married. Sylvie thought her blizzard act had re-created Artaud's famous 'cruelty' with Zen perfection, and it was crazy, yes, but was it brilliant crazy or just crazy and pathetic?

But she can't talk about this to Jerome. Sylvie's art is one of their fundamental fictions. Instead, she talks to him about Berlin. How insignificant she feels around his friends. How he makes no moves to make his friends respect her. She's wounded by this, by all the times she's stood next to him at openings and parties in LA, New York, Berlin, and the person who 'they' are talking to won't speak, won't even bother to make eye contact with her. And now they're on their way to Haugsborg… Has she become so insignificant that Jerome can't do a simple thing like blow off Josef Peichl just because she asks him?

"You know I didn't want to join you in Berlin. I only went because you promised if I came to Europe, you'd help me find a baby."

Jerome wishes only to be left in peace. Her relentless arguments make him feel like he is being bashed to death by hummingbird's wings.

"Oh Sylvie, you know that you are not *in any way* maternal."

"You don't know that!"

"If you were serious about a child, you'd understand that raising one costs money. And Josef's paying us well for this short drive."

"He isn't paying *us*, he's paying you, Jerome! And what? A big 500 dollars? For fuck's sake, how much money do we need? I just made $8,000 renting the East Hampton place for just three months—"

"Another of your famous schemes. What makes you think East Hampton is your money? We never could have bought it if my mother hadn't sold her condo in Netanya. That money was a gift to me, from my family! Do you think we could have built the second floor if I hadn't spent my sabbatical teaching in Los Angeles? You don't even have a job! You have no way of getting one. You can't even support yourself, so how do you expect to have a child?"

"Well I can always teach—"

"Hah! Teach what? Teach *filmmaking*? You have no credentials, you antagonize the feminists, you don't even know where Austria is. Who in their right mind would hire you?"

Jerome remembers how the Nazis launched a massive medical research program after annexing Austria in 1938, the year Jerome was born in. Vienna's Jewish scientists and doctors had made Austria world-famous for advances in technology. In 1939, the Nazis opened an Institute for Bio-Eugenic Research in Austria, at Grasz Hospital. The Final Solution was still in its early planning stages.

A special, hand-picked team of Nazi doctors went to study there, including the notorious Mengele. From there, Mengele went to Auschwitz.

"That's not the point!" protested Sylvie. "Don't you see, Jerome—I'm still your wife. How can you respect yourself if you never think about my *feelings*?"

"Ahhh, feelings," Jerome smirked. "Your feelings are what you really care about. You see? You never really wanted to have a baby. The child is just a symbol that you use. A means of testing, how much you are able to control me."

At night, Jerome recalled, Mengele and his team of Nazi doctors toured the Auschwitz barracks to make 'selections' of the physically unfit, who would be taken to be gassed the next morning. *Arbeit ist freitag*, yes. But not everybody knows the gas chambers were not the full extent of the camp's horrors. Auschwitz became a clinical testing ground for bio-tech experiments developed hypothetically at Grasz (*under the mentorship of Jewish scientists and doctors*). How long will it take a human limb, exposed to extreme cold, to atrophy? Select a prisoner, and place him in a bathtub full of ice. The results of this bizarre experiment helped Nazi generals assess how long their soldiers could withstand the Russian winter.

"This is not a test!" she screamed someplace far outside him. "This is my life. Jerome, I hate you now. You were never serious about going to Romania. All these years since I had the first abortion you swore to me that we'd eventually have a child. You lied. You never wanted it, not ever!"

Not all the Nazi medical experiments had such direct and practical applications. There was one, Jerome recalls, in which technicians combed the camps and Warsaw Ghetto for twin Jewish children. Twins, with their identical genetic structures, were at a premium. One could be used as an experimental subject, the other kept as a comparative control. For example, inject one twin with gasoline, the other twin with water. Observe the effects upon the skin and body temperature of the gasoline-injected child. Jerome cannot recall what the results of this experiment were used for.

Silent, drifting back uneasily into his survivor pose, Jerome thought about his father's death in light of these experiments. Did he die in transit? Starve? Was he gassed upon arrival, or did he become the subject of one of these unthinkable experiments? Jerome remembers reading that the Nazis skinned the corpses of their victims, boiled up the flesh and mixed it with synthetic DNA to learn if human flesh could be used as soil for the farming of synthetic organisms.

Why, Sylvie wonders, does Jerome torture himself by reading every piece of Holo-porn? He'd never been a prisoner himself. Why does he let these simulated memories of the camps define his every action?

"I don't know why you married me," she finished softly. "I was 27 when we met. What kind of monster would marry someone so much younger, someone who expects to have a child, if he didn't want to have a baby?"

Since the ending of the War, survivors of the Jewish Holocaust, their families, and later on, descendents of American slaves have debated the ethics and the efficacy of reparations. Can monetary sums ever be attached to human life? Once atrocity is quantified, is it accepted? Accepting Josef Peichl's 'gift' allows Jerome to keep these thoughts alive. Thoughts that make him hate himself more deeply.

"Oh Sylvie, don't you get it?" Jerome finally shouted back. "It's not like I *set out* to marry you. I had lots of other girlfriends. I didn't want a life with you, especially. But you were so persistent.

You invaded my life, piece by piece, you took over, until finally I just gave up and relented."

Jerome's arthritic leg is cramped within the tiny space between the driver's seat and gas pedal. His hip replacement aches. Outside, the Czech Republic countryside has become considerably more urban. Steely clouds are gathered in the sky above the parking lots and warehouses. It's going to rain. They're just outside of Brno now. Like Sylvie and their dog, Jerome is trapped inside this crappy tin box car that has become a metaphor for their marriage. It's headed, where? To Brno now for lunch, and then eventually Arad.

But first they'll go to Austria.

CHAPTER 12: DEPECHE MODE

DEPECHE MODE

THEY GOT COMPLETELY LOST, then, driving into Brno. Squalid, claustrophobic, Brno was everything Jerome had dreamed the East would be. It was the dirty underside of Havel's economic miracle. Construction sites, abandoned since the Dubcek era, form a second wall around the medieval city. Late summer weeds grow thick on vacant lots and highway medians. The town exudes an atmosphere of possibility for random pointless acts of violence. Unlike the former East Berlin's cute and clever leftist slogans, graffiti in the town has been reduced to spray-painted names of foreign bands: Depeche Mode, The Cure and Public Image Ltd.

After missing the single highway exit into Brno's old city, Jerome and Sylvie are trapped on the peripheral road for another 20 miles. It is about to rain. Sleek new BMWs and ancient Skodas dart around the road.

Eventually, they circle back and find the Brno Public Square behind a web of cobbled alleys. Outside the cathedral, market vendors are dismantling their displays and packing merchandise back in vans. By now it's 3 p.m.—too late for lunch, too early to have dinner. Since leaving Prague, they've been driving for six hours. They decide to take a walk, discover ancient Brno. Sylvie gingerly lifts Lily from her back-seat nest and puts her on the curb. Once outside, the dog will not do anything but sniff and tremble. The dog can't pee, and Sylvie wonders if she's been traumatized by their fight.

Tacitly, the pair agree that it's too late to drive to Haugsborg. Jerome wants to take a look around the market. With its displays of tube socks, key chains, sneakers and root vegetables, it has all the authenticity Prague lacked. Though he still intends to visit Josef Peichl in the morning, Jerome hopes that shopping can offset the bitterness between them. They'll comb the dismal market for authentic local merchandise, just like in the old times. Sylvie tries to rally to this consolation prize, but the offerings of the Brno market don't inspire much enthusiasm.

The Brno vendors mostly have the same gray-market orphaned merchandise she bought in Echo Park from Benjamin. She sees a few clay jugs between the china bags, but these are mass-produced, made only for the tourists. Instinctively, she looks around for hardware. She's learned over years of traveling with Jerome and setting up their houses that it's only in the hardware stores you still find truly local merchandise. Candy pink mosquito nets in Guatemala; plywood rat traps in Oaxaca; terracotta bean pots in the eastern villages of Quebec. It occurs to Sylvie that this kind of foraging for Third World décor accessories—for many years the sole domain of vacationing academics and their wives—has recently been professionalized by buyers from Pier Nine and Ikea. Vaguely, this thought depresses her.

There isn't any hardware in the Brno market, but Jerome spots a robust kerchiefed peasant selling strings of garlic cloves and dried red peppers. Her goods are laid out over cobblestones on a blanket.

Of course! These things would look fantastic hung between the copper pots suspended from the antique hand-hewn beams of any hi-tech kitchen. *But which kitchen, in which home?* Sylvie grumbles to herself. It's not as if they actually have one. Each time she rents one of their places, she has to clear all of their belongings out. *If we'd only had a child we would have had to live somewhere.*

Meanwhile Jerome attempts to bargain with the woman, who does not speak English, French or Polish, over the price of a string of garlic cloves. Through elaborate pantomime, he gets her down from ten to seven zlotys, or is it dinars? Crowns?

Buoyed by this triumph, Jerome suggests they check out Bratislava. According to the map, it's only 40 miles away. He thinks that Bratislava may have been an important cultural center forty years ago, though he really can't remember. But there's a university and a Museum of Czech Folklore. Perhaps they'll find a nice hotel? They'll get up early in the morning, back on track to Austria.

Sylvie mopes along behind Jerome dragging Lily's leash in one hand, the string of garlic in the other. It will be no more possible to bring the garlic back with them through US Customs than it will be to bring a baby without immigration papers, but this thought does not occur to her.

Jerome turns out to be right about the hotel in Bratislava. Their room has cheerful tartan curtains, low-slung single beds, a Georg Grosz-era woodcut hung above the desk. Sylvie orders bratwurst in the restaurant and coaxes bits of it down Lily's throat. United in their love of all things Soviet, they suspend their hatred of each other and sleep blissfully in a deep reprieve.

THERE IS AN IMAGE of them Sylvie now remembers, they must have been together for two years: it's early morning and they're exiting a cheap motel in Troy, New York. They already have the little dog—she's hidden in the nylon zipper bag, slung over Jerome's shoulder. Sylvie holds onto his arm, wrapped up in a fake snow leopard coat. She remembers being very happy, stumbling down a cement path into their 1977 Ford Granada. They still haven't had a cup of coffee. It's late October. Frost is covering the ground, and it's cold enough up here near Albany to see your breath.

Jerome wears the ugly beige acrylic cardigan that his mother forced on him a year ago when Adam died. Jerome looks old and thin in his dead uncle's sweater, in the early morning light, but Sylvie finds this very sexy. She imagines them as the Whore and the Professor, an unlikely, perfect pair of grifters. No one else at this motel is traveling on business, or traveling anywhere at all.

Sylvie thinks she knows the low-life very well. She thinks she understands America. She thinks she can explain it to Jerome. She's happy, because in the picture, she has become the kind of whore she's always dreamed of being: a skinny one with crooked teeth who, for no good reason, is held in high esteem. Jerome is patient and compliant, and it excites her that in some small way she has already managed to derail his life. Together, they visit truck stops, bars and diners. They steal old furniture from vacant houses. He is a long way now from academe. With Jerome, she's finally found a way to be both bad, and in control. When she's been with other people, guys, who are *really* bad, she doesn't know how to handle it. She knows that they don't like her, and she gets too confused. Sylvie holds on to Jerome's arm just like she embraces everything he's given her: a $300 Ford Granada, and 20 dollars for the room.

LATER ON THAT AFTERNOON, they drove north and found the house in Thurman. The empty ten-roomed place was everything they'd dreamed: twelve miles from the Thruway on a two-lane road that led nowhere except to other dying towns, the house had nothing to remind them of themselves. Later on, when they moved in, they found the walls were stuffed with ancient newspapers to protect the former, subsistence-farming occupants from the cold.

In Thurman, every logging road and boundary fence contained a story. Obligingly, their neighbors recited their family histories in the unbroken narrative of Homeric myth. These people rarely went as far as Albany, or even Saratoga, a mere thirty miles away. Lost and shabby in large towns, the Thurmanites lived like kings and queens in their ancestral homeland. Here, the Bakers, Putnams, Woods and Camerons were all (at least) second cousins. Roads and glens were named for their great great-grandfathers who'd cleared the land 150 years ago. Across the bridge where the Schroon and Hudson rivers met, Jimmy's Peak faced Mountain Number Nine. As everyone in Thurman knew, Jimmy's Peak was named for one James Cameron (great-great-grandfather of Pearl Cameron, who ran the store) who'd hid out there an entire winter when the colonists won the War of Independence. James, a Scot, had sided with the British. He was afraid of being lynched. To Billy, Pearl's adult son who lives alone in an unfinished log cabin up on Cameron Road, it was as if these things had happened yesterday.

In Thurman, history was a lot like hypothermia: a warm and loose embrace into a dreamy state that turns out to be inertia. While all their former friends stayed busy "getting" something in New York—great sex, mature relationships, a movie deal, a poetry spot on MTV—in Thurman, tomorrow had a way of turning into never. By entering other people's disappointment, Jerome and Sylvie found it possible to alleviate their own.

As ghosts, they found they could remain superior to other people. They liked to play at being Keats and Mary Shelley. Even on Jerome's salary, they lived much better than the local hicks. Sometimes, after reading Arthur Waley, Sylvie made believe that they were Chinese poets, exiled to the provinces from the court. For amusement, they took aimless drives around the southern Adirondack countryside that lulled them even further into Thurman's torpor. Sylvie liked to point and name the barnyard animals they drove past. "Horse!" she'd say, in the thin voice of a three-year old, hoping to charm and entertain Jerome.

But their most sublime form of communication took place through the medium of their dog. At age 7, Lily had been close to death when Sylvie rescued her from the pound. Like Jerome, she was a survivor. Her happiness could not be simple and intuitive. It was something more heroic, conditional and willed. Like Jerome, Lily had a huge capacity for sentiment. Like Sylvie, the dog suffered strange somatic illnesses that couldn't be appeased by offerings of chew toys, bones or food. Supremely grateful for her rescue, the dog had not completely overcome her sorrow. Jerome and Sylvie sensed the deepest *weltschmerz* behind her rheumy eyes.

In the months following the War, Jerome recalls his mother opening the mail at their apartment on rue des Poissonniers. Letters she'd sent to relatives in Poland, hoping they were still alive, came back from by the Red Cross with the word "Deceased" stamped on the envelope. This happened eighteen times. He'd been, what, nine? Weeping uncontrollably for her family, telling stories about babies being bayoneted in the Ghetto while their helpless mothers watched, his mother chose to systematically contaminate him with grief.

Jerome wanted more than this for Lily. To amuse the dog (and also Sylvie) he made up new words to describe their private universe. He didn't realize then that sentiment was actually a balm for horror. Happy words, for things they liked. One of their favorite words was "woofy," a term coined for things that were as adorable as their dog. Afternoon snacks of Stilton cheese and fresh-picked apples, rose trellises against old clapboard houses, hand-embroidered pillowcases, blackberry bushes on the road... they spent long afternoons adding items to this list.

Time, in Thurman, might have gone on like this forever, had Sylvie not turned 35. That birthday, Jerome let her pick out her own gift. She'd found the most amazing Chinese ceramic rabbit in an antique store on Lower Broadway during one of her Movement Therapy visits to New York. Bunnies were an important item in their pictographic alphabet, and this one, with its creamy-orange porcelain, was completely woofy. Significant, substantial, stately, it was everything that they were not. Jerome happily looked on as she unwrapped the rabbit from its tissue paper box, but Sylvie felt a queasy wave of doubt. This time next year, when she turned 36, would she unwrap its mate?

JOSEF PEICHL's bed floats like a white cloud in his large private room at the Haugsborg Sanitarium. A nurse in an old-fashioned white uniform leads Jerome and Sylvie down the hallway.

There is no video surveillance, just the murmuring of voices above an electronic hum of diagnostic and condition-monitoring devices. Impressive, how the Austrians have preserved the building's 19th century character while equipping it with everything that's new in medical hi-tech. It's as if by doing this, they can make the international uniformity of medical technology appear as a unique product of the Austrian national heritage.

Three weeks after receiving triple bypass heart surgery, Josef's hard at work, chain-smoking Marlboro Lights and talking on the phone. He finishes up a call and waves them in. After exchanging a few pleasantries about the restrictions placed upon his freedom, Josef motions for Jerome to take a seat.

Taking five fresh hundred dollar bills from his zippered leather purse, Josef explains that he needs Jerome's help in bringing his Romanian Media Revolution project to a wider audience. Based upon a conference that he organized a year ago in Japan, the Romania book in fact mirrors his own personal theories on mass media. As a filmmaker and a scholar, Peichl has long recognized how *the cinematic gaze can be deployed* to *separate reality from the actual.* Only the media, in this sense, can function as *both the subject and sublime object of the revolutionary gaze*, as the Romanian Revolution has so synchronously proved. The book is coming out in Germany next fall from Merve Verlag, but it's important that these ideas reach an English-speaking audience. Towards this end, could Jerome get Jean Baudrillard to write an introductory essay? Baudrillard will be well paid, of course.

Peichl's proposition takes Jerome's breath away. He'd expected to be pumped for his own ideas on semiotic theory. At worst, he'd expected to be pitched to publish this ridiculous diatribe. But he'd never imagined Peichl saw him as an unofficial agent for Jean Baudrillard. As French theory's wandering pimp.

Sylvie observes Jerome sitting like an alert young Irish Setter at Josef's bedside, unable to sense his deep disgust. He laughs when Peichl laughs, he discreetly pockets the fresh currency. Why doesn't he tell Josef to get fucked? Watching the two men transact their business, she imagines how she must appear in both their eyes. At 35, she's shrewish, sharp and haggard. There is a certain energy in this. There is a tightness in her chest. She senses its potential. This time, she won't comment on her husband's self-erasure. She'll refrain from lecturing him about assertiveness or accent elimination. She no longer sees the point.

She and Jerome don't speak until they get back to the parking lot. Lily's sprawled out underneath the tree where Jerome tied her leash. Asleep, she's made no efforts to chase squirrels or escape. She's hardly touched the cup of water that they left for her.

Jerome unhooks the leash, strokes Lily's head.

"Drinky, drinky," they both plead.

CHAPTER 13: END GAME

END GAME

THEY GET LOST driving out of Haugsborg. It's late, they're trying
to avoid Vienna. To make up lost time, Jerome decides to take a
web of secondary roads southeast through Slovenska, a new
nation that has recently seceded from the Czech Republic, which
was the former Czechoslovakia. Jerome speeds down unsealed
Slovenskan byways at 70 mph. Driving through a stop sign, he
swerves to miss a cattle truck. "But I didn't see the sign," he
protests when Sylvie screams, as if this is a rational defense.

He wants to stop someplace and eat, thinking surely Sylvie
must be hungry? *What's the point,* she says, *of eating?* They're
way out in the country, and it's nearly dark. The landscape
churning past outside the car is different from the landscape in
America, but the dog's asleep in the back seat and Sylvie can't be
bothered noticing what those differences are.

Eventually they will reach Romania, although at this
moment, driving through Slovenska, it seems possible that they
will not. There's still the whole of Hungary to get through, and
it's already August 12. In just two weeks, Jerome is due in Paris.
Sylvie and the dog have tickets to fly back to JFK from Berlin-
Tegel on August 31.

They'll return on Thursday morning, but the East Hampton house will be rented through the end of the long weekend. She'll take a cab to Port Authority from JFK and ride to Warrensburg on George Putnam's Trailways bus. From there, she and the dog will catch a ride to Thurman. Thankfully, the August tenants will have left the house in order, but when she picks up the phone to call Jerome in Paris there won't be any service because she forgot to pay the bill before she left a month ago.

Jet-lagging, she'll wake up at 6 a.m. and drive five miles down to Stony Creek to use the nearest public phone. Her annoyance will be momentarily transcended by the sunrise. She'll see slices of pink light shot through holes of cloudy sky. Swirls of mist will rise above Zaltz Pond behind the abandoned summer camp, water rapidly evaporating, proof that nights up here have already started dipping down to 40 degrees or so.

In the warming September morning, Hap Emrick will be sweeping off the porch of his general store. Standing in the parking lot outside the tavern, she'll watch Hap stop to light a cigarette. Hap will wave to her across the creek, and water churning over rocks will roar. It will be early afternoon in Paris. Jerome will be at his mother's rue Enghrien apartment, expecting her to call. She'll stretch out the payphone receiver towards the creek so Jerome can hear it, too.

On Sunday afternoon she'll pack the car and drive down to East Hampton, but the tenants won't be gone 'til Monday evening so she'll stop at a motel. Curling up with Lily on the bed, she'll turn on HBO—a treat!—and watch an episode of *Confrontation*, which seems to be one of the season's hot new shows. *Confrontation* is apparently a program about crime victims meeting their assailants on blind dates arranged by the producers. In this particular episode, the *Confrontation* crew brings a paralyzed ex-New York City high school teacher up to Comstock Prison to visit with the unrepentant youth who shot him in the face. Said youth is scheduled to be paroled next month, and *Confrontation*'s female anchor asks the victim earnestly if there's "anything he'd like to say"? Tears stream down the fleshy white male victim's paralytic face.

Confrontation rings a bell with Sylvie. Thirteen years ago, she'd attended a performance of that name staged at the Robert Miller Gallery to celebrate the opening of Louise Bourgeois' new show. *Confrontation*, in that case, consisted of some 70 spectators looking at each other through gaps in a plank fence while her ex-girlfriend Liza Martin stripped.

It occurs to Sylvie this new TV show might be the *only* cultural legacy created by her generation in late 1970s New York. And sure enough, when *Confrontation*'s credits roll, she recognizes names of several experimental filmmakers she used to know from the old non-profit Film and Video Workshop. People who can probably now afford to rent her house. Sylvie will realize that instead of moving forward, she's simply gotten dumber and at the same time, more repelled by everything around her. She'll think there might be something about that era—the late 1970s in New York—that never quite came out. The lump within her chest will rise again, she'll think: *it needs to come out now.*

Back in East Hampton, there will be a form rejection letter waiting for her from the New York State Council on the Arts film panel. The grant she wrote for her and Fran to shoot five more scenes for their *Sadness at Leaving* movie pilot will have been turned down. A hurricane that swept the beach two weeks ago will have struck a tree that hit the house, but she won't be able to call anyone about it because the phone is dead. This time, it will be the tenants who forgot to pay the bill.

Biding time, she'll ride her bike to Maidstone Beach. The sky will be a very fragile kind of blue with blackbirds sweeping through it, a golden light will be reflected on the choppy little crests of waves in Maidstone Bay. Lying on the beach grass, she'll read a story by June Goodman and she'll feel somewhat on the brink of something: *Oh, this is what it's supposed to be.*

Later, filling out another funding application, the image of her useless diligence will move her practically to tears. Writing in her diary, she'll wonder if there is something else beyond the films, something the films have been excusing her from doing? *I don't know,*—the notebook breaks off with that comma—and she won't begin another one for several years.

IT'S IMPOSSIBLE for Sylvie and Jerome to know how lost they really are on the back roads of Slovenska. There's no one around to ask, and even if there was, they don't know what the language is ... Slovenskan? One thing is sure: they won't arrive in Budapest tonight. So much, thinks Sylvie, for visiting the famous spas. She doesn't bother to berate him. What's the point of even fighting? They're not a couple, never were. If they'd been a couple, fighting would have brought them closer. Their fights wouldn't simply take the place of everything they couldn't say. Her rage, at least, would have had a target, she would not be simply arguing with a ghost. They would have already *had* a child, not been zigzagging through Eastern Europe on this crazy pretext neither of them believed.

Jerome senses Sylvie's rage but it bewilders him. How can he be blamed? He's made no promises. He's spent the best part of his life shuttling between the endless needs of Ginny, Sylvie, Laura. What more can anyone expect? He is exhausted. With his left foot to the floor of this crappy tin box Ford Festiva, his plastic hip aches constantly. He'll probably have to have another surgery next year and *that* will be another two months wasted. He hasn't opened his Toshiba since they left Berlin; his text on Death is nearly four months late. In two more weeks he'll have to catch the train to Paris to see his mother one more time before returning to New York and then—the beginning of another academic year.

All of us are here to die, Robert Anthelme wrote after being freed from Dachau. (How did Anthelme reach this level of despair? He wasn't one of the despised. Jailed for his activities in the French Resistance, he wasn't even Jewish.) *That's the objective the SS have chosen for us. They haven't shot us, they haven't hanged us, but systematically deprived of food, each of us must become the dead man they have aimed at.*

You have to choose your death, Jerome thinks to himself. *Yes. That is the only way of having freedom.* If he could just explain this, make her understand—

But now she's sobbing. When he reaches out to touch her shoulder she pulls back against the Ford Festiva door.

"Jerome, don't touch me!"

He knows she often gets this cranky when she's hungry. Luckily he's saved two rolls this morning from their breakfast back in Bratislava. And there's a jar of peanut butter in the hamper underneath the hatch.

"Sweetie, let's stop. I can fix you up a peanut butter sandwich."

For a long time she says nothing. When she does, her voice is very hard.

"Jerome, I hate you."

Panicking, he insists that dinner's on the way. "There must be something coming up—a bar, even a quaint *petite auberge*—"

"Jerome, there's nothing here! We're lost! A quaint *petite auberge* my ass!"

He grips the wheel much tighter. Now she's mimicking his accent and his voice.

"You should have thought of that when you insisted that we 'pay a visit' to that asshole!"

Why has she become so vicious and so angry? It's all his fault, they haven't eaten dinner. And maybe Sylvie's right… there may not be a restaurant anywhere. They're hurtling down a two-lane road in a country that still does not officially exist, they don't know where they are, his eyes fill up. Survival is the thing that he does best, but now he isn't even doing very well at that.

She sees his tears. She pounces. "What Jerome, so you're upset? But you have every reason to be happy. Haven't you gotten everything you want? Your Berlin friends, your stupid Hitler film, your big 500 bucks?"

But Jerome has never wanted anything at all. She is so monstrous in her anger, can't she understand this simple thing? He *has* no wants or needs. She says she hates him, but there's really no one there to hate. *This is what you get*, he thinks, suddenly supremely pleased. She doesn't get it. Obviously she's not as smart as he once thought. The air outside is riotous with the hay and cow-dung of Slovenskan summer. Jerome keeps his eyes locked on the road.

LATER ON that night there was a cabin in a field of daisies. Sylvie remembers this: Jerome had seen it first, through the wash of yellow headlights on the road. Pulling over onto a patch of gravel, the cabin seemed to be part of some old fashioned Soviet vacation camp. Jerome took a flashlight out from underneath the seat and Sylvie followed him while he explored. A group of cabins, scattered in a jagged horseshoe around a field of meadow grasses, thick with paint, a chestnut brown. Lily got out of the car all by herself and ran around, her red coat burnished in the daisies, as Jerome pushed on the door of the first empty cabin.

It opened easily enough, but there was no electricity in the cabin. They gathered blankets and a hurricane lamp and candles from the car. Sylvie made up the narrow bunk with sleeping bags and blankets. Jerome blew the candle out. She fell asleep against his chest. In the morning, sunlight beamed in through a window that they hadn't seen the night before.

Outside, dew beaded on the meadow grass and daisies. A small hill rose behind the camp. They got up and packed the car. Everything about Slovenska seems much better in the morning, so when they pass a turn-off sign for Korovoce 12 kilometers away, they decided to take the detour, have some coffee and explore.

KOROVOCE SEEMS to be a market town for the surrounding farmland. Underneath a summer sky, 19th century rural archetypes drive shiny Renault Clios to transact their business: the butcher and the baker, the pharmacist and notary, all set up in pastel stucco'd buildings grouped around a village square. Dirty and road-weary, Sylvie and Jerome park and walk around in search of coffee. Holding Lily in her arms, Sylvie imagines Thomas Hardy's classic novel: Michael Henchard with his wife Susan and their baby, wearily approaching Weydon. Hopefully a happier fate awaits Jerome and Sylvie here.

They find an old-fashioned tabac and order two espressos. Lily curls up beneath the bar at Sylvie's feet, and no one seems to mind. Next door there's a bakery. Jerome goes out, buys six fresh rolls. Haugsborg and Romania both seem a long way off. They order two more cups of coffee and relax.

As they're sharing the third roll, Sylvie looks out the plate-glass window and sees a woman passing by with a small dog. Incredibly, the woman's dog is practically identical to Lily. They've never seen a dog before with Lily's unique breed proportions: the sensitive dachshund face, the long cocker legs, the silky reddish coat, the floppy ears. She tugs on Jerome's sleeve and points, and *Yes!*, Jerome agrees, *There's Lily's twin.*

Swooping Lily up, they rush outside to introduce her to her Korovoce cousin, but by the time they reach the sidewalk, the woman and her dog are halfway down the road. They decide to take a walk. Perhaps they'll find a butcher shop and buy a bone for Lily? Jerome clips Lily's leash onto her collar and takes Sylvie's hand.

As they walk beyond the central square, they notice Korovoce's stucco'd houses change to stone. It's like the Breton countryside, with its web of pietons and walkways winding through snug villages with scalloped slate on gambrel roofs. Tea roses blossom wildly behind wrought-iron gates and rough stone walls. They'd been to Brittany six years ago, it was the first trip to France they'd taken with their dog. Sylvie tugs on Lily's leash—*Remember?* But now her spine is stiff with age, she has difficulty walking. Jerome scoops her up. Sylvie gives the dog a little kiss and looks up at Jerome. *Double-snout—remember?*

Jerome raises Lily's small thin body towards his lips and plants a kiss on one side of her muzzle, while Sylvie leans in to kiss the other. Their heads meet above the top of Lily's nose.

They walk until they reach the country. Barns replace garages, tidy gardens turn into split-railed yards. Two dogs wander past them on the road.

THE LEAD DOG is a German shepherd mix. He's followed by a small red dog that looks astonishingly like Lily... and like the woman's dog they saw at the *tabac*. What kind of strange coincidence was happening here? At home, Lily's mix was utterly unique, but here she seemed to be part of an entire *breed*. Was Korovoce her ancestral home?

Jerome quickly sets her down and props her up on her hind legs so she can get a better look. "Midor, Midor," he calls out to the other dogs, "Come meet your cousin." Lily bares her few remaining teeth and growls as the two dogs lope past her down the road.

Sylvie reaches for Jerome. "What if Lily had a child?" she wonders. For the first time since arriving in Berlin, she is gripped by an enthusiasm that floods through him with her gaze.

Well yes, of course she knows that it's impossible for Lily to have an *actual* child, or puppy. She'd been spayed before she left the pound. At age 13, she was less biologically equipped for motherhood than Sylvie. But then, the epiphany that visited Sylvie all those months ago at Deer Leap Pass returns as a reprise. Because of course—they could *adopt* a puppy. This concept moves her practically to tears. Consciousness moves ever forward. She forgets about Romania, the nylon zipper-bag, the child.

"Yes," Jerome blissfully agrees. "We can try to find a puppy."

Sylvie forces back a sniffle and Jerome's blue eyes fill with tears. The subtext of their many fights is suddenly on the table. When Lily dies, there will be very little left between them. Without her, there will be no audience for their routines, no happiness except Jerome's for Sylvie to lament and engineer. But if Lily had a puppy!—if Lily raised and trained the dog herself, in her remaining twilight years—there would be a bridge between their history and the future. Lily's sufferings, her sensitivity, would not have been wasted. With this canine continuity, everything that happened to them up until this point would be redeemed—

A small but neatly fashioned kennel loomed to Jerome's right just up the road.

Built like a breezeway in between a ranch-style house and its garage, the kennel was a slab of poured cement surrounded by a chain-link fence. Behind the fence, two full-grown replicants of Lily jumped up on their hind legs and barked, as if to guard their litter of some six or seven puppies. At ten weeks old, the red-haired puppies looked like little Lilies.

Bravely, Jerome walks up the driveway to the kennel holding Lily in his arms. Her Slavic cousins growl and bark. Lily's long ears tremble. She's scared, but knows she's safe in Jerome's arms.

But then a man comes out of the front door and speaks to them in rapid Czech, or was the language now Slovenskan? He's in his early 60s, lean with a straw hat—perhaps he's a retired farmer? Clearly, he wants to know who these strange people are and what they're doing in his yard. Sylvie stands behind Jerome, expectant, eager. Her heart sinks, realizing that they probably have no common language. It's so important now, for them to make themselves understood.

"*Regarde, regarde,*" Jerome calls to him, holding Lily out

before him. The man, apparently, does not speak French. Sylvie, normally so shy addressing foreigners, leaps in to pantomime. Jumping up and down, she points at Lily and then at his caged puppies. She does this several times. "Look!" she says in English. "We want to buy a puppy." The man looks at her quizzically, says something in Czech. Sylvie tugs at Jerome's sleeve, defeated. Suddenly he remembers what the universal language is. He takes out his wallet, waves a wad of deutschmarks, florints, dollars. The farmer shakes his head firmly, holds up his palms for them to stop. He speaks again in Czech. Jerome puts away his wallet. A pause. Everybody smiles.

In perfect French, Jerome makes a second brave attempt.

"Vous voyez, monsieur, notre chienne est très agée. Elle va bientôt mourir et nous l'aimons beaucoup. Aussi, nous aimerions en avoir une autre, une nouvelle petite chienne…"

But the dog man doesn't understand a word of French. Sylvie's never felt so close to something, yet so far. The farmer interjects a string of angry-sounding words in Czech.

Sylvie grabs hold of Lily to present her to the dog man. "Here," she pleads. "Don't you see? This is our dog. Her name is Lily. She's 13 years old, and she's—probably going to die soon. Last spring she had a tumor and the vet swore it was benign, but I think he lied, because—look at her chest, it's already started coming back—"

The dog man shakes his head and sighs. He has no idea what these strangers want. Are they trying to sell their pet to him? Then why did the man want to give him money? He already has nine dogs, he doesn't need another.

Jerome fumbles in his backpack for a notebook and a pen. He's actually very good at drawing. All those months when

Sylvie hovered on the brink of suicide, he'd drawn cartoons to cheer her up. Pictures of the three of them. Pictures, Sylvie'd cooed, of Lily. Quickly, he sketches out a picture of their dog wearing a broad smile, surrounded by a sea of puppies.

"Agghhh!" the dog man laughs, and claps him on the shoulder. Firmly, he takes hold of Lily, unlocks the chain-link gate, and throws her in the kennel.

"Nooooo!" Jerome and Sylvie scream together. "We do not want to give her up!"

But the dog man obviously knows better. If the pair of them want puppies, well then—with his entire sinewed body, he mimes the motions of a male dog, humping.

Sylvie and Jerome look sideways at each other. Instinctively, they step apart. They haven't fucked in what? six months? Faithful to their distrust of each other, they are celibate.

Meanwhile Lily cowers against the chain-link kennel fence. Back arched higher than a cat's, the dog wishes she could disappear. When the Slovenskan male comes up and sniffs underneath her tail, she lunges out and bites him.

Clearly this is not going as well as anyone had planned. Tactfully, the three avert their eyes to give the dogs some privacy. When they finally turn back to see what's happening in the kennel, the dogs are doing everything except for fucking. They sniff and growl, they lick and bite. Lily rolls onto her back, but the Slovenskan male is bored by her submission. Nose in the air, he trots back across the cement kennel to his mate, who has observed the whole performance patiently.

Sylvie is humiliated. Shamed by her dog's sexual dysfunction, she's forgotten how impossible it was for Lily to get pregnant. She's forgotten what they really wanted was to buy a puppy. The idea that they could just stride into Slovenska and grab a little foreign dog suddenly seems silly. The dog man steps into the cage and hands Lily back. Chastened, Jerome clips on her leash. They thank the man, and the three of them return to town. They'll be in Hungary that night.

Afterwards, they never mention Korovoce.

CHAPTER 14: WORSE

WORSE

LIVING IN LOS ANGELES in 1998, Sylvie Green applies for, and receives, a travel grant to go back to Romania from the art school that she's teaching at. She has long ago stopped making films. Since she no longer believes in art, she's found it possible to become moderately successful in the art world. This is what it means to 'come of age': to find a cover story that fools everyone except yourself. She finds that she can use this cover story as a protective shield. Safe behind it, she can confront the things that happened to her in New York, the years she's wasted. In LA, she knows a lot of New Age people. They tell her that *the universe is filled with light and love. If there are any imperfections, then they must be with me and my perceptions.* Since belief is now completely arbitrary, she's cautiously impressed by how effectively such people use these platitudes to give color to their days.

Sylvie still believes that poverty is structural, that the ease of certain countries relies upon the misery of others. She wonders, Do the wretched countries *choose* their fate? And if not, how is that fate chosen? She wonders when the interrogative 'who' turns into 'how'?

Nine years after the Romanian revolution, Sylvie wants to see Arad again. She arranges to retrace part of the trip she and Jerome took all those years ago, flying into Budapest, catching buses to

Szegd, and from Szged to the Romanian border. She wonders if Arad has changed. Yes, it has, she finds: but only for the worse. The border town of Nadiac is as bereft and dreary as she remembered it. Throughout the trip, she keeps a diary. She gets off at the Central Terminal in the City of Arad.

April 22 1998: Walking through the streets, An Encyclopedia of Deformities... the Woman with the Penguin Walk—her legs are bowed so close she stumbles on her toes. The Penguin Woman barely keeps from falling by balancing her entire weight between both legs on a cane... the Mole Woman, whose large brown facial mole curves from her right eyebrow like a crescent moon, down around her cheek... The Furrier with One Glass Eye whose good eye wanders while he's showing me some inexplicably luxurious mink Russian military hats... the Club Foot People, the People with Splayed Feet, whose withered paralytic feet drag behind them like loose slippers... and everywhere, of course the Hunchbacks of all ages and both sexes...

In Arad, Sylvie soon meets a young journalist, Stefan Korilescu. Tall and 22, Stefan speaks fluent English (as well as Russian, German and Romanian) and works as an investigative reporter for a new weekly newspaper called *Librere Prensa*. Foreign visitors are still rare, and Stefan wants to write a piece on Sylvie's visit. He takes her to the *Librere Prensa* office to meet his editor. They catch a taxi to an office tower ten minutes from the city center. There is no parking lot, and the security guard behind the lobby desk is fast asleep. Still, many of Stefan's colleagues on the newspaper speak English and the young photographer who takes Sylvie's picture has magenta Kool Aid hair. Sylvie takes this as a sign of hope, until she sees the girl is missing several of her teeth—

Stefan's editor agrees that he can take some time off from the paper, show the American around.

First stop is a visit to the Museum of Romanian National History. Stefan tells her it's important that she see this, because foreigners need to understand the *Romanian national character*. Sylvie finds this odd—Stefan is the son of doctors, he's visited Berlin, he is obviously a sophisticated person. And on that Wednesday afternoon, the Museum turns out to be closed, although after much banging on the wood and iron door, a kerchiefed peasant docent emerges from her slumber. When Stefan shows his press ID and Sylvie offers her a wad of lei notes, the peasant turns on the lights and lets them in.

The entrance hall is lined with dioramas featuring taxidermied birds and mammals… *Wildlife of the Carpathian Mountains*, Stefan tells her. And this region called "Carpathia," located somewhere in western Transylvania, turns out to be key. "The Magyars robbed us of Carpathia," Stefan explains.

The second exhibition room outlines the history of Hungarian aggression. *Our Dacian-Roman roots are thrust deep into the Carpathian soil, which is the cradle of our nation*, translates Stefan. Apparently the Magyars first annexed Carpathia eight hundred years ago. A medieval tax collector's ledger records the quantity of goods extracted from Romania's noble peasants under Magyar rule: *five hens, two sheep, a wine barrel…* Still, eight centuries seemed a long time to hold this kind of grudge. "As a race," Stefan continues matter-of-factly, "the Magyars are even greedier than Jews." After this, Sylvie was much less shocked to see the Museum's comparative display of Dacian and Magyar human skulls, with color-coded arrows used to indicate the phrenologic proof of Magyar cowardice and impotence. In LA, Sylvie had often driven past the sign for the Museum of Tolerance in Baldwin Hills. This was turning out to be a Museum of National Hate.

Later on that night, Sylvie has a drink with Stefan and his *Librere Prensa* colleagues. Several of them ask her what she thinks of Celine Dion? Celine's *Titanic* theme appears to be a kind of anthem here, the brave acceptance of one's destiny aboard a sinking ship... A single bootleg of the album is being shared around the office, dubbed several generations down. "We are the most homogeneous race in southeast Europe," Stefan drunkenly confides. "This gives us optimism for the future." A taxi-driving friend of one of Stefan's colleagues tells Sylvie that Romania's biggest problem was the gender-blurring that occurred throughout the Ceausescu era, a period no one much recalls, because the "revolution" happened in their early teens. The driver's mother was a teacher, but he forbids his wife to work. Earning twice what the *Librere Prensa* writers make, the taxi driver has a cell phone that gets passed around the table as if it were a magic object. The friends get drunk, can't find a taxi, walk home through the fog.

The next day, Stefan has a press conference to attend and Sylvie decides to read about the "revolution" in the Arad Municipal Library. But the library only keeps its newspapers for three years, and she's directed to the larger Timisoara Public Library. Timisoara is thirty miles away. She finds a cab to take her, but then waits two hours for the librarian. Finally, he returns and shows her fading, yellowed papers. There are banner headlines in December of the revolution's triumph. In February, there are photographs of demonstrators being clubbed in Bucharest by miners. The library doesn't have these documents on microfilm. Sylvie asks if she can make some Xeroxes, but the library doesn't have a photocopier. The librarian gives her the bound books and directs her to a stationary store several blocks away.

Returning to Arad, she tries to mail the cardboard box of photocopies to herself back in Los Angeles. The driver takes her to the Central Post Office. After waiting there in line, she's directed to the Parcel Office in a building several doors away. But the Parcel Office isn't authorized to handle *foreign* parcels. She's told she'll have to bring it to the Satellite Foreign Parcel Office. The clerk has no idea where this is located—best to ask them at the Central Office. This time the driver stands in line, and returns with an address out in the suburbs several miles away.

After several missed directions, Sylvie and the driver reach the Satellite Foreign Parcel Office, which looks something like Jerome's mother's living room. A vase of plastic flowers sits atop a wooden table with a broken leg. Sylvie and the driver wait in line, only to be told that foreign parcels must be wrapped in "regulation sacks." The clerk holds up a sample, a draw-stringed muslin bag that looks a little like a pillowcase. Fine, says Sylvie. Then I'll buy one. But the regulation sacks are not for sale. She'll have to have one made up by a tailor, but there aren't any tailors in the district…

Driving back downtown, Sylvie sees a donkey cart, two girls carrying water in a plastic bucket, and an old man with a sheep pelt wrapped around his shoulders like a jacket.

"Find out," she wrote that evening in her diary, "what makes the prognosis for Romania so uniquely hopeless. At what point does entropy become negative? Stasis can't stay still forever, it eventually spirals down…" She tries to wash her hair, but there is no hot water at the hotel.

BACK IN LOS ANGELES, Sylvie phones her friend, the Romanian art historian, Sanda Agalidi. She asks if she can come and visit around 5:00 tomorrow afternoon? No, the woman hedges, 6:30 would be better, because *I am not so good with the transition between day and night.* Drinking tea in Sanda's small Echo Park apartment, Sylvie wants to talk about how strangely things had ended up with

Stefan. At first he'd wanted to be paid for his translation services, and then he didn't, and when Sylvie'd handed him a $100 bill 'for Xeroxes,' he'd stormed off and walked away.

"Ahh, Romania is in a state now of absolute paralysis," Sanda explains. Sanda travels back to Bucharest each summer to spend a few weeks with her aging mother. "They know what is available, but they are not able to have it. They don't know what they need most, money or respect, because they need everything. The state used to be in control, but now it's nothing. Romania is still full of demons of a very diverse kind."

Sylvie asks Sanda, *What do you remember?* and scribbles in her notebook while her friend recalls her first trip back to Bucharest in 1988, after fleeing on a student visa.

"Walking at night on streets with flashlights because there wasn't a street light; trying to avoid holes in the pavement, this in the middle of the city. People standing in small lines at stores waiting to buy anything, from cigarettes to bones. Endless homages to Ceausescu on TV, it was an anniversary year or something. Being stopped many times on the street by the Security Police—there were searches going on all the time. Large areas of the street dug out, for the Metro that was never finished. Churches I knew had been demolished… so was the house my parents lived in before they were moved into the slums.

Walking on those streets that were eerie, dilapidated, unreally real. The air was yellow. My friends were troubled, but completely helpless. Was this a comedy? Their humor could not match this occasion.

The search at the border; harsh, frightening. When I came back to LA I tried to write something for the LA Weekly but was told they were not interested in such reports.

The whole thing was weird, nightmarish to the point that it kept on happening to me visually each night for months after. The Aparator

Patriei slums my parents were moved into was shocking: unfinished, shocking, although they still had their old furniture and books; all the old things."

"But that was eleven years ago. Surely things have gotten better?" Sylvie insists.

"No, only worse," her friend replies. She takes another sip of tea.

"It is difficult to remember. But it is also difficult to forget."

IN MID-AUGUST 1991, Sylvie and Jerome will arrive at the Hungarian border a few hours after leaving Kosovoce. The Hungarian countryside will charm them. They'll see contented barnyard animals grazing along roadsides everywhere they go.

They'll spend two days in the resort town of Lake Ballaton. Sylvie will want Jerome to photograph the quaint old railway station with its shuttered windows and lace curtains. They'll wander through large parks with lush perennial gardens and marvel at the sorbet-colored buildings dotted all around the town. They'll take a lot of tourist photographs, and Sylvie will insist the colors here remind her of her favorite children's books: *Babar the Elephant, Maggie Goes To Town*. They'll meet an interesting French couple in a restaurant near the lake, and eat Hungarian goulash on red and white checked tablecloths in the Paprika Capital of the World.

Jerome will spend some of Josef Peichl's money treating Sylvie to a five-star luxury spa hotel (though not that much: the exchange rate brings the tariff down to $75). While Sylvie enjoys the mud treatments and baths, Jerome will take out his Toshiba laptop and finally get back to work on *Death: The Interrupted Life*. Before leaving, they'll steal two thick terry bathrobes, which in New York, Jerome will note, would cost more than the hotel.

In Szged, for only $20 a night, they'll take a room at the once-grand Hotel Tesla. They'll marvel at the crystal chandeliers, the curving staircase in the lobby. The hotel will remind Jerome of reading Proust, and he'll recall, to Sylvie's great delight, Proust's descriptions of Balbec, the lobby of the Grand Hotel illuminated from the boardwalk with its primitive electric light. They'll visit the Szged market, and as they drive south towards the Romanian border they'll be amazed to see a line of gypsy caravans camped out along the road. They'll break out their first pack of Kents, and Jerome will take some photographs of Sylvie holding Lily next to the gypsies and their horses.

But when they cross the border into Nadiac, they'll notice the barbed-wire walls and searchlights that separate Romania from the rest of Eastern Europe.

Immediately, they'll feel Romania to be a prison. They'll notice that the lines of those attempting to leave Romania are much longer than the line of people waiting to get in.

They'll notice that the Romanian peasants are unnaturally short, as if their growth were stunted. Riding past on donkey carts in dirty clothes, with twig brooms and hand-made sieves, the peasants will look like extras in a corny epic film set in the Middle Ages. Or perhaps more accurately, they'll look like the villagers in the Soviet Russian version of *King Lear*.

But the countryside in Nadiac will not remind them of a medieval Book of Hours. It will be dry and dusty, with open sanitation trenches and unfinished concrete residential towers. Rats will run around outside in uncovered piles of garbage. Even though the buildings are unfinished, this will not have stopped thousands of homeless people moving in.

In Nadiac, they'll stop to ask directions at a store but no one will speak English. They'll notice there is very little in the store to buy. Outside, a group of men will sit and watch a black and white TV, plugged into the store's lone electric outlet. The soccer match they're watching will be bootlegged from Bulgarian State TV.

When Sylvie and Jerome reach the City of Arad, they'll pull into the parking lot of the International Hotel Astoria. As Sylvie holds their little dog and argues with her husband, they will both be being watched by two dozen idle taxi drivers. The boldest of these men will finally approach them. They'll be grateful when this man, who calls himself Rodescu, speaks to them in English. He'll say: *I think I know why you are here.* Immediately, they'll know exactly what this means, but instead of being alarmed by it, they'll feel well-understood and cautiously relieved.

They will not trust this man, but neither will they distrust him. With no familiar points of reference to hold onto, they'll find themselves incapable of thinking beyond the next five minutes. When the man proposes that they follow him to his house, they'll do it gladly, grateful to have found a room.

Rodescu's house will be luxurious by local standards. They'll note the electric stove, the fridge, the working toilet. His affluence will reassure them. *Whatever this guy's hustle is,* they'll think with satisfaction, *it's obviously working.* They'll sit down in the kitchen, and Alina, the man's unmarried 28-year-old daughter, will come in. Alina will lead them to her bedroom, with its frilly bed and sewing machine and Christian evangelical posters. She'll say to them: *You will stay here.* They'll notice that the photos on Alina's dresser are all pictures of herself, in different dresses. They'll agree to pay Rodescu $35 a night to sleep in Alina's bed.

Over dinner of fried schnitzel, Alina will explain how fortunate they are God led them to her father, instead of to the thieving gypsies. "The gypsies sell their babies to Americans for $5,000," she will say in outraged broken English. "But I know how to do things in the proper way."

She'll boast to them about her contacts in the local orphanage. "My friends are honest," she will say. Alina guesses she'll be able to complete the whole transaction for about $1,000 US dollars. She proposes that they pay her in installments, by the day.

Every day, Jerome will give Alina a fresh pile of German deutschmarks, for "expenses," "for her time," and "for the room." And so they will be cheated, but not that badly. Jerome won't think much about where the money's going. He'll be relieved that staying at Rodescu's house, he finally has the time to start working on his essay. They'll never see the inside of an orphanage, but neither will they be arrested. Every night, Alina will come into their room and say *Be patient. Wait until tomorrow. There have been delays.* There will be missed appointments, complications. She will claim to *fear surveillance*, but she'll promise them protection by God's will.

Nights, they'll leave Rodescu's house and walk around the city. The entire power grid in Arad City will shut down at 9 p.m., but they'll find a boulevard café that boasts a private generator. Here, they'll observe Arad's haute-bourgeoisie: corpulent misshapen men, ugly wives and daughters wrapped like Christmas gifts in tightly ruffled dresses… people not unlike Rodescu and Alina. They'll note a strange and toxic feeling of malevolence that seems to hold them all together.

Bored at the Rodescu home, by the third or fourth day Sylvie and Jerome will take a drive to Vinga, a village 15 miles away. Here, they'll watch the Vingan men sit sullenly outside the church, drunk and playing checkers. Mules will defecate in muddy Vingan streets. There won't be anything else to see. When one of the

Vingan men gets up and waves a bottle in Jerome's face, they'll give him a 10,000 lei note and drive away.

By the seventh day, Arad's omnipresent atmosphere of brutality and fear will oppress them. They will crave a good meal. Having already spent Jerome's entire German stipend, they'll make excuses to Alina that they have to go away. Enormously relieved, Alina will protest her sorrow. She'll be pleased at her success engaging these two 'foreign guests' for an entire week... though really, what recourse could Jerome and Sylvie ever have, what could they say?

After making life-long vows of friendship with Alina and her family, Sylvie and Jerome will drive back to Berlin. He'll leave from there for Paris.

Their Romanian adventure will become a well-crafted story to tell at dinners in New York and LA. They'll find ways of telling it that obscure the purpose of their trip. They won't say much about the orphan. They'll concentrate instead on their *impressions* of Romania. They'll cast themselves as two adventurous, sophisticated travelers, shocked beyond their Third-World savvy. They'll mention Anton Chekhov when they talk about Romania's rural squalor; they'll joke, *they finally understood just why the sisters longed for Moscow*. Few will care enough to question them.

But sometimes, on bad days when they are alone together, Sylvie and Jerome will remember their trip to Romania *as it really happened*. When Sylvie is overcome with shame at having come so close to being a Third-World baby grabber, when she tries to understand the falseness of their project and what it says about their lives, Jerome will try and comfort her.

"It could have been worse," Jerome will say.

CHAPTER 15: BETTER

BETTER

THE DOG WILL DIE, and Sylvie will know she has to leave then. Still, it will be another several years before she leaves Jerome. Eventually, a friend will offer her a part-time job teaching at an LA art school. She'll see it as a chance. She'll take it.

Jerome will stay in New York. Just before his 60th birthday, he'll enter therapy. In between these sessions, he starts having (or remembering) very vivid dreams. Sometimes he writes these dreams down in a notebook:

I'm in a restaurant with Sylvie and I give a 20 dollar bill at the counter, expecting to get some change. But we're kept waiting and Sylvie leaves. I think of leaving too (Sylvie always leaves large tips) but I wait, because the dinner only cost 6 or 7 dollars.

I find myself in a kind of Roman theater with many people lying down wrapped in white togas. The light is overexposed, white on white, like the amazing pictures by Gunther Brus, the elegant Aktionist work I saw in Vienna. Faces are white too. These people are all friends of Sylvie's and they're making fun of me, or being critical. I feel kind of lost, don't know what I'm doing there and what they expect of me. It's some kind of carnival. One of them says: "this man has no heart. He has a heart in radium."

It's getting late and I have to go back downtown to the East Vil-
lage, but other people, young people, offer to share a cab with me,
and I gladly accept.

And then he adds:

I had this dream at my mother's place in Paris on November 24,
a Sunday, after talking to her about her father, who took refuge in
Radom when the Germans were about to occupy Warsaw. In Radom
he was put into a transit camp with his own father, and both were
eventually sent to their deaths on a transport, destination yet unknown.

I immediately thought that "radium" was Radom. But radium
is also used in atomic bombs, and I remember reading things about
Chernobyl. But "heart in radium" also makes me think of the Tin
Man in The Wizard of Oz, *the man who has no heart. He is white*
too, and clownish.

So the statement is contradictory. At once I have no heart, and I
have a heart in radium/Radom. So the second accusation may well be
my own answer to the first. Yes, I have a heart, but it is in Radom. I
only feel for things that connect me to the camps. The statement was
a statement of fact, but polemic. It may have to do with the conversa-
tion I had on the phone earlier that day with Sylvie, she was angry
and she told me that I have no heart. My answer is that I have a
heart, but it is caught in "radium." And to prove that I have a heart,
I answer with this dream. Yes, I have a heart, I have an unconscious,
because I dream and play with words in a meaningful way. The heart
also connects to my past: the tuberculosis and infection of my heart
("your cells have a memory," the homeopath said) after too strong an
emotional fight with Ginny and Laura.

Back to the problem of remembering things and dreaming. My
inability to dream has to do with the camps. They infect me. I try to
tear them away from my chest, but I can't. It is where my heart is,

and I have to keep bleeding. But this 'bleeding heart' is a heart, and is all that I have. Whatever I can do will come from that.

The same year Jerome enters therapy, his old friend Henri Lachmann hangs himself in Paris in a suburban park. Like Jerome, Henri had been hidden as a child throughout the War. Because Jerome has decided, now, to take an active interest in his past, he goes to visit Henri's widow Marielle the next time he's in Paris. He brings a tape recorder to record their conversation. But when he turns it on, though he is normally a great interviewer, Jerome can't think of what to say. Finally, he simply asks: "What do you remember?"

Marielle considers this. In the days before his death, Henri seemed neither more or less depressed than usual. He'd recently obtained a part-time job teaching sociology to Algerian immigrants at a night school. This post was a far cry from the brilliant future once imagined for him by his doctoral dissertation supervisor, Henri Lefebvre. But then again, Henri had never finished writing his PhD. His life had trailed off into something much more inconclusive, he'd never been that interested in pursuing a career. A few weeks before her husband's suicide, Marielle recalls, their youngest child moved out—but happily. Surely it could not be this?

"You know," Marielle recalls, "there was a strange way Henri used to talk. He was never good at making plans. I mean—he never talked about himself as if there was a future, the way most people do. There was this funny tense he used, as if the future had already happened. He always said, *I would have been.*"

ALONE AND WEIGHTLESS in Los Angeles, Sylvie buys a '67 Rambler and rents a house in Highland Park. She goes to the gym and finds that working out transports her to a teary, universally empathic state. Without Jerome, she is simply sad for sadness now. Her trainer screams at her to eat.

Sylvie doesn't like the landscape in LA. She doesn't like the art. She doesn't like the west coast Jews, who hardly seem like Jews at all. Her female colleagues dress like aging sluts. She doesn't like the clothes. In New York, she'd seen the people she'd loved and admired most die of poverty and heroin overdoses, suicide and AIDS. The drag queens Nan Goldin photographed in the 1980s were mostly dead of AIDS and Hepatitis-C. There'd been a battle to hold back the flood of gentrification on the Lower East Side of New York City. This battle had been lost.

The LA art world Sylvie moves around in is free of arcane references and ambiguity. There are no alternate hierarchies of glamour here. Those who work outside the gallery system are simply *losers*. Any artist any good will be professional. All it takes is social skills and an MFA from the right school. Her new art world associates wear Bermuda shorts and barbecue on Sunday afternoons. Talking about one's art is considered unprofessional. Sylvie digs her nails into her arms to stay awake while people talk about their living rooms—is yellow now passé?—and how to grow tomatoes. No one flaunts ambition in your face. Everyone is either *married*, *single* or *divorced*. Though most of them are married. Things coast along.

It occurs to Sylvie there is a great deal of money in LA, and very little competition. In some ways, LA is as provincial as the small New Zealand city she grew up in, but with vastly higher stakes. No one cares enough to question anyone too much. She sees it might be possible to benefit from this.

Nothing important that happens to Sylvie happens in the city of Los Angeles. Everything happens in her head. In the months before she left Jerome, she'd started writing love letters to a man who didn't love her. In LA she continues writing to this man, and then she just continues writing. For the first time, it seems that everything she wants to do can now be broken down into small, achievable goals. She embraces everything that's practical and finite.

A therapist in Beverly Hills gives her excellent advice about success in business: *Never put anything important into writing. See each transaction through the eyes of your opponent. Assess what people want, and try to give it to them. Then you will be left alone. Never say no to anyone. Instead just say, I'll think about it, and then stop returning calls.* Sylvie follows this advice. It works.

It occurs to Sylvie that she'd be less lonely if she started having sex. But no one in the LA art world ever fucks (or even flirts) unless the sex is used in order to pursue mature and serious monogamous relationships. Since everyone knows that she's still married to Jerome, she's not a candidate. She wonders if she can overcome her loneliness by turning sex into a goal, like other business? She answers personal ads in the newspaper, dials the Telepersonals Dating Hotline on the phone. This works. It is the shortest line between two points. She's surprised to find that in *this* world she can be belle of the ball, so long as she's not pursuing a committed and mature relationship.

Giving blowjobs in the parking lot behind the House of Pies, finger-fucking on a stranger's couch, she is amazed by how completely sex annihilates the need for context. None of the men she meets this way see 'chemistry' as a requisite for having sex. There is no dating, no auditioning for the girlfriend role. They encourage her to be a slut. She finds she can be anyone. It's all light-hearted, girlish fun. Through this lens, sex becomes a recreational pursuit, like playing chess. Appearance, common interests, politics become completely immaterial. She finds this very liberating. So long as they are skilled and serious about the game, nearly anyone will do.

BUT SOMETIMES, when she's having Great Sex in Los Angeles (a thing Jerome encourages her to do) her mind wanders backwards in its hazy pre-orgasmic state to the torpid years they spent in Thurman. Pictures flash into her mind: a frozen waterfall; a walk along Schroon River; the plaid blanket in a room they stayed in at the Tupper Lake Motel. Eventually she comes, or else her partner does, and she's slammed back into the present, breathless, grateful and amazed. She'd never known that sex could be this easy. Another goal achieved. She forgets the orgasms quickly. It's only in the pre-orgasmic drift that she revisits the expectant emptiness she felt throughout those years of living with Jerome.

She recalls a lonely drive they took when Lily was still nine, before the tumor. *It would have been* an autumn Sunday afternoon, frayed and aimless, like so many of their days. Jerome's anxiety would have been escaping like a poison gas through a crack beneath his office door, and Sylvie would have been concerned about another weekend ending without a happy, memorable event.

This time, when she asked Jerome if he'd come out for a drive, he would have sensed her deep unhappiness and turned off his computer. Together, they would have settled on a destination: *Let's try and find the Town of Day!* Day was a mythic hillbilly outpost in the southern Adirondacks, mentioned by their Thurman neighbors in tones of deep disgust and horror.

Guessing Day was someplace north of Hadley, Sylvie would have packed a thermos and a map. They would have stopped at Emrick's General Store to buy the Sunday paper, and seen a toothless bearded trapper striding off Hap's front porch with a case of beer and groceries. Surely this was proof that they were getting closer!

They would have driven north along the Sacandagua River after leaving Lake Luzerne, and the landscape would have changed. Tidy village homes gave way to abandoned company houses from the shut-down Corinth mill. They would have passed the River Bar and Grill, a business Sylvie dreamed of purchasing. She'd wait tables while Jerome cooked and tended bar. But then again—perhaps he'd like to be a French TV producer? If he'd been anything but what he was, they would have been rich enough to have a child, or poor enough to breed instinctively.

As the stark, abandoned countryside slipped by, the numbness they'd both felt all weekend would have given way to pleasure. Feeling alive for the first time in a long while, Sylvie would have begged Jerome to apply for the part-time sorting job at the Thurman Post Office. It paid 11.53, top dollar in their town. He'd have to pass a civil service test, but if he studied hard—"Alright," Jerome would have punned, "I'll be a man of letters."

Holding Lily on her lap to get a better view, Sylvie would have stroked the wide-wale corduroy on the pants Jerome was wearing. She would have rolled the window down to test the air. They would have both agreed, *the bottom of the air was cool.*

APPROACHING EDINBURGH, they would have followed road signs to Northville, a lovely old colonial town they'd never known existed. Beached amid the poverty of the southern Adirondacks, there was no apparent reason for the town's existence. Jerome's thoughts would have drifted back to Paris, as they did in every dying town. He'd think of how it was before the War: the smell of rain, the cobbled streets, the Les Halles open markets. Comfortingly, they would exclaim how glad they were to leave New York. If they'd never left New York, they'd never know that towns like Northville still existed.

They'd stop in Northville, share a grilled cheese sandwich and a bowl of soup at the Town and Country Diner. They'd see an antique store, and Sylvie would have found a teapot fashioned like an ear of corn for five dollars. Jerome would buy it, and she'd bring it home to add to her collection of retro corn-inspired kitchenware and china.

But by the time they left the antique store, it would have been 4 o'clock already: too late to find the Town of Day. The air would be distinctly cold, and Jerome would think about the Trailways bus he had to catch to teach on Tuesday. And then another Parent-Teacher day at Laura's school on Wednesday... the text he'd promised to François was nearly six months late, and now he wouldn't have a chance to look at it again 'til Friday. Nauseous and defeated, he would have tried not to spoil their nice Sunday afternoon. And so he'd hand the map to Sylvie, ask her if she'd like to find them a new route back home to Thurman?

Sylvie would have felt Jerome's panic ricochet around the car as they turned off 418 onto the back road over Seventh Mountain. This route, she thought, would come out near Zaltz Road and take them nearly home. But the Seventh Mountain Road would have turned to dirt and gotten narrower.

While Jerome navigated ruts, they would have weighed their options: should they turn around? But suddenly, the road would dead-end at a grassy clearing, and there, they would have seen a herd of deer, grazing in the early twilight.

Jerome would have turned the engine off, and Sylvie would have covered Lily's mouth to stop her barking. The small herd would have stayed there, eating, oblivious that they were being watched, or else not caring. Two weeks from now, deer hunting season would begin, but these animals didn't seem to know it. The deer were caught, and probably doomed, yet they remained serene, safe and protected in their unknowing. Jerome's chest would have pulled tight, tears would have welled up in his eyes. If only he could be like the deer... if he could have stayed like that, suspended—

Back home, Sylvie would have made tea in the corn pot. They would have lain in bed with Lily's tiny body in between them, kissed each other over her gray muzzle, until Jerome finally picked the dog up and put her down—

Sylvie has already been living in LA for several years when she finds the picture Jerome took the day that she got pregnant at the Pennsylvania reservoir. She finds it in a carton full of files and papers that they'd boxed a million years ago, before the first round of year-long tenants moved into their Thurman house, the place they'd never managed to shape up into a home. *All my dreams*, a poet wrote, *the bluest smoke.*

The photo is a strange artifact: a souvenir of possibilities that never came to be. Sylvie is no longer remotely like the woman in the picture. But you can tell by looking at the photo how much, then, she wanted to get pregnant. Desire pulsing underneath a mask of deep repose. When she finds the box, Jerome and all that she imagined for them has been lost to her for a long time. *Take me anywhere, but take me now*—it is a picture of complete abandonment.

The woman in the picture is inescapably immersed in an expectant emptiness… the same emptiness that Sylvie likes to simulate by having recreational sex in Los Angeles. Safe in Highland Park, cheerfully pursuing a career in an art world that no longer matters much to her or anyone, she sees a link between her present life and the photo. Sylvie understands that her anonymous and finite, 'discrete' sexual encounters are to true romance what the blank and open LA landscape is to the old European grid of history, warfare and causality. There are no ancient tribal feuds, no wounds, no blood.

It is less absolute, perhaps. But better.

Afterword by Mckenzie Wark

Fur and Trembling

"My entire state of being's changed because I've become my sexuality: female, straight, wanting to love men, be fucked. Is there a way of living with this like a gay person, proudly?"
— Chris Kraus, *I Love Dick*

"Now they were painting, cleaning, and in three weeks they'd be gone again. What kind of life could they believe in? What kind of life could they afford?"
— Chris Kraus, *I Love Dick*

Sometimes reading Chris Kraus is like archaeology. Somewhere beneath the surface of the text are some rich fossil layers. Call it the hyperreal strata of the Anthropocene. Some of it smells like the New York of a certain era, all speed-sweat and peroxide. On top of that layer is something else, something that filled the niche when those punk creatures went extinct. Once there used to be whole separate ecologies of art and fortune. There were poets, performers, artists of a sort. They made their own rules for glory. Then they went away, and after that comes pedigree creatures, sired by great names for brilliant careers.

As someone who only became a New Yorker in 2000, I find this has its unsettling quality. I got there too late for any of those parties. And yet as an invasive species I keep finding myself grazing next to down-town royalty mentioned in Chris Kraus books. The playwright Lenora Champagne is a neighbor where I live in Queens. The musician Eszter Balint, who grew up in the Squat theater, was a playground mom I met when our kids went to the same school. Kraus: "Unlike most of their contemporaries, they aren't dead, or wildly famous, or living in tract homes in Denver."[1]

Among other things, Kraus has written the *Domesday Book* of the lost wilds and commons of New York. "All of New York's mystery has long since been depleted."[2] This is perhaps the case with a lot of the cities of what the Situationists so usefully called the *overdeveloped* world. Kraus: "There is no longer any way of being poor in any interesting way in major cities like Manhattan."[3] As late as the winter years of the eighties, other lives, other communities, other values still survived in neglected corners. But is that still possible? "It's only rarely that the overwhelming sadness of the city galvanizes into anything like rage. And when it does, this rage is quickly channeled into new career-paths in the art world."[4]

As people get older they start to think its all over and the good old days are gone. As a Kraus-like character says of LA: "There are no alternate hierarchies of glamour here. Those who work outside the gallery system are simply *losers*."[5] And yet the actual Chris Kraus could still celebrate the brief and brilliant life of the Tiny Creatures

1. Chris Kraus, *Summer of Hate*, Semiotext(e), Los Angeles CA, 2012, p. 190
2. Chris Kraus, *Torpor*, Semiotext(e), Los Angeles CA, 2014, p. 202
3. *Torpor*, p. 24
4. *Torpor*, p. 85
5. *Torpor*, p. 286

scene in LA's Echo Park: "What all these people do best is collage. They're all on speed...."[6] So while her books are in part like archaeological records, they are also blueprints for how to turn your own quirk and smarts and boredom into its own scene, with its own intensities, if only for a time.

Perhaps this is not the least reason Kraus' books have a following. They are about working the inside-out margin. As the Kraus-character says in *Summer of Hate*: "She saw no boundaries between feeling and thought, sex and philosophy. Hence, her writing was read almost exclusively in the art world, where she attracted a small core of devoted fans: Asperger's boys, girls who'd been hospitalized for mental illness, assistant professors who would not be receiving their tenure, lap dancers, cutters and whores."[7] Her books are theory-books, but ones which—uniquely—describe and analyze the means of production of theory, its extraction from situations, from lived time. Her books are read by thinking people who feel their lives have situations, not to mention predicaments. They are especially for those who are "aware of the cost of the freedom to *think*."[8]

It's a classic demystification move, all the more stunning for being the obvious one nobody else was willing to make: Rather than theories of subjectivity or the body, how about an assaying of *this* self, *this* body, of its affects and effects, but rendered with a certain cool detachment? The example might be *this* woman's history. This coming of age story, in a New York that was somewhere between the punk and postmodern moments it would now rather forget. But the method can be modeled, repeated, set to work elsewhere. This isn't memoir or nostalgia or the bourgeois novel. This is Castiglione's *Book*

6. Chris Kraus, *Where Art Belongs*, Semiotext(e), Los Angeles CA, 2011, p. 25
7. *Summer of Hate*, p. 16
8. *Summer of Hate*, p. 159

of the Courtier for those who lack titles, inheritance, provenance, but have the wit and patience needed for survival in the Anthropocene.

One of Kraus' genres is picaresque, with herself and her friends as the rascals, rogues and outcasts of late imperial America, a world no less venal than that encountered by Fielding's *Tom Jones*. Let's just consider for a moment the epithets that attach to the Kraus-like characters in her various books: She is a journalist, a New Zealander, a Marxist; but then also a gutter-rat, a weird girl, hunched and introspective; a strange and lonely girl, most intelligent and useful; a small boned, thin, weightless, gamine, crazy and cerebral girl; tall and anorexic, an innocent, de-gendered freak; plain-faced, thin and serious. As her character ages, she becomes default androgynous, a Hippy Intellectual high school teacher, an old punk girl, even punk grandma; shrewish, sharp and haggard, a female monster, a rakish, crazed witch; a hag, ruthless and brittle, who will say of herself with pride: "I'm a kike."

It's a hard corner to work. These are not the attributes of heroes. "What do you do with the Serious Young Woman (short hair, flat shoes, body slightly hunched, head drifting back and forth between the books she's read)? You slap her, fuck her up the ass and treat her like a boy. The Serious Young Woman looked everywhere for sex but when she got it it became a an exercise in disintegration."[9] So what, then, is the *concept* of that experience?

In the archaeological record of New York there was actually a band called *Theoretical Girls*, but it was Glenn Branca and a bunch of white guys. The girl is not supposed to *have* theories. Yes, there may be "Good Girl academics."[10] But they are supposed to do

9. Chris Kraus, *I Love Dick*, Semiotext(e), Los Angeles CA, 2006, p. 178
10. Chris Kraus, *Aliens & Anorexia*, Semiotext(e), Los Angeles CA, 2013, p. 103

feminist theory, preferably Lacanian, and confine themselves to theories of the gendered subject. There are also still lady novelists, but they are supposed to corset themselves to threading the depths of their own interiority.

What is distinctive in Kraus is coming up with a method—actually a series of methods—for conjoining *this* woman's experience with the world. One could even call it a certain kind of objectivity, not so much a deep as an expansive one, where showing the means of production of theory becomes a metonymic part of the theory, sparing us the expansive metaphors about the role of the intellectual in history. Instead, impertinent questions: who decides who gets paid to say or write what about whom?

There were some missteps along the way to Chris Kraus becoming 'Chris Kraus.' Those of the early video works I have seen I thought were actually pretty strong, particularly *How To Shoot A Crime* (1987), which juxtaposes interviews with a dominatrix or two against actual crime scene footage. The shot of a decomposing head is now indelibly seared on my brain. While S/m may be a theater of *decreation*, squeezing subjectivity out and leaving trembling flesh, there's a hard yet fascinating boundary between decreation and death. Still, this work failed to find recognition, particularly Kraus' feature film *Gravity & Grace* (1996). Her self/diagnosis: "Too punk to be a formalist, too intellectual to be underground... she'd been a fool to think she could be some kind of female Guy Debord."[11]

I Love Dick (1997), Kraus' first published book, is among other things a record of the breakthrough into a method for being a theoretical girl. "Because most 'serious' fiction, still, involves the fullest possible expression of a single person's subjectivity, it's

---

11. *Torpor*, p. 125

considered crass and amateurish not to 'fictionalize' the supporting cast of characters.…When women try to pierce this false conceit by naming names because our 'I's' are changing as we meet other 'I's', we're called bitches, libelers, pornographers and amateurs. 'Why are you so angry?' he said to me."[12] In the old New York, Barney Rossett's Grove Press published the literary dudes who traded on *obscenity*. Perhaps in their wake there would be a way to make headway by challenging the notion of *privacy* they left alone. Their women were not supposed to write about their chiseling for money or their nurturing of 'careers.'

The conceit of *I Love Dick* is that Kraus finds a way in to writing by addressing letters to an actual person, but one who also functions as a kind of blank screen. If you wanted to get all Lancanish about, it: she is writing to the phallus, the master-signifier. Whatever. The interesting stuff engages neither pole, tiny-self or Big-Other, but is elsewhere. "If I could love you consciously, take an experience that was so completely female and subject it to an abstract analytic system, then perhaps I had a chance of understanding something and could go on living."[13] And: construct a conceit for writing that appeared both everyday and shocking at the same time: "Because emotion's just so terrifying the world refuses to believe that it can be pursued as discipline, as form."[14]

In writing about the work of others we usually write something about our own. Kraus is clear in her follow-up book, *Aliens and Anorexia* (2000), about why her work both is and isn't feminist, as that term is deployed by others as a marker of genre: "Perversely, all this literature is based on the unshakeable belief that the formation

---

12. *I Love Dick*, pp. 71–72
13. *I Love Dick*, pp. 235–6
14. *I Love Dick*, p. 196

of a gender-based identity is still the primary animating goal in the becoming of a person, if that person is a girl."[15]

The problem of 'the girl' is neither erased nor entirely inescapable in Kraus. In her book of art essays *Video Green* (2004), she writes of someone else's work: "It is a self-portrait fashioned from a Deleuzian sense of self, or from the identities held by adolescent fans (same thing): a belief that who you are is never any more or less than who you love, than who has made you larger."[16] Note in passing the neat hi-lo switch here, from French theorist to fangirl pride, but also self-belief as escape-hatch from the cramped space of that shadow double of The-Name-of-the-Father, the slip-of-a-girl.

You could say that Kraus zeroes in on a fatal flaw in high theory: that it wants to talk about difference, or the minor, or the margins, but it still wants to do so from a position of strength, from the point of view of some universal abstract spokesmodel. Perhaps Kraus reverses the procedure: she starts rather from an apparent weakness, from the less-than-ideal girl, who should not only not be seen much but not heard at all. She makes this the aperture through which to see and feel worlds. Not a universal abstract world, but still, more world than most high theory wants to let in.

The 'I' who writes and speaks in *I Love Dick* and *Aliens & Anorexia* is not exactly the confessional first person, baring the soul of a novelistic character or autobiographical self. Its more the 'I' of the New York poets of the late twentieth century. Its an 'I' that scans both perceptions and feelings as modes of clocking situations, more analytic than lyrical. Curiously, the three people who 'I' think managed to translate this method beyond the St Marks Poetry Project ghetto were all women: Chris Kraus, Eileen Myles, Patti

---

15. *Aliens and Anorexia*, p. 160
16. Chris Kraus, *Video Green*, Semiotext(e), Los Angeles CA, 2004, p. 197

Smith. One as fiction for the art world, one as lesbian performativity, one as pop Rimbaud for the provinces.

Torpor (2006) changes up the game again. The character Chris Kraus becomes Sylvie Green. Two techniques emerge from the margins of her writing: parataxis and metonymy. "Parataxis is a strange literary form.... Old epic stories that had once been handed down by tribal elders pass into the hands of storytellers. Flashing back and sideways, holding back the outcome of events, these tellers fracture old familiar and heroic tales into contradictory, multiple perspectives. It becomes impossible to move the story forward without returning to the past, and so the past both predicates the future and withholds it."[17]

One usually thinks of parataxis as a poetic form, juxtaposing short phrases, and sometimes Kraus does this. But in *Torpor* it works also on bigger units, and the emphasis is more on holding back the outcome of events, preventing either personal or historical time from falling into a neat sequence, where each unit of time forms the next. "To organize events sequentially is to take away their power."[18] It is to restore at least a weak power over time that *Torpor* breaks time into situations which can be combined and recombined, to find ways that time, if it can't be changed, can at least be known and endured.

Maybe parataxis is the condition on which modern history now becomes accessible in writing. It's a way out of the bind of refusing neat causal order on the one hand and on the other throwing all the fragments, good, bad or indifferent, into the dustbin of history's end. "Each fragment of reality contains a little bit of poison. You

---

17. *Torpor*, p. 88
18. *Torpor*, p. 143

must be careful when ingesting it, never swallowing it whole. You must prevent yourself from reaching false proscriptions of causality. When there is no longer any *Why*, reality is best experienced in tiny poisoned morsels. In this way, toxicity insinuates itself into the body of the receiver-host, who then becomes a carrier." Kraus is an aesthetician of history under constrained circumstances.

Torpor has its metaphors, but maybe only one that's structural. The shifts from one block of time to another in *Torpor* are links along metonymic chains: from part to whole to part again. Sylvie brings along a bear which would have belonged with the orphan, which would have belonged with Sylvie and Jerome, but actually the little dog Lily belongs with the Sylvie-Jerome whole, but they would be part of another whole of those who are in a certain sense orphan people, but then Romania is a whole orphaned country, once the IMF are done with it, and as such Romania is a part of all those fringes of Europe that are disaster zones, orphaned from history, and so on.

Each of these part-objects in the text is something invested with intense emotional affect and yet also estranged, and not least from its locus is time. Parts of the book are written in what would be a future anterior tense, if this were French. Being English, is some more slippery tense, which as an indifferently schooled antipodean I cannot name but recognize from certain books. "Tenses situate events relative to their closeness or their distance from the speaker. Rules of grammar give the empty space of human speech some shape. The simple past: *We left*. In more complex tenses, 'have' and 'had,' the helping verbs, help to separate the speaker from the immediacy of events. *We had left*. *Had* forms a little step between what happened and the moment when you're telling it."[19]

19. *Torpor*, p. 163

That gives it the distance, but there is also its intensity of affect: "There is a tense of longing and regret, in which every step you take becomes delayed, revised, held back a little bit. The past and future are hypothesized, an ideal world existing in the shadow of an *if. It would have been.*"[20] This is a sort of folding of time. The apparently flat post-historical time of the late twentieth century spectacle can, with the right grammatical origami, still yield a certain shape. For whom did affect wane? For the universal subject of high theory. There are other subjects, other affects, other theories.

For *Torpor* is a book about the late 80s and early 90s. It's the time of America's 'first' Gulf war, the fall of the Berlin wall, the Balkan wars, of Vaclav Havel's 'velvet revolution' in what was then Czechoslovakia, and the more sinister 'media revolution' in Romania.[21] It's an era when the cold war appeared to end even if other kinds of wars were only just beginning. It's a time when the military industrial complex will have morphed into the military entertainment complex.

It's a time when people still got their world news images from CNN. It's a time when CNN still had news. MTV was still a music video channel. The PC had taken off, as had Apple's MacIntosh computer, but email was still something of a novelty. AOL had just started popularizing dial-up internet. The world wide web was just beginning. Google did not yet exist. The cd co-existed with vinyl records and cassettes. Movies still came on video-tape from the video rental store. Nintendo has just brought back the computer game as a popular form.

Analog and digital co-existed. Nobody really knew what the future of media was supposed to look like, but anybody who could

20. *Torpor,* p. 163
21. See Andreij Ujica and Harun Faroki, *Videograms of a Revolution,* 1992

talk a good game was an 'expert.' "*The Digital Dialectic*? To Jerome, who hasn't even heard of email yet, this sounds like some high-tech form of finger-fucking."[22] The myth of Silicon Valley, triumphantly disrupting and pivoting, destroying all of the old social and media forms, had not yet come into existence. The ten years after the fall of the Berlin wall was a time in search of an over-arching story.

The cold war narrative did give way—to what? There will be, and still is, endless talk about postmodernism, post-structuralism, post-Fordism, biopower, neoliberalism, cognitive capitalism, late capitalism, communicative capitalism. That all of these supposedly new concepts work by just adding modifiers to the old ones should give the lie to their temporary quality, their shallow grasp on what may or may not have transpired in the late twentieth century. Such (non)concepts proceed as if there was a *locus solus* from which to work the structural binary, to turn a big pivot between discrete, opposed terms that the master-thinker leverages with his big Archimedean fulcrum. It doesn't really work. High theory lost its bearings, or its marbles. Perhaps for good.

There's two good metonyms for this in *Torpor*. The first is the rather savage but entirely just portrait of Félix Guattari, hosting his mates to a marathon viewing of the Romanian 'media revolution' on his big-screen TV: "He was at once the bourgeois host and the countercultural savant, presiding over an ideological slumber party."[23] Lacking the requisite finish-school French, Sylvie follows only the topics of conversation: "Words like *fin*, *histoire* and *idéologie* circled around the loft like dead air in a sick building."[24] The Guattari boys have not found a way to fold the flat plane of the

22. *Torpor*, p. 184
23. *Torpor*, p. 102
24. *Torpor*, p. 104

spectacle, to give it dimension, shape. As a woman, Kraus would be excluded from the high-minded talk anyway, but she does notice the girl who will slip out to buy heroin.

The second metonym is the orphan. Kraus' books tend to be constructed around missing objects: letters to an unresponsive Dick, the film which fails to come together and find its audience in *Aliens & Anorexia*, even the absent psycho sadist killer of *Summer of Hate* (2012). And then there is the most powerful talisman of all: the orphan of *Torpor*. As Sylvie says of herself and her husband, Jerome: "Were they both not orphans, in a certain sense? She'd wept when Marx's application of Hegelian dialectics onto human history had been first explained to her."[25]

At first, this seems like a bit of parataxis. What does Marx have to do with orphans? The proletariat, by definition, are those who have nothing but their own offspring. To be orphaned is to be somehow below or outside the proletariat. One could even, for example, think of the intellectual as the proletariat's orphan. Of it in spirit, but not by blood.

Sylvie's mad plan to adopt an orphan is among other things an attempt at the metonym made flesh. Sylvie and Jerome are "full-grown intellectuals," but also "two rootless cosmopolitans."[26] The orphan would be a small part of all of the oppressed. But the orphan role would have to do more work than that. "Bad History could be symbolically redeemed with a single (happy!) act of synthesis."[27] The rescue would not only redeem the history of the cold war and capitalist exploitation, but also the unspeakable past of the Holocaust.

---

25. *Torpor*, p. 89
26. *Torpor*, p. 29; p. 21
27. *Torpor*, p. 90

If there is a metaphor, perhaps even a symbol, it's something small, something everyday: it's the blue zippered nylon bag in which Lily the dog is carried across borders, over seas, into hotels and homes. Sometimes she is drugged to feign death and evade border guards. It is at once what makes her flight possible, but it also presages her coffin, her grave. And as Sylvie knows, the blue zippered nylon bag will not hold the orphan. It won't hold a metonym, let alone history.

"It could be argued that an anoetic memory of the Holocaust hovers over the French mid-century discovery of formalism."[28] Perhaps theory's linguistic turn was more a swerve away from thinking that for which historical thought really had no language. One of the more remarkable things about *Torpor* is its portrait of Jerome, recognizable from Kraus' earlier books as Sylvère Lotringer, "French theory's wandering pimp."[29] But there is more to Sylvère than the pimping, and it is signaled by that tainted word 'wandering.'

Like Alexander Trocchi's *Cain's Book*, I take Kraus' books to be selectively true. As she writes of the Kraus-like character in *Summer of Hate*, "Having no talent for making shit up, she simply reported her thoughts."[30] This omits the care that goes into the editing of those thoughts, and the care that goes into finding a rhetorical form through which observation, inflected by affect, can become a concept of its own situation. All the same, I take Jerome to be a portrait of Lotringer, one of the most interesting figures in *American* letters of the late twentieth century. He was the Barney Rossett of the era after Barney. Where Rosset brokered Samuel Beckett and William Burroughs into American literary consciousness, Lotringer gave us Jean Baudrillard and Paul Virilio.

---

28. *Torpor*, p. 192
29. *Torpor*, p. 248
30. *Summer of Hate*, p. 15

Jerome sees himself as an agent provocateur, a producer, a broker-spy. But his own book never seems to get written. A study of Celine, Bataille and Weil, it would be called *The Anthropology of Unhappiness*, or *Modernism and the Holocaust*. In a curious way it did actually get written, through Lotringer's imprint Semiotext(e). Lotringer is a kind of meta-author, an author not of books but of authors, English-language authors. It is Lotringer who is the 'author' of Paul Virilio, Jean Baudrillard and one or two others as 'writers' of English literature. Ones who, in the era of the linguistic turn, did something very different in the wake of semiotics than the high theory of Yale deconstruction. All the authors he authored signaled through the flames.

"Jerome caressed his fantasies of Auschwitz the way that Humbert Humbert groped Lolita's pre-pubescent body."[31] One could read Lotringer's whole corpus as an attempt to make present, but indirectly, that which in France formalist literature and structuralist theory had elided. The selections, the editing, the formatting of Semiotext(e) books rewrote the codes of postwar writing as being not about the failure of communism and the turn to the sign, but about something else.

"There was a pervasive feeling among Félix and all his friends that change would always happen for the worst. Born before the triumph of the spectacle, his was the last generation to whom things would really *matter*. In his heart, Félix still felt personally betrayed by the victory of consumerism over communality."[32] But for Jerome, "it could be worse." It had been worse, actually.

The Kraus character points out that some of the actual editing had been done not by Jerome but by herself. In *Aliens & Anorexia*,

31. *Torpor*, p. 190
32. *Torpor*, p. 107

Kraus has even written her own alternate version of one of the missing chapters, not only of Jerome's book, but of much of the Semiotext(e) oeuvre: Simone Weil. Hers was a much more nervy, embodied, genuinely committed version of that which the 'Bataille boys' mostly just talk about: corporeal *decreation*.

Like any great publisher, Semiotext(e) has had many lives. Alongside its *Foreign Agents Series*, which packaged European theory into little black dime store paperback-sized conceptual stealth-bombers, there is also a *Native Agents Series*. This started out with first-person non-confessional narrative, but broadened out into a range of writerly tactics for getting a fresh grip on language as the theory-effect started to fade. My personal favorite book in the series is *All The Kings Horses*. Originally published in 1960, its by the Chris Kraus of the Situationists— Michèle Bernstein.

Sometimes, to take three steps forward, one has to take two steps back, to look in the archives again. It's a retrospective version of the "*Who's Peaked?*" game played by Jerome and his pals.[33] One with a similar kind of cynical clarity. Why is Simone Weil relatively neglected, compared to her contemporaries? Or in a different register: one finds in Kraus an insistent questioning of the priorities of canonization. Why Karen Finley and not Penny Arcade? Why Cindy Sherman and not Hannah Wilke? Predictably enough, Kraus' own writing has had an influence, not just on certain writers but also certain editors. She has enabled some new kinds of writing, which speak to the present in a way that other modes of theoretical text no longer can. But there is also an effervescence of Kraus-lite in certain corners of the literary market.

---

33. *Torpor*, p. 172

After *Torpor*, Kraus published *Summer of Hate*. It's the early twenty-first century, and another George Bush has started another Gulf war. On a sojourn in Mexico, Catt Dunlop (the Kraus-character), and an Eileen Myles character find they can finally breathe and say what's really on their minds without trembling: "Isn't it weird, how nothing coming out now even mentions what's going on?"[34]

Torpor had the quality of a settling of accounts, among other things with a certain kind of French writing, which from Flaubert to Perec still got a certain mileage out of an ironic mode. *Summer of Hate*, by contrast, is an American novel: it starts off noir-ish, but ends up almost as social realism. It's rather like the films of Laurie Collyer: the struggle of the (mostly) white working class in America, not against the ruling class, but against the poisoned landscape that late capitalism has made. Or perhaps it's not late capitalism, perhaps it's early something else. Not exactly capitalism any more, but something a bit worse.

The no-future sensibility of punk is now the general condition, which is also one of no-past. "It occurred to Catt that the epistemological groundwork for the war in Iraq had been laid by Paris Hilton's anal sex video."[35] The provenance of images is now completely unknowable. Once they exist, they exist. Meanwhile, everyday life is increasingly ruled by what used to be called the 'repressive state apparatus.' Police-talk infects language: people make *statements* about *incidents* involving *individuals*, present their *items* as *evidence*. Heat storms are rebranded as mere heat waves. There's no need any more for an official 'ideological state apparatus,' just marketing consultants. "Information was immediate: there was no longer any need for the apostles."[36]

---

34. *Summer of Hate*, p. 194
35. *Summer of Hate*, p. 27
36. *Torpor*, p. 105

Now that the New York where bohemia met the demimonde is apparently extinct, all that remains are the fringes of the art world. At its center, the art world has become a market for financial instruments that take a singularized commodity form. Like any contract, art still needs the signature; but the artist, not so much. There is little room for the self-created monsters of the past. "Whereas modernism believed that the artist's life held all the magic keys to reading works of art, neoconceptualism has cooled this off and corporatized it. The artist's own biography doesn't matter much at all. What life? The blanker the better. The life experience of the artist, if channeled into the artwork, can only impede art's neocorporate, neoconceptual purpose. It is the biography of the institution that we want to read."[37] We no longer have dark pasts; we have shiny resumés.

I take neocorporate neoconceptualism to be a joke style name, about as dignified as the contemporary art world deserves. But whatever its problems, the art world might be in better shape than what happened to high theory in the humanities academy. As part of researching this essay, I put my favorite Kraus-quotes on my Facebook wall. This is the one that got the strongest reaction: "What put me off experimental film world feminism, besides all its boring study groups on Jacques Lacan, was its sincere investigation into the dilemma of the Pretty Girl. As an Ugly Girl it didn't matter much to me. And didn't Donna Haraway finally solve this by saying all female lived experience is a bunch of riffs, completely fake, so we should recognize ourselves as Cyborgs?"[38]

God is dead; theory is dad. What that quote got as response was defenses of the Lacan cult. What used to be the theory-world

37. *Video Green,* p. 21
38. *I Love Dick,* p. 181

now appears to be organized as a series of father-cults. You can criticize the Lacan cult, but only among followers of the Heidegger cult, and so on. The academy has not crossed into the no-dads world yet, one of the perhaps necessary stages or variants after the punk or cyberpunk no-future. This is perhaps because The-Name-of-the-Theorist functions like brand or genre, as a way to manage uncertainty in the marketplace.

And so there just might be a bit more room around the inside-out margins of the art world than the academy to find ways to know the world. "The story of international contemporary art is now the story of global dislocation. Everybody's following the money, and the party, and few are ever rewarded. Exclusion keeps the dislocation moving."[39] Perhaps there's a way to work on and in its margins as a metonym for the marginal life now to be had in this time after capitalism, this time that's just like it but worse. The rage of which the art world is the exclusive agent could be ported back into textual form, where some cooler methods might convert the neoconceptual back into actual concepts.

I think *Torpor* marks a turning point in Kraus' work. It can be read either as concluding a trilogy of books, starting with *I Love Dick*, then *Aliens & Anorexia*. Or it can be read as of-a-piece with *Summer of Hate*, and a turn in Kraus' writing toward a kind of novelistic style, where items and individuals are the building blocks of metonymic sequences of understanding wholes through parts, but where the wholes to be grasped are not the old totalities of high theory but other kinds of objects dictated by the encounter with particular parts: twelve-step culture, a courthouse in Phoenix or Albuquerque real estate.

---

39. Chris Kraus, *Kelly Lake Store & Other Stories*, Companion Editions, Portland OR, 2014, p. 34

In *Summer of Hate* the Kraus character is put on the spot at a public speaking engagement. "Wondering if she'll have to summon French theory for the rest of her life to explain her brief, girlish adventures, she performs as expected and deflects the question."[40] The joke is that those adventures were never really particularly transgressive or shocking. It was just that the privacy that protected the space around the male artist or writer had been breached. Having brokered the topic of thought's intimate relation to life, perhaps there's no going back. We really are going to have to think about what kind of life we can believe in—and afford.